RETURN TO SILENT HILL

THE OFFICIAL MOVIE NOVELIZATION

RETURN TO SILENT HILL

THE OFFICIAL MOVIE NOVELIZATION

By
John Passarella

Based on the screenplay by
Christophe Gans
Sandra Vo-Anh
William Schneider

TITAN BOOKS

Return to Silent Hill: The Official Movie Novelization
Print edition ISBN: 9781835413319
E-book edition ISBN: 9781835413326

Published by Titan Books
A division of Titan Publishing Group Ltd
144 Southwark Street, London SE1 0UP
www.titanbooks.com

First edition: January 2026
10 9 8 7 6 5 4 3 2 1

A CIP catalogue record for this title is available from the British Library.

EU RP (for authorities only)
eucomply OÜ, Pärnu mnt. 139b-14, 11317 Tallinn, Estonia
hello@eucompliancepartner.com, +3375690241

Designed and typeset in ITC Novarese Std by Richard Mason.

Printed and bound in the United States.

For Andrea, who rescues caterpillars
to ensure someday they'll become butterflies

CHAPTER 1

Cruising in his black Mustang with the top down, wind blowing through his shoulder length brown hair on a beautiful New England day, James Sunderland had the two lane road to himself. At least it seemed that way. He hadn't seen another car in a while and the world opened before him. The road had been cut through the procession of mountains rising on either side of him, along with an abundance of pine trees like a gathering army awaiting orders to march. Civilization seemed far away, more concept than reality. And despite the weaving road beneath the humming tires, with its occasional hairpin turns, James pressed down on the accelerator, gratified by the immediate and throaty response from the Mustang's engine.

Of course, in hindsight, he should have known better.

He heard a *thump* in back and glanced over his shoulder. His easel had slid across the back seat and now leaned against the side of the car at a forty-five degree angle, like a broken ship's mast. He'd packed carelessly, rather than in haste, propping a half dozen blank canvases on the back seat, along with a large sketch pad, his right-handed palette, and a wooden oil paint box set, roomy enough for over a dozen tubes, several brushes and a few small bottles of solvent. Fortunately, the travel kit had a sturdy latch to keep the potentially messy contents contained. He'd tossed some miscellaneous supplies—pencils, erasers, charcoal sticks, clean rags, and a can of linseed oil—in a box and stashed it on the floor behind the driver's seat.

While the open road hadn't exactly called to him, he had to admit he'd been in a bit of a creative slump, to the point where the brick walls of his studio apartment seemed to be closing in. He recalled the day he'd been bemoaning this lack of inspiration along with the encroaching cabin fever while catching a cup of coffee with his friend Leo, a photographer for the local paper by trade, who often needed to satisfy his own creative itch by way of a change of scenery. Leo mentioned a few out-of-the-way spots along the New England coastline he'd discovered on a recent business trip and hoped to revisit again when he had the time. Intrigued, James decided to take the information as a sign. Sometimes undiscovered open spaces were just what the muse ordered.

A dark shape in the middle of the road caught his attention. He gave it a wide berth but shook his head when he realized it was a dead porcupine, the left half of its body remolded by unforgiving tire tread. He drove on, while the gruesome reminder of mortality awaited its final disposition by the hands of a road crew or the beak of a vulture.

Left hand atop the steering wheel, James leaned to the right to open the glove compartment, where he kept a nondescript tin filled with a few pre-rolls. The tin was right where he'd left it. Unfortunately, it was empty. Of course, he had some pre-rolls stashed in his studio but he'd traveled too far to turn back now.

Sighing, he patted his pockets, looking for the pack of cigarettes he'd yet to throw away. Kept promising himself he'd quit—until the inevitable backslide. His own nicotine mortality had been foreshadowed through his uncle Frank, who'd passed out during a coughing spasm and split his head open on the corner of a marble countertop. During the subsequent hospital stay, Frank learned he had stage four lung cancer. The perils of nicotine addiction hit closer to home when James left a partially extinguished cigarette butt too close to a rag damp with linseed oil. If not for the dusty fire extinguisher mounted to the back wall of his apartment since he signed the lease, he would have been enveloped in a studio flambé until nothing remained but the charred brick walls. Because he would have attempted to save his finished paintings and any works-in-progress, despite the risk to himself. That's how he was wired.

His groping fingers found the crumpled pack of cigarettes in his left jacket pocket. Judging by feel, only half the pack remained. When they were gone, he promised himself, he wouldn't buy another pack. He'd already cut back a lot, weaned himself down to one pack every few days. Sitting there, one hand on the steering wheel, he tried to convince himself to crush the pack in the ball of his fist and go cold turkey. "Ah, hell," he said at last, "in the grand scheme of my life, one more cigarette won't hurt."

He gave the pack a practiced shake and plucked out the first cigarette that presented itself. He pushed in the console lighter, then stuck the unfiltered coffin nail between his lips before he could change his mind. Moments later, he took his first puff in days. Any residual tension he'd been feeling began to melt away. "Last one," he told himself. "Might as well enjoy it."

Through an exhaled stream of smoke, he saw the winding road in front of him presented a blind turn, which probably meant another hairpin. Without a cop or any other vehicle in sight, he'd been traveling well above the posted speed limit, so he had limited time to account for the turn. With a brief tap on the brake pedal, he placed both hands on the wheel, confident the Mustang could handle the curve, and enjoyed the rush as the world spun on its axis around him.

Smiling, he came out of the turn a bit wide, tires squealing in protest, kicking up some gravel on the right shoulder. Other than a few additional thumps in back as some canvases and his box set tumbled to the floor, no harm done. He straightened out in his lane and saw the road continued to weave ahead of him. Compared to the sharp turn behind him, nothing too concerning. Invigorated, he took another deep puff of his definitely-last cigarette and pressed down on the gas pedal.

The confines of his brick-walled studio seemed worlds away. When he returned home, he needed to thank Leo for the suggestion to get away, to get out of his own head. Meanwhile, he had to be getting close to those out-of-the-way scenic spots Leo recommended. Which meant he needed the driving instructions Leo had scrawled on the coffee shop napkin. Worried the ink might smear, James had decided not to put it in his pocket. But where had he stored the napkin? Glove compartment—or in the box set? Possibly in the box with the rags and linseed oil. No—

He reached for the glove compartment again as he was coming out of a wide turn. The right front wheel dropped into a pothole with a jarring impact, shaking the Mustang's chassis. Muttering a curse, he tightened his grip on the steering wheel, but the cigarette tumbled from his lips, landing above the knee of his jeans. Before it could fall to the floor and possibly set the floor mat or carpeting on fire, he reached to pick it up, glancing down to avoid grabbing the lit end.

Sudden roar of a powerful engine—

Shriek of a truck horn—

Startled, James looked up in time to see he'd drifted into the lane of an oncoming logging truck, its massive grille bearing down on him with deadly speed, the white cab and the face of the driver nothing more than a blur of imminent doom. James spun the Mustang's steering wheel hard right, avoiding the head-on collision by the width of a few layers of paint. He half-expected his side view mirror to explode like a grenade, slicing his face with shrapnel. As James veered away from the rolling wall of braced logs, the Mustang trembled in the truck's wake, the backwash hitting his face and blowing debris in his eyes.

In his frantic attempt to avoid the logging truck, James hadn't dared brake, and the sharp right turn had steered the Mustang too far in the opposite direction, risking a collision with a line of trees on the right side of the road. He struggled for control of the rear-wheel drive sports car, whipping the steering wheel back again, swerving from the shoulder toward the oncoming lane. No vehicles ahead, but out of the periphery of his vision, he noticed movement and the blurred outline of a rundown bus stop.

Before he rolled the car or crashed into something else, he slammed on the brakes and felt the Mustang immediately fishtail, a complete one-eighty, painting a layer of burning rubber on the blacktop. He came to an abrupt stop, punctuated by a loud crunch beneath the left rear tire.

"That can't be good," he whispered to himself.

But it could have been a whole lot worse.

As if to echo this sentiment, the receding truck horn blared again.

Almost as an afterthought, he switched off the ignition. Instantly, the car shuddered to stillness. Not so easy for the driver. After a few calming breaths to slow his racing heart, he realized he'd lost track of the damned cigarette. A moment later, he located it on the mat, between his shoes and stomped on it with more force than necessary.

Looking up, he noticed something in the rearview mirror: a young woman standing several yards from the Mustang, staring back at him, mouth agape, her face frozen in shock.

Oh, God, was she alone—? Did I—?

Refusing to consider the horrible thought attempting to blossom in his mind, he climbed out of the car on shaky legs.

A few hesitant steps later, he looked past the rear of the Mustang and saw what he'd hit—a turquoise suitcase, nearly split in two, clothes scattered everywhere—and sighed with relief. Then he met her stunned gaze and wondered how close he'd come to hitting her. Too damn close. "Shit."

As they stood facing each other, he had a moment to take her in. Long, wavy strawberry blond hair, unzipped pale gray suede jacket over a light pink, floral print camisole, an adventurously short jean skirt with a gold waist chain through the belt loops, and brown leather ankle boots. In short, she was stunning. Realizing he'd been staring at her a bit too long, a hasty apology spilled from his mouth. "I'm so sorry." He spread his hands. "Are you okay?"

As if a spell were broken, she looked down at her broken suitcase and its scattered contents, her initial shock replaced by equal parts embarrassment and anxiety. "Yeah. No. I'm fine. I'm fine," she blurted out as she crouched, beginning to pick up the closest articles of clothing.

He approached her, went down on a knee beside her, ostensibly to help with the cleanup, while making sure she hadn't suffered any injury, either from his car or the broken suitcase. "You're sure you're okay?"

She looked at him, finally registering his presence, close enough for him to stare into her pale blue eyes, which took his breath away.

"I think so," she said, with a quick nod and a fleeting smile.

James smiled back. Together they gathered the remaining clothing, some items smudged with road grit. But she didn't bother to shake off the dirt or fold anything, merely stuffed them in the scuffed turquoise suitcase with haste. She sighed when she spotted a broken makeup case, then scooped up the pieces and shoved them in the corner.

On the shoulder of the road, James noticed an undamaged

second suitcase, along with a matching toiletry case and, once again, thought it could have been worse. He crossed the road to where she crouched and handed her the rest of the clothing he'd collected. Without any examination of their condition, she added the last items to the unruly mound. With one quick glance around to make sure she had everything, she flipped the lid of the suitcase closed, pushed down on it and tried to engage the lock.

"The latch is broken."

With a sigh, she rocked back, resting on her heels and staring at the suitcase as if deciding if she should abandon it or hoping it would magically repair itself. Feeling responsible—justifiably so—James kneeled across from her, spun the suitcase around to face him and tried to force the latch to grab but without success. It nearly broke off in his hand; at this point he was almost sabotaging her. He started to form an apology but the hiss of air brakes interrupted him.

A blue and white bus rolled by them, passing the rundown rest area building to stop beside the covered plexiglass shelter. Beneath the bus's row of tinted windows were the printed words, Intercity Coach. With a metallic squeal, the doors opened expectantly.

"Shoot," she said. "There's my bus." Standing, she rushed toward the bus, waving her hands overhead. "Hey! Wait!"

James looked down at the suitcase and shook his head. He pushed the wobbly lid closer to true, then grabbed the hanging latch and tried to hook it over the metal lip. He felt it grab, providing enough resistance to hold the lid closed, if only long enough to get it stowed on the bus.

"Wait!" he called.

He wrapped his arm around the suitcase, keeping pressure on it against his side and ran halfway to the bus before remembering her undamaged luggage on the shoulder of the road. She had started to run toward him, away from the accordioned bus door, but stopped confused when he veered away. At the side of the road, James managed to slip his fingers through the combined handles of the suitcase and toiletry kit, but first he had to set down the damaged suitcase. With those in hand, he reached for the handle of the broken one and prayed the damaged latch would hold long enough to see her on her way.

She backed away, returning to the open bus door, keeping her eyes on his progress. But close is never good enough. As he jogged toward her, the jostling of the bags proved too much for the damaged latch. The lid flipped open, dumping all her belongings on the road a second time. James stopped to recover and nearly tripped over the mound of clothes. She ran toward him to help, but it was too little too late. James was close enough to hear the bus driver grumble, "Got a schedule to keep, lady. Catch the next one." The door squealed shut and the bus pulled away, belching a black cloud of acrid smoke from its tailpipe.

Shoulders slumped, she stared at the departing bus. "What a jerk!"

Clothes bunched around his ankles, James stood and shook his head. "I'm officially an asshole," he said. For the first time, he took in their surroundings. The grungy rest area building looked abandoned, comprised of little more than unsanitary restrooms, judging by the overturned trashcan, scattered litter and a forgotten, orange-striped construction sawhorse. On the near side of the bus shelter a poster advertised Toluca Lake. Behind them, at the near edge of the rest stop, a mounted tourist information map for Pale Ville National Park was a poor substitute for an official welcome center. Not knowing how long before the next bus arrived, he couldn't leave her here alone. Of course, that wasn't his call, but he could certainly make the offer. "Look, I can give you a ride if you want," he said, hoping for a casual tone. "Where were you heading?"

Turning her back on the receding bus, she looked at him, down at the suitcases and clothing, then back up at him. She blew a loose strand of hair away from her mouth, then tucked it behind her ear for good measure. "Into the city," she said, with a hint of resignation. "Where were you going?"

"I was heading up to the pass," he said.

She shrugged. "Guess it wasn't meant to be."

They stared at each other in silence. James couldn't blame her for not jumping at the chance to get in a car with a stranger, especially a stranger who had demonstrated a profound lack of driving acumen in such spectacular fashion. He dropped to a knee and stuffed her clothes back into the broken suitcase, closing the lid yet again despite the futility of the gesture. He stood, but she avoided eye contact, staring off into the distance. Emotions flashed across her features, a slight tremble in her lips, a furrowing of her brow, barely suppressed frustration, if he had to guess.

"So, what are you gonna do?"

Another shrug. "I can just head back into town, I guess."

She walked toward the guard rail. He followed, tracking her gaze down to a town at the base of a valley, surrounded by dense forest, bordering a pristine lake. Toluca Lake, he presumed, based on the transit shelter sign.

Beside her, he said, "Didn't even realize there was a town here. What's it called?"

Without looking away from her destination, she spoke in a voice tinged with resignation. "Silent Hill."

They stood in silence. She seemed unwilling to move, unable to end this moment that hung between them. He realized she'd come a long way to reach this bus stop. A return trip would be more difficult with the broken suitcase.

"There's a trail down that way—" She pointed beyond the guard rail, to a narrow deer trail, steep and no doubt treacherous with more than a few switchbacks of its own. He was certain of one thing. There was no way in hell he'd let her return home on that trail.

His gaze was drawn beyond the trail and the town, to the sparkling lake, a rush of movement as boats and jet skis crisscrossed each other in front of a beautiful, gleaming white resort hotel perched on the shore. Compared to the soulless, abandoned rest area, the hotel seemed vibrant, full of life, brimming with excitement and potential.

"Wow," he said. "That's some hotel."

"That's the Lakeview," she said. "The view of the lake from the rooftop—"

James smirked. "Pretty enough to name a hotel after."

She turned to look up at him, brow furrowed, ready to snap back at him. "You nearly run me down and now you're giving me a hard time?"

Palms up, James said, "I'm sorry."

But she'd seen his smile and, after a moment of feigned indignation, flashed an engaging smile of her own.

Chagrined. "Guess I deserved that, didn't I?"

"That and more."

"I'm James, by the way."

"Mary."

"Seriously, lemme drive you home, Mary. Save you a sprained ankle—or two." He took another considering glance at the steep deer trail.

"I don't even know you, James."

"Then let's make it formal," he said, offering his hand. "James Sunderland. Pleased to meet you."

Playing along, she took his hand. "Mary Crane."

"So, it's settled?"

She laughed. "That's not what I meant, and you know it."

He spread his hands. "Then I'm just gonna have to stand here and watch you go down to make sure you don't fall."

"Seems like appropriate penance for screwing up my day."

She stared at him, considering. Then, without a word, she walked away from the guard rail and the trailhead back toward her spilled luggage. After picking up the undamaged suitcase in one hand and the toiletry kit in the other, she strode toward the Mustang. James watched her, dumbfounded, but couldn't keep the smile off his face. He'd driven all this way for a fresh view, a dash of inspiration. Instead, he had the feeling he'd lucked into something much more remarkable.

She paused beside the car. "So? You coming or what?"

He snapped out of whatever spell she'd cast on him and hurried to pick up the damaged suitcase, taking care not to dump its contents for a third time, despite a sleeve and a pant leg dangling from the side gaps like vestigial appendages. Since his painting gear took up the back seat, he popped open the trunk and placed the bad suitcase inside with a show of care. After slamming the trunk shut, he made a beeline to the passenger door and held it open for her, figuring it was never too late to show her he was a gentleman, first impressions be damned.

She placed her bags at the foot of the passenger seat then slid into the car. "Thanks," she said.

Circling the front of the Mustang, he climbed into the driver's seat and paused before turning the ignition, taking a moment to study the fine details of her face, already imagining her as part of his art, sketching her, painting her. He recognized more than one kind of inspiration.

As she returned his smile, the wind picked up a bit, a sudden gust causing her hair to swirl around her face. She brushed it back, glancing up as the sky darkened, the sun blotted out by a cluster of dark clouds. Seconds later the wind grew fierce, the nearby trees swaying with the force of it, leaves swirling across the ground, along with a few empty plastic bottles, soda cans, and fast food wrappers spilled from the overturned trashcan.

James started the car, anticipating the need to raise the convertible top before the inevitable downpour could drench them where they sat. Tree branches clacked together, and the wind had begun to howl.

"Silent Hill summer storm," Mary said, fighting to be heard over the wind. "Doesn't happen often. But when it does—"

She was losing the battle to keep her long hair away from her face. It seemed to undulate back and forth before her, almost as if she were underwater.

CHAPTER 2

The chatter of a dozen conversations around him held no interest. Other than a clear word rising here and there in sharp relief, all the pointless, endless discussions amounted to nothing more than unintelligible white noise competing against the barrage of bass-heavy tunes blasting from the jukebox. Even so, it was better than the silence.

Anything was better than the silence.

Nietzsche's warning rang in James' head: *"If you gaze long enough into an abyss, the abyss will gaze back into you."* He'd do well to heed that warning. And he'd tried. God knows, he tried. But what do you do if the abyss follows you? If the abyss is inside you, slowly consuming you, creeping into every waking thought, until nothing else remained?

"Drown it," he mumbled. As he felt the welcome darkness closing in from the edges of his awareness, his head lolled back against the seatback of the padded booth, his hands dropped from the tabletop to his sides, plopping his cellphone on the bench seat. Comfortably numb, he'd welcome the slip into oblivion. The floor seemed to shift under him, his body tilting sideways—

His head snapped forward. Eyes straining wide, he attempted to rouse himself from the debilitating fatigue. He raised his right hand from the seat, almost knocking his phone on the floor, and scratched the stubble on his jaw. Noticing the empty pint glass in front of him, he grabbed the amber beer bottle beside it, but only a drop or two remained. That was a problem.

Took him another moment or two to notice his cellphone buzzing, locate the screen and check the caller ID: M

Six missed calls.

Probably had him on speed-dial at this point.

He caught movement out of the corner of his eye, looking up from the phone as his server approached. In her forties, she wore a sleeveless top and red leather skirt to match her long red hair. Her outfit seemed more a concession to her place of employment rather than a personal choice. She had the hardened edge of someone who recognized they'd become stuck in a rut yet continued to power through, while refusing to take bullshit from anyone. She'd introduced herself when he'd first arrived, but he couldn't remember her name. Hell, he couldn't remember the name of the bar.

Her plastic serving tray held a glass of bourbon he hadn't ordered but wouldn't refuse if she mistakenly left it on his table. Without a word she picked up his empty beer bottle and the pint glass as well, placing them on the tray. The bottle was done, but he needed that glass.

"Think it's time to go," she said. It wasn't a question. She flashed a pitying smile, as if about to say more but thought better of it.

"Alright," James said, nodding slowly. Maybe he'd had enough after all. "Alright."

Getting out of the booth from behind the square table proved more difficult in practice than in theory. He edged his way out, only jostling the table twice—maybe three times. Standing, on the other hand, involved coordination and balance, both of which he seemed to be lacking at that moment. The wood planking beneath his feet tilted at a forty-five degree angle, so naturally he tumbled to the floor. His outstretched palms saved him from a complete faceplant, but he was suddenly aware of the groups of faces watching his bumbling progress toward an upright position. Private conversations ceased. Patrons at the bar engaged in a trivia contest looked his way.

The server signaled to the bouncer sitting at the far end of the bar.

Afraid he'd become the evening's entertainment, James hurried to right himself, reaching for the table's edge, but mistakenly grabbing the serving tray, flipping it out of the woman's hands. The tray landed upside down on the bench seat, but his empty glass and beer bottle and the glass of bourbon fell to the floor, shattered glass and bourbon spraying in a starburst pattern at his feet.

"Jesus," the server exclaimed, gingerly backing away from the mess.

"Sorry," James said, mostly upright at this point, and tapped his chest. "That's on me."

Stone-faced, the bouncer crossed the bar like a heat-seeking missile. The man looked fit, maybe ex-military, wearing a long-sleeved black shirt with the cuffs rolled back to expose muscular forearms, and gray trousers.

James tried to shake him off. "My bad," he said. "It's all good, man."

Ignoring James' protestations, the bouncer grabbed him by both arms and hoisted him upright, inducing another wave of dizziness. He turned to the server. "This asshole's all settled up?"

"What? Asshole?" James said indignantly. "Who's being the asshole here?"

He shoved the man so forcefully James lost his balance and stumbled backward, crunching glass underfoot. Wobbling slightly, he regained his footing and reached for his phone, as if the matter was settled. But the bouncer was having none of it. Before James could make another move, the bouncer lunged and spun him around, putting him in a choke hold. In the large mirror above the booth, James saw his own frightened reflection, trapped as the man's forearm tightened around his throat—and panicked.

Instinct kicked in. Fight or flight, but never surrender. He flung his head backward, hard, and smashed the bouncer's nose. The man uttered a curse, staggered a step back, then slipped on a puddle of spilled bourbon, releasing his grip on James as he fell to the floor. But the victory was short-lived.

A second and a third bouncer appeared, flanking James, both dressed in black, one wearing a plain black baseball cap, the other sporting a shaved head. Each grabbed him by an arm as the first man climbed to his feet. With a slight nod, the initial bouncer led the way to the back of the bar. The backups dragged James with them, knocking over a few chairs in the process. Several bar patrons in their path scattered, clearing the way to the rear door.

With a trickle of blood sliding from one nostril but as stone-faced as ever, the first bouncer swung the door wide and stepped back as the other two hurled James into the alley onto a pile of black trash bags haphazardly arranged around an overflowing blue dumpster. An abandoned sofa cushion nearby would have offered a better landing spot, if not for the sour odor of vomit wafting from it.

A second later a cellphone struck the underside of a bald automobile tire perched atop the mound of garbage bags, rebounding across the alley, just out of reach. The bouncer had thrown it, probably intending to hit James.

Before they closed the bar door, James heard baseball-hat bouncer say, "Should be right at home with the rest of the trash." The other two chuckled as the bar door slammed shut, immediately cutting off the sound of excitable conversations if not the pounding bass of the music. Other than that small mercy, only the throbbing in his head held the silence at bay. He scrambled for his phone, then fell back with it clutched against his chest, the effort having exhausted him. He closed his eyes against the pale glare of the alley lights, and the dull pain in his side from where he was sure one of the bouncers had given him a complementary shot in the ribs.

He just needed to rest for a minute…

…Pins and needles in his hand woke him.

Confused, he examined his hand—which held his phone, vibrating like an angry hornet trapped in his palm but unable to sting. Squinting, he looked at the display. M again.

How long had he been out? How many additional calls had he missed. Regardless, this time he decided to answer. "Yeah," he mumbled, his mouth full of cotton, head still throbbing.

"He lives." The calm, cool and professional voice he remembered. A dozen missed calls and yet not a hint of impatience in her tone. "How are you?"

Clearing his throat, he took in his surroundings, the dim lighting, the surfeit of trash bags, an inquisitive rat surveying the week's haul, and the vomit-infused sofa cushion, which added a certain *je ne sais quoi* to the overall ambience.

"Great," he said finally. "Just so, so great."

"You've been drinking again."

It wasn't a question. Either he was slurring his words, or the missed calls had been a tell. Maybe his general phone demeanor when he'd had a few… or more than a few. But he'd accepted the call. No point in lying about it.

"It felt like we were moving in the right direction, James," she said, as patient and understanding as ever.

"I know," James said after an uncomfortable amount of silence. This was on him, not her. His failure. It would be easier, maybe, if not for the damned silence.

"How long can you keep doing this to yourself?" she asked.

Nodding, even though she couldn't see the gesture, he picked himself up from the garbage, a process that took longer than it should, but accomplished in one go, a slight stagger but no fall. With the phone's mic pressed to his chest, he glanced down at the stubby-tailed rat and whispered, "It's all yours."

He veered away from the dumpster and its flotilla of garbage bags and stumbled his way down the alley, away from what M would call his latest bout of self-sabotage. But it was hard to walk away when the abyss resided within you.

"Here's what I need you to do," M continued. "Get home. Drink some water. Get some sleep. Reset. And come to your appointment tomorrow ready to do the work."

Again, James nodded, finding words momentarily difficult.

"James?" she called through the tiny speaker.

"Tomorrow," he agreed. "Sure. I'll be there."

She let out a small sigh. He could almost imagine her slight smile. "Take care of yourself. Please."

After promising he would, he disconnected the call and shoved the phone in his hip pocket. He stepped out of the alley, and somehow it felt like stepping back into the world, back among the living. Still hours before dawn, the sky uncomfortably vast above the glare of streetlights. He gazed upward into that higher abyss a moment before lightning forked across the sky, fracturing the unrelenting darkness for a second or two. The subsequent rumble of thunder felt like a warning.

Occasional flashes of lightning followed him home, becoming more frequent as the grumblings of thunder grew in intensity. He was a mere block away before the rain arrived, dashing his small hope that he'd complete the trip before the gathering storm had a chance to hurl wet indignity upon him to complete his day. In seconds, a few tentative drops transformed into a torrential downpour. Only the driver of the white Jeep that drove by fast enough to spray a rooster tail of water across his legs, witnessed his inebriated attempt at a sprint to his front door.

He stumbled up the stairs to his studio, supported by the railing and a tactical lean against the wall. Exhaustion clung to him like a straitjacket.

As he unlocked his studio door and heard the heavy rain battering the skylight, he was grateful the roof wasn't leaking—yet. The night was no longer young, but the storm showed no sign of relenting. Normally, he'd flick on the overhead lights, but his throbbing headache and gritty eyes preferred the darkness. Besides, he knew the layout of his studio like the back of his hand, despite letting his natural inclination toward clutter go unchecked for longer than he cared to admit.

He'd always had multiple easels in various sizes to accommodate various canvas sizes, many freestanding bookshelves and end tables, most picked up at sidewalk sales or thrift shops, with painting supplies stashed hither and yon. Completed, in-progress and abandoned paintings leaned against any free wall space. Finished works hung here and there, mounted on the white brick walls. Some had been there for years, while others awaited a commercial disposition. Various studies ripped from sketchpads also adorned the walls, affixed at eye level with pieces of masking tape. Some eventually became finished pieces. But most never gave him the spark to continue. When he grew bored of them, he'd rip them down, crumple them into tiny balls and toss them in the nearest trashcan.

Lately, he'd been forgetting to close the drawers of end tables that held his painting supplies, half-read books, and other odds and ends. Paint-spattered rags remained draped over the seats of wooden stools or across the back of second-hand chairs. And while he had a storage cabinet for rolled-up paper canvases, most ended up on the floor with scattered brushes, some he hadn't even bothered to clean after their last use.

Small sculptures atop most of the bookshelves and tables gleamed in the reflected city lights, their details hidden in shadow. Most of these he'd purchased for inspiration or merely as decoration, because they spoke to him, but a few were the result of his own humble attempts at working in a different medium.

Soaked to the bone, he dropped into the scuffed leather armchair in the center of his studio without bothering to remove his jacket. Before him stood his largest easel holding one of his largest works, partially draped with a white drop cloth. Even in the darkness, the light cast down from the skylight attempted to illuminate the subject of the painting. But his gaze refused to focus on what was right in front of him. It was more than enough to know it was there, haunting him whether he acknowledged it or not.

He reached down beside the chair to a liquor bottle standing on the floor. Couldn't remember if it held whiskey or bourbon or vodka. Didn't really matter. He grabbed the bottle by the neck and brought it to his mouth, disappointed to find it empty, but not surprised he hadn't bothered to toss it in the recycling container. He clutched it to his chest and let his eyes track across the soft folds of the drop cloth to the textured pigment—

Wincing in pain, he pressed his right hand to his forehead,

massaging the space above his grainy eyes. Not enough sleep, too much alcohol. Maybe his therapist was right. He reached over the side of his chair to set the empty bottle back on the floor but let go too soon and it fell on its side rolling away from him with enough momentum to carry it to the door.

"Ah, hell," he said out loud. He really needed to throw the damn thing away before he tripped over it in the dark and broke his neck. Despite his exhaustion, he needed a small victory. He pushed himself out of the armchair and started toward the door. Something white gleamed in the dark. Something that hadn't been there when he returned home a few minutes ago—

A white envelope slipped halfway under the door.

He couldn't remember if the exterior door had locked behind him. And he hadn't heard anyone in the hallway. Maybe the envelope had been there the whole time, and he'd just missed it. Relying on his powers of observation lately was not a safe bet.

He picked up the letter. On the front, someone had written '*James*.' Nothing else. No stamp. No address. He flipped it over and read the return address:

Woodside Apartment Complex
Katz Ave
Silent Hill

Carefully, hands trembling slightly, he opened the envelope and pulled out the single sheet of paper. Before he could even read the handwritten note, his gaze was drawn immediately to the name at the bottom, *MARY*.

Holding his breath, he practically lunged at the door and flung it open, stepping out into the hallway, looking both ways. Nobody. He listened carefully for the sound of footfalls, the telltale squeaks a few of the stairs inevitably produced under the slightest pressure, but all he heard was the steady pattering of rainfall, its own kind of white noise, keeping secrets from him. He heaved a sigh. Whoever had stopped at his door was long gone.

Closing the door, he stepped back inside the studio and leaned against it, needing support as he pulled his cellphone out of his pants pocket. He scrolled through his contacts list until he found Mary's number and tapped the dial icon. A moment later he heard a recorded voice, "The number you have called is no longer—"

Before the operator's voice could finish, he disconnected the call.

Shoving the phone back in his pocket, he walked back to the armchair, but the idea of sitting and staring at nothing until he passed out had lost its limited appeal. He couldn't sit. He couldn't sit still and do… nothing. Mary had sent him this note through some sort of courier because she couldn't deliver it herself. With her phone out of service he had no way to contact her. At least not remotely. There was nothing he could do here, alone in his studio.

Walking to the counter he lifted his car keys from the wall hook and made a fist around them. Knowing Mary needed him produced an emotional alchemy that sloughed off the layers of exhaustion and alcohol-induced cognitive impairment. Instead, he felt reinvigorated for the first time in… a long time. Awake and able enough not to be a threat to himself or anyone else during the long drive back. He really had no choice. He had to return to Silent Hill.

Back in his Mustang, he navigated his way out of the city, windshield wipers on high, thumping back and forth across the windshield with the sound of an insistent heartbeat. The heavy rain had reduced city traffic enough that he soon found himself on the highway. Once the lanes opened, he steadily accelerated, first reaching, then topping the speed limit to eat up the miles. He squinted each time a pair of blinding headlights raced toward him from the opposite direction, the glare fracturing his view through the rain-streaked windshield. The mild headache they induced was a small price to pay. He was making good time.

He must have read Mary's letter a half dozen times before getting in the car. By this point, the words were imprinted on his memory, and he recalled them as if spoken in her voice, calling to him…

"James. So much time has passed. I know that."

Time since he'd last seen her. But he remembered the time they first met, how a similar storm had changed both their lives, how a chance encounter had become something much deeper.

"But I'm asking—I'm begging you to please come back. To our place. Something's happened. Please, James. I need you.

"Love, Mary."

Lightning flashed…

…in the night sky outside the windows and glass balcony doors of his Lakeview Hotel room, briefly illuminating Toluca Lake below, now absent any boats or jet skis, but nearly frothing under the barrage of torrential rain.

Safe from the storm, ensconced in the golden light cast from a lamp across the room, they lay beneath the sheets of the queen-sized bed, the combined body heat of their naked bodies banishing the chill brought on by their discarded wet clothing. Mary stared up at him as if truly seeing him for the first time. He saw himself reflected in her light blue eyes. And it felt like the start of something he could not have imagined living his life without. He cradled the nape of her neck in his right hand and lowered his lips to hers, a gentle caressing motion. But their need to explore each other was too new and too urgent for their motions to remain tentative. The kiss became deeper as his hands caressed her body. Then he cupped her breasts in his palms, thumbs exploring her nipples as his lips traced down her midriff. But soon she grew impatient, and rolled on top of him, her thighs straddling his hips as the sheets fell away. Much like the storm, she seemed like a force of nature. As she found a trembling rhythm, she closed her eyes, focusing on the pure sensation, head back as he held her hips.

She shuddered, a moan escaping her lips as lightning flashed again—

—blinding him.

A single halogen headlight swerved out from behind a rumbling intermodal truck and veered directly into his lane. For a moment, the light anomaly confused James. Then he realized it belonged to a motorcycle. The rider had been stuck behind the larger vehicle as it struggled up the steeper grade, and decided to pass in the pouring rain, but misjudged the speed of the Mustang and nearly wiped out. James instinctively hit the brake pedal and immediately felt the fishtail as his rear wheels began to hydroplane. He spun the steering wheel, turning into the skid and regained control. The trucker gave them both a prolonged blast of his horn in disgust.

The next several minutes passed without mishap. Just ahead, he recognized the hairpin turn he'd taken at excessive speed that first trip, long ago, and recalled the logging truck that had almost pancaked the Mustang. His first trip to Silent Hill, though he hadn't known that at the time.

The weaving road ahead brought him to the neglected rest area and the bus shelter promoting Toluca Lake. A lone flickering streetlight provided enough light to reveal an empty parking lot, but he expected no less. He continued past the bus stop and took the exit that led down to Silent Hill. A glance toward the passenger seat and he remembered Mary sitting there, as if it were yesterday, smiling back at him, her eyes inviting and curious about what would come next, with his painting supplies in the back seat, and her luggage stowed in the trunk.

Blinking lights cast a glare through the windshield, drawing his gaze back to the road and—

—he slammed on the brakes. Again, the Mustang protested with a skid across the slick road surface. He stared in disbelief.

A row of cement barriers blocked his path. Scattered around them were several reflective orange and white traffic barrels topped by blinking amber lights. Beyond that stood a chain link fence braced with sandbags and topped with razor wire, effectively blocking foot traffic.

Frustrated, he put the car in reverse, looking over his shoulder as he retraced his path up the narrow road until he had enough room to make a U-turn and make his way back to the rest stop. He drove across the parking lot and came to a stop near the Pale Ville National Park sign.

His mind returned to the day he met Mary. How they stood at the edge of the lot, in front of the guard rail and watched the boats and jet skis tooling around the lake. And he remembered how he talked her out of hiking down the deer trail into Silent Hill. She hadn't needed much convincing, but tonight she needed him—and he had no other option.

Switching off the ignition, he opened the door of the Mustang, determined to take that trail back to her. Honestly, it hadn't looked terribly dangerous, not if one was careful, but he hadn't wanted her to risk it and, besides, he owed her at least a ride into town. A little rain wouldn't—

Lightning crashed directly overhead. And with it, the intensity of the rain doubled, with torrential sheets sweeping across the hood of the car. Gusting winds rocked the Mustang's chassis as if it were a ship on a storm-tossed sea.

No choice but to wait it out.

He glanced at the dashboard clock: 3:58 AM

And the long day finally caught up to him, his second wind long gone. He reclined the seat a few notches, made himself as comfortable as possible and closed his burning eyes. Once the roaring of the rain diminished, the deer trail would be passable. Not yet, but soon. The storm couldn't possibly maintain this ferocity for long. He could wait a little while longer… just a little longer…

Like the lowering of a dark shroud, sleep claimed him, but not before Mary's words echoed in his mind. "*Something's happened.*"

James… awoke… to… a… world… of… ash……

CHAPTER 3

James awoke slowly, a bit disoriented, tightness in his neck and shoulders, legs cramped and stiff. He started to stretch, but his elbow struck something. As he leaned back, a tickle in his throat became a deep cough. He opened his eyes as he pounded on his chest twice, but the cough wasn't productive. And then he remembered. He'd stayed in the Mustang to outwait the storm. Must have fallen asleep and—

He checked the time on the dashboard clock: 7:18 AM

Early morning, but—

"The hell?" he muttered, staring at the windshield. Before he'd had a hard time seeing through the pouring rain. Now the windshield was covered with... gray dust, like a coating of snow. He switched on the wipers to clear his view, which only deepened his confusion. A thick fog limited visibility. Worse, the gray dust continued to fall from the sky, coating the windshield anew, smearing with each swipe of the wiper blades.

Mystified, he climbed out of the Mustang and looked around. The fog was everywhere. After running his hand across the cold hood of the car, James examined his palm. Coated with the gray... ash. He smelled his fingers, and they seemed to carry the memory of something burned and lost. The ash clung to his hand as if it had begun to seep into his flesh and corrupt it. Suddenly, he wanted nothing more than to be rid of it.

Striding across the parking lot, he decided he'd finally check out the neglected rest area's restroom. The door hinges creaked in protest as he passed through. Immediately, the heavy tang of aged urine assaulted him. Layers of yellow grime covered the walls and urinals, rust corroded all the fixtures and, here and there, wall tiles were cracked or missing. Remarkably, the fog had oozed its way into the restroom itself, blurring the edges. Inadequate lighting buzzed and flickered overhead, as if protesting his presence inside the building. He stopped at the nearest sink and stared into the fly-specked mirror. Brushing at the ash covering his hair and shoulders, he noticed that he wore exhaustion like an old cloak, his face lined and haggard, eyes red-rimmed and weary. Had he aged a decade in the last year?

He turned the hot water faucet: nothing. Same with the cold. Why was he not surprised? A grungy roll of toilet paper on the edge of the sink helped rid his hands of the ash. Reaching into the pocket of his leather jacket, he pulled out Mary's letter to read it one more time, even though her words had seared into his brain before he left his studio. After the frantic drive, the ferocious storm, and now the rain of ash, he needed to anchor himself; seeing her words, written by her hand, was a balm. But when he unfolded the damp paper, he discovered the rain had caused the ink to run, her words slowly dissolving, as if she herself were slipping away, for good this time.

He couldn't let that happen.

After tucking the folded paper back in his pocket, he left the restroom, strode across the parking lot and made his way to the trailhead. The fog would make the descent challenging, but he only needed to see far enough ahead for his next step. One benefit of the deer trail's narrowness was his ability to use tree branches for support when the footing was dicey. And the visibility was sufficient for him to avoid tripping over tree roots, rocks and vines. Gradually, he lost track of time, his methodical progress taking his mind off other concerns as he focused on getting to the bottom in one piece.

The steep passages became less frequent, and he began to think he was close to the valley floor. And while the shallow sun scattered the fog high in the trees, nearer to the ground it remained a concern, gathering in opaque waves that made progress more difficult. He pulled out his phone and turned on its flashlight, swinging it in a low arc to reveal any treacherous footing.

Crack!

Looking over his shoulder, he tried to determine the source of the sound. Instinct told him it had emanated from behind him, farther up the trail, but the fog tended to muffle sounds and could play tricks with his ears. He waited several moments, unmoving, listening, alert. A rustling sound moved through the underbrush, soon falling to silence. Probably an animal, no doubt having as much difficulty navigating through the fog as James. After waiting a few more moments and hearing nothing, he forged ahead, grateful as the trail began to level out, but he kept his cellphone's flashlight on to avoid any pitfalls.

Soon an indistinct shape resolved out of the fog. At first, he thought it was a vine-covered storage shed. Then, as he strode closer, he saw it was open, possibly a gazebo with a square four-column canopy. But the canopy covered a round stone well, which sat in the center of a raised stone platform. Noting the mechanized pump attached to the well, James turned the faucet. The pump chugged to life and clear water gushed from the spigot. Setting his phone down on the edge of the well, James cupped his hands under the water and brought it to his lips. As he tilted the cupped water into his mouth, he noticed a sign under the canopy, in the grip of ivy. But he could make out the words:

DANGER!
Do NOT Drink the Water

Coughing and sputtering, James spat the water out, wiping his mouth with the back of his hand. Thankfully, he hadn't swallowed any of the contaminated water before reading the sign. But it had been a close call.

"Something's happened."

Until he knew exactly what had happened in Silent Hill, he needed to proceed with caution. He stared at his hands, first covered in the weird ash that continued to fall from the sky, and now still wet and dripping from water that might be crawling with bacteria, toxic chemicals or—

Unbidden, the haunting image came to him…

In his studio last night, under the weight of the rain, running in rivulets along the skylight, the reflected city lights cast a pale beam of illumination across the massive canvas in the center, the focus, the eye of the storm, partially draped and concealed, but equally exposed to view—forcing him to look. Yet he refused to comply. His gaze skipped past it, over it, beyond it, never confronting what was right before him.

In this moment, he acknowledged the lie. A lie he'd told himself, that he wouldn't look, hadn't looked at his own creation. But now the image flashed before him, as if exposed from the darkness of his mind by a strobe light. He'd painted Mary's face on that undeniable canvas, a Mary he had never known, so disturbing to him, he'd been unable to finish the work. But unlike the studies that no longer spoke to him, that he crumpled up and tossed in the trash, he couldn't let go of this work. The face of Mary on that canvas was emaciated, hair lifeless, cheeks hollowed, where only the whites of her eyes showed, and the fingers pressed to her rouged lips were wet, but with blood. And he knew that the lips were wet with that blood, smeared across them.

He had looked at that image. In fact, he'd been unable to look away.

James shuddered, unsure why such a frightening version of Mary had flashed in his mind. Perhaps he'd ingested some of the foul water, after all. No sense dwelling on it. He'd returned to Silent Hill to help her, not stand around imagining the worst.

Wandering away from the contaminated well, he sought his way with the aid of his cellphone's flashlight. The terrain seemed alien in the fog and falling ash. Not that he'd ever spent much time in this area of Silent Hill. And he'd never entered the town via the deer trail. But he had expected to get his bearings by following the familiar landmarks. Instead, anything that might have helped him find his way back to the Woodside Apartments was rendered invisible by the blanket of fog coating the town.

Fortunately, the path ahead remained relatively straightforward, bordered by pine trees on the left and a split rail fence on his right, and no unexpected forks. Continuing to proceed with caution, he soon came upon a dual-swing, wrought-iron gate braced by old stone pillars, damp to the touch and filigreed with pale green moss. The left side of the gate had fallen out of true and dragged against the ground, but the right side swung open despite a low squeal of protest from rusty hinges.

Beyond the gate, the trees fell away exposing a grassy meadow. He turned slowly, in a full circle, light facing outward, trying to pierce the veil of fog to locate the continuation of the trail or at least find the boundaries of the meadow. Drifting wisps of fog seemed determined to obscure the way forward.

Murmuring voices carried to him, but the fog kept the speakers hidden as well. Yet the longer he listened, the harder it became to tell from which direction the voices emanated.

"Hello?" James called. "Hey. Is somebody there?"

Again, he held himself still, straining to hear the voices. He couldn't make out individual words, but there were multiple speakers, all female, and—he heard the whisper of a child speaking so quietly he could almost believe he'd imagined it. The fog made it all too easy for his imagination to run wild. He began to wonder if he'd heard the voices at all. More than likely his mind was filling the sensory gaps with nonsense.

He whispered to himself, "Get a grip, James."

Footfalls shuffled behind him.

He whirled around, shining his light for all the good it—

A young woman appeared out of the fog, early thirties if James had to guess. Pale features untouched by makeup, shoulder-length dark brown hair disheveled, baggy clothing worn and frayed. She wore a dark gray, long-sleeved sweater over light gray pants. Between her bland, unassuming appearance and the lack of any color in her wardrobe, she could have been the physical manifestation of the fog. But she seemed real enough, holding her hands up before her eyes to shield them from the light of his cellphone.

"Oh. Hey," James said, almost as unsure of her as she seemed of him. He lowered the light. "Sorry, I didn't mean to scare you—"

"Was gonna say the same thing," she replied matter-of-factly, walking off to the side to hoist a sandbag from an orderly pile of them. "Grab a bag?"

"What?"

She waved a hand across the row of sandbags, as if explaining a simple concept to a slow student. "Careful," she warned. "They're heavy."

When in Rome, he thought and shrugged. Switching off the flashlight, he shoved the cellphone in his pocket and picked up a sandbag. He followed her since she appeared to know where she was going.

"I'm James, by the way."

"Angela," she said, with a glance over her shoulder as she navigated her way between cement headstones.

James belatedly realized the wrought-iron gates had been the entrance to the Silent Hill cemetery. *I should have known that,* he thought, but couldn't pinpoint why. "I can't believe how lost I am," he confessed. "Used to know this place like the back of my hand."

"Easy to get lost with all this—" She moved her head side to side since she couldn't gesture with her hands full. A few moments later, she dropped her sandbag on a pile of others already two feet high.

"Where's it all coming from?"

She turned to face him. "Started with the fires in the summer. Tore through the forests."

As James wove his way between headstones, he felt a sudden chill race down his spine and stumbled, almost dropping the sandbag right there. He took a moment, staring at the bag in his arms, before proceeding. Once he neared the row of sandbags, he saw that beyond that barrier, the cemetery was flooded, headstones partially submerged. If the flood zone spread much farther, Toluca Lake would swallow the dead.

"Some are still burning," Angela continued. "Then came the rains."

"Right..." James replied absently, laying his sandbag down beside hers as he stared at the half-submerged gravestones, reflected in the stagnant water. "Do you know how I get into town from here? I need to find someone."

"You won't," she said, again matter-of-factly. "Sorry to say it. The floods overran the water treatment plant. When your water gets contaminated, people don't tend to stick around."

James stared at the devastation. A stone angel sculpture leaned precipitously, the soil beneath it eroded by the flood waters. Made sense that the well water was no longer potable. But that sign had been posted for a while, which meant any remediation plans had been delayed or discarded.

"How long did you live here?"

"Short while," James said. "This is nothing like I remember." He took a deep breath. "Look—I'm still gonna try and head into town."

"If you knew this place like it was," she said, "you won't like what you see."

Her attempts to warn him off fell on deaf ears. James was not about to be dissuaded from finding Mary, regardless of what had changed in Silent Hill. If anything, he was becoming impatient to be on his way.

"Is there any way you can tell me which way I should be walking?"

Placing both hands on her hips, she looked him in the eyes as if weighing his determination by appearance alone. "I'm not doing a very good job of talking you out of this, am I?"

James flashed a smile. "Afraid not."

She sighed, gave a little shake of her head. "You see that chapel?"

James looked in the direction indicated and, surprisingly, the fog had cleared enough that he could make out the outline of a building in the distance. He nodded.

"Go past it," she continued. "Walk about... five hundred feet, then you go right. Shouldn't take you more than ten minutes."

"Okay," he said. "Thanks."

"You don't find who you're looking for, you can always come back and find me."

"Sure," James said, humoring her. Unless she was the cemetery caretaker and lived nearby, she would be long gone before he ever returned. He turned toward the chapel, now no more than a shadow in the fog, and strode toward it.

Before he'd walked more than several steps away, he thought he heard her talking to herself. "I can already tell," she whispered, "he won't leave before dark."

James turned to take one last look at her, but she'd already wandered off to gather another sandbag and been swallowed by the fog. Returning his attention to the path ahead, he followed the bank of the river. But as soon as he left Angela behind, the whispering voices returned. He wondered if Angela heard them too. Did she speak to them? Did they answer her? He had the sense they followed him, but whoever they were, they remained hidden by the fog. A couple times, he tried to walk toward the source of the murmuring, shining his light left and right, but discovered no one. He reminded himself to stay on the path, and not let anything distract him or lead him astray. He couldn't get lost again. And since their words were unintelligible, nothing more than random murmuring, they were easy to ignore, though slightly unnerving. Once they realized they couldn't get a reaction out of him, they fell quiet, leaving him in the eerie silence of a world with soft edges.

As Angela had estimated, he reached the chapel within ten minutes, its shadowy presence in the fog slowly gaining substance. Beside the chapel, was a field of long grass, coated in ash that continued to fall from the sky. Like the rest area overlooking Toluca Lake, the field had been neglected for a while, cluttered with trash and overgrown with weeds.

Nothing like he remembered...

CHAPTER 4

A dazzling late summer sun blazed against the white walls of the chapel and bathed the meadow beside it in golden light. James had stood his easel in the meadow with a medium-sized canvas on it to capture the chapel in the late morning light but had changed his plans when Mary agreed to pose for the painting. Now her face occupied the foreground while the chapel became part of the background.

Initially, they had planned a picnic outing, although it was more of a spontaneous decision than a proper plan. Mary had loaded the trunk of the car with a picnic basket, a bottle of wine, and a blanket. Then they had stopped at the Grand Market for premade mixed salads, fresh fruit, assorted nuts, and blueberry muffins. But James always carried art supplies in the Mustang in case inspiration struck. After they had set out the blanket and enjoyed most of the food, James had the urge to capture the chapel, perhaps to remember a perfect day.

"What about me?" Mary asked playfully. "Don't you want to remember me?"

"Oh, I could never forget you," James replied. But she was serious. "You really want to pose for this? Here? Now?" She nodded quickly, smiling.

With the painting drying in the sun, they lay on their backs in the long grass. Butterflies and diurnal moths fluttered in lazy arcs among the wildflowers. While dragonflies darted here and there, intent on unknown agendas, foraging birds provided musical commentary to the proceedings. James stared up into the deep blue sky, his left arm under Mary's shoulders as she curled against him. He couldn't remember a time he'd been happier.

"You look a million miles away," she said, her breath tickling his ear.

"Not true," he said. "No place I'd rather be than right here with you."

"Aw, that's sweet," she said, wrapping her left arm across his chest and giving him a squeeze as she gave him a peck on the cheek. She wore a short-sleeved sundress with an open neckline, white with a crisp floral patten, perfectly suited to the summer meadow.

He turned toward her, staring into her twinkling blue eyes.

"What?" she said, rising slightly, abruptly self-conscious. "Do I have a piece of spinach in my teeth?"

He chuckled. "Your teeth are fine," he said. "I was thinking..."

"First time for everything."

"Harsh."

"Sorry," she said, unable to suppress a grin. "I meant to say, 'What were you thinking, good sir?'"

"Better," he said, nodding.

"Well...? Don't keep me hanging."

"What if I moved here?"

"To this sleepy little burg?" she asked, surprised. "No museums. No clubs. Zero anonymity."

"I'm just as shocked as you are."

She drew back slightly, assessing him. "You'd really want to move here?"

"I would."

With a slight frown, she asked, "Why?"

"Well, there's this girl," he began. "She's not much to look at but—"

"Oh, really—?"

He leaned in, placed a hand on her cheek, and kissed her, stilling her feigned protest. She returned the kiss for a few moments but pulled back before it developed into something more serious. He sensed concern in her eyes, noticed her lips pressed together, hesitant about voicing her thoughts.

"You don't think we're ready to live together?"

That caught her attention. She pulled farther away, sitting up and turning to face him from a less vulnerable position. "Now you want to live together?"

"You can't keep me locked up at the Lakeview forever."

She looked away, staring off into the distance, gathering her thoughts before she returned his gaze. "It's a big step, James," she said. "You don't even know me."

"You say that like it's a bad thing," James replied.

"This place…" She furrowed her brow. "It changes you."

Cold feet. James understood. Moving in together was a big step in any relationship. But he was certain he could win her over. "It's okay, Mary. I can handle it."

"There are parts of me, James. Parts of me you haven't seen."

The playful banter completely gone, she stared into his eyes, locked in, her demeanor charged with emotion, almost as if trying to impart an unspoken warning. Everyone had a few bad habits or idiosyncrasies that wouldn't cast them in the best light early in a relationship. That was human nature. But he couldn't imagine finding out anything that would change his mind about her. He was all in.

She took his hand in both of hers. "What if who I am scares you?"

James smiled and shook his head. "It won't," he said, brimming with more confidence than he had ever felt. "I promise you. It won't."

And with that, the tension drained from her face. Though he had no reason to doubt his power of persuasion, James believed Mary wanted him to have faith in her, and in what they were forging together. He had no issue carrying that responsibility.

Smiling, she grabbed the lapels of his open long-sleeved shirt and pulled him in for a kiss, this one delivering on the impassioned promise of the first. With his hands on the back of her shoulders, warm from the sun, he pulled her down to the picnic blanket and felt the luxuriousness of her body pressed against his.

A moment later, he felt a drop of moisture strike his cheek. He swiped at it with his fingers and opened his eyes, looking at Mary, then at his fingers—smeared with blood. Concerned, he eased her back slightly to examine her face. "Mary—"

She looked a question at him before noticing the blood-smeared fingers he kept away from her sundress, then her own fingers went to her nose.

"Here, I got you," James said, pushing himself upright while she sat back on her heels. "Tilt your head back. I got you—"

James retrieved an unused cloth from his wooden paint kit nearby, dabbed at her face to clear the blood, then pinched her nose to stop the flow. He shook his head, chuckled softly.

"What's so funny?" she asked, sounding as if she were congested.

"This is not how I expected that to go."

She laughed, testing her nose by dabbing it with the cloth. "Gotta keep you on your toes, mister," she said. "Besides, I wouldn't be too concerned on that account, if I were you."

"And why is that?"

She ran a hand through his hair, cupping the back of his neck as she held his gaze. "The day is still young," she said mischievously. "And we have all the time in the world."

CHAPTER 5

The smile triggered by the fond memory of Mary's and his summer together slipped away as James confronted the new reality, embodied by the fog-shrouded field and falling ash. He proceeded along the path to the official entrance of the town, pausing to read the white-lettered green sign, its paint flaking away, the wood worm-eaten.

Ahead, through the omnipresent fog, the outlines of buildings along Market Street began to emerge. A few steps along the paved street, he stopped again, looking around. Not a person in sight. "Hello!" he called, though the fog muffled his voice. "Is anybody here?"

"Something's happened."

Mary's words. A warning without an explanation.

How is this possible? It made no sense: a small town once

filled with life but now seemingly deserted, if not for the self-appointed caretaker of the cemetery, and the murmuring ghosts of those displaced from their final resting place.

Yet, he remained determined to forge ahead. He couldn't give up on Mary until he'd exhausted all other possibilities. He'd search the entire town if necessary. If she'd left, she would have found a way to let him know, by note or by messenger. Why ask for his help, ask him to come here, if she'd planned on abandoning Silent Hill?

James walked down Market Street, veering from one side to the other, peering in shop windows, looking for employees or customers—anyone who might have information about what had happened to the town or, more specifically, if anyone had seen Mary. Odds were, anyone he'd meet would know Mary Crane, or at least know of her. She'd warned him once about 'zero anonymity' in Silent Hill and, considering who her father was and what he'd meant to the town, she might almost be considered a local celebrity.

Everywhere he looked, he found signs of abandonment and neglect. He wiped ash from the display window of a flower shop, cupped his eyes and peered through the glass. All the visible plants and flowers were dead and rotting, a few vases overturned or broken.

A nearby deli had become the restaurant of choice for Silent Hill's fly population, with hundreds of them swarming over rotting meat and moldy bread. The door was unlocked, but he had no desire to unleash the stench swirling inside. He rapped on the door, waited for a response, shook his head and walked away.

By comparison, the bookshop across the street appeared relatively normal. But all the books, whether on shelves, tables or in window displays, were coated in a thick layer of dust that rendered the volumes untitled and anonymous. In a few spots, books had fallen to the floor in random piles, but those were equally blanketed in dust.

James found the door ajar, so pushed it open to look around. The fog had crept inside here as well, rendering the far corners of the store amorphous. The layer of dust on the floor by the counter and down the main aisle was undisturbed. Nobody had been inside this place in a long time.

He stepped outside again and walked down the middle of Market Street. No need to use the sidewalk when there was no vehicular traffic. Cars parked on the street all wore a thick coating of falling ash, long abandoned by their owners. He passed the Silent Hill movie theater, a second-run venue at the best of times. The marquee advertised midnight shows of *Jacob's Ladder* and *The Tenant*, but the security grille had been pulled down and the aluminum bars wore the familiar thick coating of ash.

James cupped his hands around his mouth and turned in a slow circle as he shouted, "Hey! HEY!"

Silence.

"IS ANYONE THERE?"

He dropped his hands to his hips and shook his head. Had everyone left town, as Angela had suggested? Or were they hiding, holed up somewhere, awaiting assistance maybe, from the county or state.

He continued along Market Street with only occasional glances at closed shops and their darkened windows. Nobody was 'open for business.' But something up ahead caught his attention. Temporary fencing, some sort of blockade and scaffolding, with tarps draped over certain sections, falling in others. Then he saw the red sign with black lettering and the familiar trefoil symbol:

As James stared at the sign in confusion and more than a modicum of fear—*what the hell happened here*?—he heard the sound of shuffling feet. Almost relieved that he wasn't the only person in the entire town, he turned around. Finally, someone—

What he saw did not seem human.

At least, that was his first, brief impression. It walked on two awkwardly splayed legs, as if learning to mimic human ambulation, but it had no arms, its face turned away from James. With each step, its body seemed agitated, trembling uncontrollably, as if suffering in silent torment.

As quickly as James glimpsed the armless creature, it disappeared into a nearby alley, beyond the scaffolding and barricades.

"Hey!"

James rushed after the figure, whoever or whatever it was, and turned into the alley. Too narrow to accommodate any motor vehicle larger than a motorcycle, the alley was strewn with litter and overturned trashcans. Ahead, a mound of trash moved left to right, something tunneling under it, accompanied by a chittering sound. Forced to watch his footing, James lost sight of the armless figure at the far end of the alley. Though he blamed his overactive imagination, it seemed as if the walls above him were closing in, forcing him to turn sideways to continue. In red paint, someone had sprayed a message on the soot-stained brick wall at eye level: *Run away*!

A nearby trashcan, lying on its side, started to roll in front of him as something crawled its way out. The size of a New York City rat, it had a chitinous body and six segmented legs, freakishly fast as it scuttled across James' shoe toward the wall on his left. Then, reconsidering its retreat, it spun around, dropped from the wall and rushed James.

"What the fuck!"

Before he could react, it had scrambled over his shoe again, but this time began to climb up the leg of his jeans. Repulsed, he swatted it from his leg with a backhand sweep of his hand, not wanting to touch the damn thing. It struck the wall and fell to the ground, scrambling for purchase. This time James didn't hesitate. He stomped on it with the heel of his shoe, repeatedly, until the broken legs and the wavering antennas stopped twitching.

On the lookout for more of the creepy insects, James edged his way down the rest of the alley, glancing in all directions the few times he heard chittering nearby. He recalled what people said about roaches: for every cockroach you see, a hundred more are hiding. Not wanting to find out if that were true for whatever the hell he had just squashed underfoot, he exited the alley—

—and found himself in a small yard.

"The hell…?"

Again, he heard the shuffling sound of the armless creature and caught another glimpse of it a moment before it was swallowed by the ashen fog. "Hey!" James called again as he followed it onto Main Street.

He couldn't remember a time when Main Street had looked so desolate. Not a soul in sight. Back when he'd lived in Silent Hill, long after midnight, when only a bar or two remained open, he would have found a few shift workers and insomniacs walking on Main Street. Now he saw no one.

Frustrated, he shouted into the blanketing fog. "Is anyone there?"

A shifting black mass on the side of the road broke apart—a flock of black birds shrieking as they took flight, alighting on nearby wires and rooftops. On the ground where they had clustered, James saw the gutted and eyeless remains of a massive rat, entrails strewn across the pavement. Above him, shifting foot to foot, the scavenger birds waited impatiently to resume their meal.

James gave the decomposing rat a wide berth and continued down Main Street in the direction the armless creature had taken. Before long, he heard music playing, faint, something classical. As he neared the source, he identified it as Bach's Aria from Suite 3 in D major, a piece he remembered listening to years ago and, for some reason, it always made him melancholy. Following the sound of the music led him to a building with more multi-story scaffolding and hanging tarps, construction buckets, and wire cases holding various lengths of unused pipes. In the center of the scaffolding was an unobstructed vaulted passageway, cloaked in shadows, its highest point still low enough that he had to hunch over to enter.

Once inside the archway, his eyes adjusted to the dim light, and he spotted a small radio—the source of the music—atop a corroded 55-gallon steel drum. As he walked toward the radio, he heard a growl. But the source of this sound was human. A pile of what he had assumed were discarded rags and blankets shifted and moved, lying on a bed of cardboard, emitting a distressed moan.

"Hey," James called as he approached. "Hey. Are you all right?"

Rising to his elbows, a homeless man with matted hair and an unkempt beard stared at James with wide, frightened eyes.

"Can you hear me? Are you okay?"

The man, who was probably in his thirties but, due to his circumstances, had not aged well, wore a knit hat, a distressed puffer vest over a stained jean jacket and fingerless gloves. His mouth moved in a feeble attempt to speak, revealing yellowed and rotting teeth. Large pustules and open sores, some of them leaking yellowish fluid, covered his left cheek and his exposed neck.

The foul odor wafting up from the man's distressed breathing caused James to keep him at arm's length. "Where'd everyone go?"

Before the man could attempt to answer, James heard a shuffling sound and looked back the way he'd come, in time to see movement, someone or something crossing in front of the passageway's entrance. At the same time, the radio squawked and squealed, with a burst of static.

The homeless man grabbed James by the collar of his jacket, his dirty fingers and blackened fingernails almost skeletal. James tried to pull away, but the man held fast and spoke in a rush, his voice hoarse from disuse.

"They're coming back. You know they're coming back. All that darkness, you can't keep it away—"

Horrified, James stared at the man's sunken jawline: greenish-black flesh, maggots burrowing in and out of pits and divots in the ruined skin. Gangrene had set in.

"Who?" James asked, unable to look away. "Who's coming back? What the hell happened here?"

James felt his gorge rise as a cockroach emerged from the man's tangled hair, scrambled across his diseased face, crawled down his neck and disappeared into his stained undershirt.

If you see one cockroach…

"Let me go," James said, repulsed. He tugged on the man's palsied hand, locked in a death grip on his collar, until he yanked it free.

"I'm gonna get some help," James said, backing away. The man was too far gone to be a source of any reliable information. "Just—stay there."

The man rose up, in a feeble attempt to stand and follow, but couldn't get past one knee. Instead, he wailed after James, "Leave. You have to leave. We should have left. Leave!"

Nodding, James turned away from the man and vacated the dim passageway and was finally able to stand upright again. He massaged the crick out of his neck and looked both ways along the deserted, ash-covered street. His phone rang, startling him.

M again.

He accepted the call.

"Hey—"

Before he could go on, she interrupted him. "I know we've been through a lot, but I wasn't expecting a no-show, James."

He'd completely forgotten his promise yesterday to come in today. That seemed so long ago—and immaterial now. "Listen," he said. "I'm in Silent Hill—"

"What?" It wasn't that she'd misheard him. The disbelief—and disappointment— was evident in her voice.

"Something's happened here—something really, really bad has happened."

"James—" disbelief and disappointment were clear in her voice. "Listen to me carefully. This is getting out of control—"

"There was a note. From Mary—she's in trouble—"

But M was unwilling to listen to his reasoning. Over the staticky connection, he heard her shuffling papers and tapping computer keys as she spoke. "I'm clearing my schedule. I need you to come back. Come in. I can help you with this—"

Phone against his cheek, James had already stopped listening. Down the street, a flickering red neon sign had stolen his attention. Winking on and off, like a beacon on a distant shore, the neon sign spelled out two words: *Heaven's Night*.

"I have to go—"

"James—"

He disconnected the call.

Mesmerized by the pull of the sign, he shoved the phone in his pocket and strode down the street with renewed purpose.

Heaven's Night was a red brick building that had been converted from a storage warehouse to a nightclub. As he neared the establishment, James picked up his pace until he stood before the twin doors with matching chevron patterns beneath a double row of transom windows. Those windows and the red brick walls were blanketed with ash, as were the metal trashcans on either side of the entranceway.

The neon sign flickered one last time, then stayed dark.

He checked the long windows on either side of the doors, attempting to peer inside, but they were hopelessly caked with ash on the outside and dust on the inside. His attempt to wipe the ash away only smeared it, further obscuring anything that might have been visible from the street. So, he returned to the double doors, gripped the doorknob on the right and pushed it open—

CHAPTER 6

As soon as James stepped through the doorway of Heaven's Night, music playing from wall-mounted speakers competed with the babble of dozens of overlapping conversations. The size of the bustling crowd nearly overwhelmed him. He'd never seen so many Silent Hill residents gathered in one place. After a few moments, he acclimated to his surroundings and stepped forward expectantly.

The golden light of the setting sun streamed through the second story windows opposite the front entrance, making every wooden surface gleam as if freshly polished and casting everyone in attendance in a warm, welcoming light. The first floor was wide and open with a central gathering space, the perimeter filled with high two-seat tables and leather armchairs. A partial mezzanine level, to the left and straight ahead, provided additional seating in front of the tall windows. Mounted high on the right, flush with the wall, was a bank of television monitors, all currently showing the same baseball game even though there were enough screens to televise every major league matchup simultaneously. To the left, the bar was a modest size, but several servers circulated around the tables on the first floor and mezzanine level to keep the drinks flowing.

James had arrived later than intended, hesitant to leave a painting in progress while dissatisfied with the current state of the work, then because he had trouble deciding what to wear to meet Mary's circle of friends for the first time. She'd told him to keep it casual, but there were degrees of casual. In hindsight, his frustration with the painting had probably been a result of anxiety over the impending evaluation by the friend group. He was determined to make a better first impression with them than he had with Mary, although he'd managed to recover from nearly running her down with his car. A casual gathering over drinks should be a snap after that.

He'd settled on a lavender dress shirt with a darker smudge pattern—open at the neck, cuffs rolled back over his forearms—paired with a black undershirt, black trousers and brown loafers, accessorized with a pair of medallion necklaces and black rawhide bracelets.

Weaving his way past small tables and the milling crowd, he noticed people openly staring at him, some whispering to others with their backs turned who then glanced over their shoulders to peek at the new stranger in town. Mary had mentioned Silent Hill was a close-knit community where privacy came at a premium, so he couldn't say she hadn't warned him. *Let them look,* he thought, reminded of the old aphorism: today's news is tomorrow's fish wrap. They'd forget about him soon enough.

Meanwhile, he spotted Mary standing among a cluster of people whose attention all focused on her, to the exclusion of everyone around them. Probably grilling her about him before he arrived. She wore a shirred, bronze-colored maxi-dress with an open neck over a long-sleeved black turtleneck with a wide gold choker. The full effect of the setting sun cast her in a warm, vibrant glow as she stood at the center of her friends' collective orbit. She took his breath away.

She must have sensed his unabashed stare of admiration, because her attention shifted abruptly, her gaze flicking from her friends to lock onto him. Flashing James a generous, welcoming smile, she slipped past her group with a quick apology and hurried over to meet him. Taking his hand, she leaned in and gave him a quick peck on the cheek. Lips close to his ear, she whispered in a sing-song tone, "You're late."

"You're lovely."

"Thought you stood me up."

"I considered leaving town."

She chuckled. "They're not that bad. Come on over. I'll introduce you."

He sighed. "The things we do for love."

She continued to hold his hand—

For moral support? Or worried I might try to escape?

—as she led him into the circle of her friends. The group of seven fanned out so they could all face the new couple, which transformed the previous circle into a semi-circle. They each flashed tentative smiles and held curious expressions, trying to act as if the situation was completely normal even though they had basically closed ranks around the couple. Everyone had a drink in matching glasses except for one woman, who held a black kitten wearing a collar adorned with a striped bow tie.

Before Mary could make introductions, James turned toward her and whispered in her ear. "There's a cat in the bar, Mary. A cat. In a bar."

She raised her glass a bit, nodding to the group, to distract from the elbow she playfully poked in his side. The unspoken message was clear: best behavior now!

She cleared her throat and said, "Everyone, this is James."

A pair of women in their forties stepped forward slightly; the first had a bleached blond punk pixie haircut and wore a black pantsuit. "James," she said. "I'm Dara. And this is Kaitlyn."

Kaitlyn, who might have been her sister or partner, flashed a smile and offered her hand, which James shook. She wore her dark hair up under a scarf, a silky black blouse with opaque long sleeves, a spider broach at the collar, and black slacks. "So wonderful to meet you."

Next up were Cal and Mitzy, a married couple. Cal was bald and fit, early forties. With his glasses, and ash brown blazer over a black turtleneck, he had a professorial demeanor. "Good to meet you," he said as they shook hands.

Mitzy appeared several years younger than her husband, had a ready smile, and wore an open ivory cardigan with fine patterned borders and floral accents over a black turtleneck and voluminous black slacks. Rather than shake hands, she gave him a welcoming nod and smile.

Two women, identical twins in their forties, had drifted back a bit, occasionally glancing awkwardly at James. They both had full bangs, but one had shoulder-length, bright red hair, while the other had longer brunette hair. Both wore short-sleeved navy blouses with Peter Pan collars, but the redhead's had three mock buttons on hers, the brunette's had a bow. As they seemed reluctant to step forward, Mary waved an arm in their direction.

"The Meyers twins," Mary said. "Don't be shy. Come say 'hi.'"

The redhead stepped forward, the brunette in her wake, and shook James' hand quickly. "Hey, there!"

"Hi!" James replied.

"Same," said the brunette, with an even quicker handshake.

Then they both drifted back beyond the others.

Lastly, Mary turned to the cat lady. "And this is Claudette—"

"Don't forget Boo," Claudette said, stroking the kitten's head with one hand and holding the cat against her chest with the other. She wore glasses—cat eye frames, naturally—a long mint green jacket over a cream-colored blouse and bronze colored slacks.

At this point, James had kept a smile plastered on his face so long, he worried it had transformed into a grimace. He glanced at Mary, eyes wide, hoping for a lifeline. She stepped close and slipped an arm around his waist.

"Well, that was—"

"A lot—" James said, then added quickly, "—of people to meet all at once."

"I think he needs something to drink, Mary," Cal suggested.

"Of course," Mary said. She looked to a nearby server, who had been standing close to the group, unlike the other servers, who continually circulated from bar to tables and standing groups, taking orders and collecting empty glasses and bottles. The hovering server immediately approached Mary.

"What can I get you?" she asked.

"My friend needs a drink," Mary said.

"I'll have a bourbon," James said when she looked at him. "Neat."

With a quick nod, the server immediately made her way to the bar, ignoring calls and hand gestures for refills from the patrons she passed. James was about to comment on her single-mindedness when Claudette sidled into his line of sight.

"So, Mary tells me you're an artist."

"Painter," James replied. "Yes."

"And you have the perfect muse," Claudette replied. With her chin hovering over the black kitten's head, she whispered, "You hear that, Boo? He's a painter."

James stared at the cat again, trying to wrap his head around its presence in a bar. "Excuse me, but is that a therapy cat or something?"

"Aren't they all?" Claudette said, smiling at him.

"Ah," Dara said, ignoring Claudette's fawning over Boo. "All coming together now."

Turning away from Claudette and her cat, James asked, "How do you mean?"

Absently stroking the spider broach at her collar, Kaitlyn

answered for her, "You wanting to move to Silent Hill. No shortage of beautiful things to paint."

"I second that—" Dara said, but her eyes were focused on the other woman, not James. She took Kaitlyn's hand and gave it a soft kiss. Kaitlyn chuckled, slightly embarrassed at the attention in a public setting.

Mary had moved close to James' side. He exchanged a look with her. *Well, that settles that question*, he thought. Focusing on the paired women again, James said, "It's a special place."

Mitzy nodded, took a sip of her drink, then looked from Mary to James. "How'd you two meet?" she asked.

Mary pressed her lips together, cast her eyes downward.

James caught her reaction but couldn't make sense of it. Maybe she'd been embarrassed to mention his reckless driving and luggage demolition. That certainly didn't cast him in the best light, and she might worry they would disapprove of him as boyfriend material. Friends could be overprotective.

"Kind of a crazy story," James said. "I was heading up the pass. Friend told me about some of the vistas." He opted for a condensed version of their meeting. "Hit a pothole on the way. Almost ran her down."

Kaitlyn looked shocked, pressing her hand to her chest, but for some reason, he wasn't sure if the reaction was genuine or overly theatrical. He didn't know these people well enough to recognize their tells.

"My God," she said. "And where did this take place?"

"Up on the highway. Near the rest stop."

Dara looked toward Mary, who had been avoiding eye contact with any of them while James spoke. "Wow," Dara said. "What were you doing all the way up there?"

James picked up on Mary's anxiety, the compression of her lips, an almost brittle smile before she spoke. He thought she worried about them judging him for reckless driving, but they seemed more concerned about her role than his. She interlaced her fingers with his and squeezed. Reflexively, he squeezed back. Her palm was damp.

"Nothing," Mary said nonchalantly, with a quick glance at James. "Was hoping to spend the day in the city—"

Dara and Kaitlyn shared a quick, subtle look with the rest of the friend group. If James hadn't been confused about Mary's reaction to the questions, he probably wouldn't have noticed it. He was missing part of the story, but recognized he needed to ask Mary when the two of them were alone.

"Instead, we went to the Lakeview," James said. "Sat at the bar." He glanced at Mary with an expectant look. She caught on and nodded, smiling. "Talked until we got kicked out."

James knew Mary hadn't told them the whole truth about why she'd been at that bus stop. One doesn't need two suitcases and a toiletry kit for a day trip into the city to do some window shopping. At the same time, she'd never told him why she'd been ready to hop on that bus. She'd obviously intended to travel a few days, minimum. Impromptu vacation? No hard plans or reservations. Just a carefree trip. Maybe. At the time, he was simply grateful she'd changed her mind about leaving.

Of course, how they'd spent their time at the rooftop bar of the Lakeview Hotel, and what came after, became a secret he chose to keep…

CHAPTER 7

By the time they'd driven into Silent Hill and arrived at Mary's apartment building, the impending storm seemed to have cleared. Not wanting their chance meeting to end so soon, James suggested Mary show him the view of Toluca Lake from atop the Lakeview. Mary had readily agreed, leaning into her role as his Silent Hill tour guide.

He had to admit the view was spectacular. They ordered drinks and sat at one of the many bisque-colored wrought-iron table sets, near one of matching patio umbrellas scattered across the terrace. They had indeed talked and joked and laughed, enjoying each other's company until sunset. At some point, James had intentionally grazed the back of her hand with his, testing the waters, and she had, without hesitation, taken his hand in hers, smiling warmly as she stared into his eyes.

A flash of lightning arced across the sky, followed almost immediately by a crack of thunder, startling them both out of the moment. Apparently, the summer storm hadn't quite finished with Silent Hill after all. And even if the bartender hadn't advised everyone to clear the rooftop during a lightning storm, the ensuing downpour provided a compelling argument. As James and Mary rushed toward the stairwell entrance, laughing at the sudden turn of events, James spread his jacket over Mary's head to protect her from the worst of the rain.

Breathless, they paused inside the shelter of the stairwell to face each other, dripping wet despite their haste in fleeing the storm: another extended moment, heady with potential, albeit less dignified, where they had trouble taking their eyes off each other. James reached out and brushed a wet strand of hair from her face. She smiled at him, invitingly. He leaned in for a kiss. She reached up, taking his face gently in her hands, and met him halfway. As she stepped closer, he wrapped his arms around her waist. And she pressed her body into his. While kissing him on the cheek, she whispered in his ear, "If you'd like to extend your stay in Silent Hill… I've heard the rooms here are really nice."

CHAPTER 8

Lost in the reverie, James was slow to notice everyone had fallen quiet. Mary and her friends stood around, absently looking into their glasses, or casting gazes across the crowded bar, people watching. Standing farther away from the others, but close to each other, the Meyer twins bobbed their heads in time with the music. Mary looked up and her eyes widened.

"Oh, here's your drink," Mary said, grateful for the interruption.

James followed her gaze and took the glass of bourbon from the server with a grateful nod and smile. If he hadn't needed a shot of liquid courage earlier, he welcomed it now. He took a sip, enjoying the sweet flavor, with hints of caramel and vanilla.

"I'm just glad I stayed," Mary said. "Whole thing felt like fate..."

Kaitlyn, Dara and the others all nodded in agreement, appreciating the sentiment. For the moment, at least, the tension between Mary and her friends had been broken. Another group of people, threading their way through the standing crowd to find a table, nodded and smiled at Mary as they passed. James couldn't help but notice the special attention they paid to her at the expense of the others. Mary was special to him. Apparently, a lot of other people shared his opinion of her.

"Our Mary," Kaitlyn said. "She's something special."

Dara placed a hand lightly on Mary's shoulder. "Knew it since she was a young girl."

"Sparkling little apple of her father's eye," Claudette said with a chuckle.

Intrigued, James asked, "You all knew him?"

"Knowing Joshua Crane—" Dara began. "It doesn't quite do it justice when you say it out loud."

This exchange caught the attention of the drifting Meyers twins, who both spoke simultaneously. "He changed our lives."

"In stereo," James said good-naturedly. "Wow."

They laughed, nodding toward each other.

"Mary's family," Dara said, her tone more serious, "they built this town. Gave us purpose."

"That's—" Mary gave a small shake of her head and turned to James. "They're being kind—"

"My life was spinning out in all directions," Cal interrupted. "Joshua Crane helped me get my head back on straight."

"Think we all have a similar story," his wife added, looking to the others for consensus.

"Only time in my life I felt like there was someone looking after me," Kaitlyn said.

Dara leaned back and gave Kaitlyn a comically appraising look. "What? I'm chopped liver?"

Kaitlyn rolled her eyes and gave Dara a playful elbow. "You know what I mean," she replied, then turned to James. "Mary's father taught us to look out for one another."

Despite their earlier reticence, Mary's friends clearly all agreed on one thing wholeheartedly. Joshua Crane was without peer. When he turned toward Mary to see her reaction to all the flattery of her father, she no longer appeared slightly embarrassed about the talk. She seemed nervous.

Claudette looked up from fiddling with the bow on Boo's collar. "We have a way of seeing things here in Silent Hill."

"And how's that?" James asked.

Mary waved a hand in front of the group. "I'm not sure we really need to get into this—"

"No, it's all right," James said. "I want to hear it."

Until now, he'd viewed Silent Hill through a Mary lens. Other than the Lakeview Hotel staff, he hadn't conversed with any of the town's residents beyond the usual pleasantries. For the most part, he'd been isolated in his long-term stay at the hotel. When inspired, he tended to fall into creative binges where sleep, food, and socializing fell by the wayside. Sometimes he'd come up for air and realize he was ravenous. Or he'd be painting for hours and only remember he hadn't slept when the sun came up. But this time, Mary had been the focus of his stay in Silent Hill, to the exclusion of everything else. And when he couldn't see her, he turned his attention to the next canvas. He had no true sense of the town where she lived, so all the talk of her father, whom she rarely mentioned herself, had him intrigued.

"We've always felt like it was us against the world," Dara said. "But don't worry—"

"I'm sure we'll find a place for you—" Kaitlyn added.

Dara nodded. "Even if you are on the outside looking in."

James was taken aback by Dara's words, and it must have shown on his face, because Kaitlyn flashed a broad smile and said, "A toast!"

Everyone raised their glasses.

"To your new adventures in Silent Hill."

The circle tightened as everyone except James said, "Cheers." They each tapped James' glass in turn. The process took a few seconds, which caused him to notice all the glasses were identical—except his. And they all drank the same dark, almost black, liquor unlike the rich mahogany color of his bourbon. Reminded him of the black vodka he'd seen people drink once on Halloween, a few years back. Maybe this group had their own special blend of whiskey flavored with black licorice.

As everyone sipped their strangely dark beverages, James took a gulp of his bourbon. Aside from the continual music playing, he noticed conversations had gone quiet and, as he glanced around, he got the eerie sense that everyone in attendance had been staring at Mary's group, more specifically at him, during Kaitlyn's toast. But the moment passed as quickly as it had begun.

Still, James wondered how a lone stranger in town was so novel a concept that everyone had some vested interest in whether the new guy was accepted in some small social circle? The idea seemed ridiculous. Easy for James to believe he had imagined the crowd's scrutiny.

When a slow song began to play through the bar's speaker system, several couples made their way to an area of the first floor reserved for dancing. Mary looped her arm through James' and gave him a playful tug. She leaned in and said, "Take me dancing, sailor."

"Have to warn you," he said. "I'm not known for my dancing."

"So… more small talk?"

"God, no," he exclaimed sotto voce.

She chuckled. "Didn't think so."

With each step they took away from Mary's circle of friends, James felt the tension dissipate, both hers and his. When they were alone together, unburdened by her friends' expectations, she became relaxed and carefree. And James no longer felt the performative pressure of fitting in or being accepted by them as a condition of being with her. They slow-danced with her arms around his neck and his around her waist, close enough that they could speak without shouting, and far enough from her friends that he could indulge his curiosity.

"Well, that was certainly…"

"Odd?" she asked, grinning.

"Interesting."

"No need for diplomacy," Mary said. "They can't hear us."

"Okay, so a little bit… yes, odd," James said. "But I guess they want the best for you."

"I've known them all as long as I can remember," Mary said. "They were my father's… acquaintances before they became my friends."

"Acquaintances?"

With a tilt of her head, Mary indicated that they should move away from a few couples dancing nearby, an area which obstructed the view of them by her friends, who had remained behind, talking to one another. Now that sunset had passed, the lighting in the bar was dim, more intimate.

Once they were swaying together in that more shadowed area of the dance floor, she continued. "More like mentees to his role as mentor. They looked to him for… leadership. Or, really, guidance. He was a… forceful man. Powerful." She sighed. "No offense, but I'd rather not talk about my father. I hear enough about him from everyone else around here."

"Sure," James said. "I get that. What about them?"

"My friends?" He nodded. "What do you want to know about them?"

"Anything," James said. "You know what they say, know your enemy."

She laughed. "They aren't your enemies."

"Know your girlfriend's besties, then."

"Let's see," Mary said. "Cal and Mitzy are married, as you heard. Cal is a lawyer, and Mitzy is a charge nurse at Brookhaven Hospital."

"Ah, sort of a Silent Hill power couple."

"Kaitlyn is a real estate agent, but she moonlights for me at the Fashion Boutique. She's a bit of a clotheshorse and loves the employee discount."

"And she's with Dara?"

"For about a year now," Mary said. "Dara is a detective with the SHPD."

"Important question," James said. "For future reference. Can she fix speeding tickets?"

Mary laughed. "I wouldn't risk asking her, if I were you."

"Noted."

"Let's see," Mary continued. "Claudette is a guidance counselor at Midwich High."

"Bet she loves take your pet to work day."

"Who am I forgetting?"

"The Meyer twins," James said. "Didn't catch their names."

"Mia and Gia," Mary said. "Don't ask me which is which."

James almost stumbled. "Wait—what?"

"I know," Mary said. "It's some weird game they play. Since they were kids. They switch names back and forth. One day Mia answers to 'Gia' and Gia answers to 'Mia.' The day after that they might switch again or stay the same. Who knows? It's like they're one person with two bodies."

"Weird is right."

"They both own and work at Glass & Mirror," Mary said. "One day I stopped by and they had set up a row of full length mirrors facing each other, so when they walked down the main aisle, it looked like there were hundreds of Mias and Gias."

"Yeah, maybe that's enough talk about them."

"Agreed," Mary said with a brisk nod. "Besides, I prefer when it's just the two of us." She gave him a mischievous smile and whispered in his ear, "Wanna get outta here?"

CHAPTER 9

"Yes," James whispered into the silence of Heaven's Night.

He stood inside the entrance, surveying the desolation. Not only was the place abandoned, but all the tables and chairs and support columns were covered in a thick layer of dust. While several tables and chairs had been overturned, other tables held cocktail glasses and beer bottles, also caked with dust. Along with the interior lighting, the wall-mounted television monitors were all dead, a few cracked. And instead of golden sunset light streaming through the mezzanine level windows, grim ash twilight provided insufficient illumination to dispel any but the weakest of shadows inside the bar.

The difference between that night with Mary and her friends and now could not have been more striking. James shook his head in disbelief. He couldn't help wondering where—

Someone screamed, a bellowing wail.

James hurried from Heaven's Night and followed the sound of the ongoing screams along the deserted street. Whoever it was, they had to be close—

Silence.

No, not quite silence. Now that the screaming had stopped, he heard classical music playing softly.

He stood outside the vaulted passageway where he had encountered the homeless man. Of course, it had to be the only person he'd encountered in Silent Hill besides Angela at the cemetery. Ducking his head, he peered into the passageway, dreading a second encounter with the diseased-riddled man, infested with vermin. For all James knew, the man was contagious...

As his eyes adjusted, he saw the man's body, sprawled face down far from his makeshift cardboard bed. But something was wrong—

"Jesus," he whispered.

The body—lying in the middle of a pool of a black tar-like substance—was dissolving. Like acid, the black fluid ate through the layers of the man's tattered clothing as well as his diseased flesh. The homeless man appeared to be sinking into the ground itself, an illusion exposed by the bubbling and hissing of the acid as it made quick work of his corpse. In the man's outstretched right hand, clutched in his skeletal fingers, was the small radio, still playing music. Beyond the man, the construction barrel lay on its side. Again, James was left wondering—

Abruptly, the music distorted, interrupted by squeals, squelches and short bursts of static.

Familiar shuffling footsteps sounded behind him.

Turning, James saw a long silhouette emerge from the fog and falling ash, naked and armless, vaguely feminine, its body trembling and twitching on splayed legs. Had to be the same armless creature he'd pursued through the alley.

"Hey!" he called. "Hey! Who are you?"

Behind him, the radio crackled again, but this time emitting loud sighs and moans. His attention torn, James glanced over his shoulder, then back at the armless creature, which continued to advance on him, upper torso contorting throughout its stumbling gait. Its head strained to the side, but its face was featureless flesh pulled tightly over a skull. Without arms, its upper torso appeared and moved like someone wearing a straitjacket—at least when it wasn't twitching and spasming. Whether it was in pain or somehow at war with its own body, its intentions seemed provocative. James wondered if it was somehow responsible for the death of the homeless man.

Needing a weapon, James scanned the immediate vicinity and noticed the waist-high storage cage beside the entrance filled with construction debris and loose sections of pipe left over from the scaffolding project. He hefted an eighteen-inch length of metal pipe with a four-way connector attached to the end—an effective club—and prepared to defend himself.

"Don't come any closer!"

Without a mouth, it couldn't answer. Without eyes or ears, could it see or hear? He had no doubt it sensed his presence; it had homed in on him and refused to stop.

A dark orifice opened vertically in the armless creature's chest, spewing a stream of the black tar-like substance at him. James dodged to the left, barely avoiding the blast. Behind him, the wall and the paint on the storage cage hissed, blistering with corrosion.

He'd already seen how the acid could dissolve human flesh. Before the armless creature could turn and attempt to spray him with more of the foul liquid, he hurled the pipe at it, striking it squarely in the chest, directly where the maw had opened. Staggering backwards, the creature fell out of sight behind a dust-caked white commercial van.

Groans sounded from the radio.

James waited a moment, undecided. One blow might have knocked the Armless down but, judging by the scuffling sound, it wasn't dead. He could simply flee the area, but if that thing snuck up on him... One dousing of the black acid would kill him, certainly mutilate him. Better to deal with it now than be caught unawares.

Backing away from the van, he circled around to the

side where the Armless had fallen. Lying on the sidewalk, disgustingly thin, it wriggled like an insect, rolling its shoulders and pushing with its feet to scuttle under the van.

James retrieved his pipe club and knelt beside the van so he could look underneath. The featureless head—like a flesh-colored bag pulled over a human face, but completely inhuman just the same—oriented on him. It scuttled away from him again, toward the opening by a displaced sewer access cover. A moment later, it fell through the hole into the sewer shaft.

For an insane moment, James considered pursuing it into the sewer system, but the risk wasn't worth it. The tight quarters and darkness would make James more vulnerable to the black acid spray. The creature might have a nest underground. There might even be more of them down there.

Crackles and squeals burst from the radio, louder than before.

Steering clear of the puddle of acid and what little remained of the corpse, James retrieved the small radio from the homeless man's extended hand, prying the fingers free of their death grip. The Deluxe radio had a yellow case, held inside a snug dark leather sleeve vented for the speakers. Small enough to fit in a good-sized pocket, it looked old, several decades old—vintage basically.

He carried the radio out of the vaulted passageway, holding it close to his ear at the sound of chattering voices, a murmuring crowd. Wholly unintelligible, but then he thought one of them spoke his name. Nonsensically, he had the urge to call back to the voice, even though the radio was a receiver, not a transmitter. But he couldn't shake the sense that somebody, somewhere was trying to contact him.

Frustrated, he looked around to assess his surroundings. That's when he saw them. Multiple contorted figures approaching, stumbling through the fog with the same splayed gait as the Armless who had escaped into the sewer. They sensed him the same way the first one had. But this time he was outnumbered. If they all had the ability to spray black acid, he didn't like his chances, armed only with a section of pipe.

He decided it was time for discretion to be the better part of valor and turned to flee in the opposite direction. Then pulled up short. More of them, emerging from the fog, ghostly silhouettes slowly gaining resolution. Had the first one somehow called for assistance, branded him a threat?

He was surrounded.

Even if the vaulted passageway was narrow enough to face them one at a time, he'd face them head on. One blast of the black acid and—

The wail of a siren startled him.

Loud enough to hurt his ears. Loud enough for the whole town of Silent Hill to hear the damn thing—if anyone had bothered to stay behind.

And yet, someone had sounded the siren. There was still a chance people were holed up somewhere. Mary could be with them. He had to hold onto that hope. But right now, he had more pressing concerns—

Flocks of distressed birds took flight, streaking across the sky and drawing his gaze upward. Something strange was happening. The dreary gray light of the ash-filled sky bled away, shifting to darkness faster than time would normally allow, as if the rotation of the planet had been set to fast-forward. And the fog ebbed, retreating from the town like a receding tide, while the siren continued to blare.

Even as the accelerated darkness descended over Silent Hill like a shroud, James looked down terrified as a strange sort of rust began to spread across the cement sidewalks, the asphalt beneath his shoes, and the walls of the buildings on both sides of the street, infecting his surroundings with corruption and decay.

With the withdrawal of the fog, the drifting ash had ceased to fall from the sky. Instead, a steady drizzle began. Surrounded by rust, pelted by rain, James stood in a transformed town suddenly plunged into darkness. Mercifully, the siren stopped.

James shoved the radio into his jacket pocket and took out his phone, switching on its flashlight. With that in his left hand, he hefted his pipe club in the right. Shining the light in a slow three-sixty revealed that the town was overrun by the Armless. The first one must have been an outlier. Most of them seemed to prefer darkness. His options were dwindling. If he stood still, they'd converge on his location and overwhelm him. He had no clear avenue of escape, so he had to make a run for it.

Navigating toward the widest gaps between the Armless, gripping the pipe in his sweaty hand, he ducked between them. The radio squawked and squealed as he closed the gap. The nearest one turned toward him, spurting black acid in his direction. If he'd been a few steps slower, he would have been doused in the corrosive liquid.

Too damn close!

Fortunately, with their uncoordinated ambulation, twisting torsos, and erratic convulsions, they lacked the ability to run. Though they outnumbered him, they couldn't keep up with him. If he stayed on the move and avoided their acid attacks, he might have a chance of finding shelter.

One lurched off the curb, uncomfortably close, causing the radio to screech again as the thing twisted toward him. With a backhanded blow, he struck it across the head with the pipe, causing it to stagger sideways as its chest maw spread open to spray him.

When a pair got too close, he swept the leg of one, hooking its ankle and upending it into its partner. Both fell to the ground before they could spray him. He turned a corner, nearly crashing into one—

"Oh, fuck!"

—before dropping to his knees as its chest orifice spread open. Black acid splashed the street where he'd stood a moment before. Rising behind the Armless, he swung the pipe in an overhead arc, striking the creature on the back of its skull, caving in the flesh. Remarkably, it staggered but didn't fall, twitching as it tried to turn around. James didn't give it the chance, raining multiple blows on its neck and shoulders until it finally crumpled and fell face forward—if it had had a face.

He should have run after the first blow, but the close encounter had freaked him out enough to unnerve him. Yet staying in place long enough to deliver the coup de grâce had given more Armless time to converge on his position. Couldn't make that mistake again.

Six behind him. Three ahead. In seconds, any of them would be close enough to spew black acid in his direction. Gritting his teeth, he sprinted toward the lesser number, dodging right as a maw gaped wide—and his radio squealed—to avoid spurting acid. He cleared the three Armless, but the side of his foot hit the curb, and his momentum caused him to lose his balance. Staggering one-two-three steps forward, his center of gravity outpaced his ability to stay upright. He crashed into a row of overflowing trashcans lined up in front of the closed garage door of an auto repair shop. Metal cans toppled over with a hideous racket, and garbage bags burst as he collapsed on top of them.

"Son of a bitch," he muttered, wiping foul-smelling goop from the sleeve of his jacket in disgust.

As he started to rise, he noticed the auto garage's shattered glass door and the cracked and stained fascia sign above it that read 'Silent Hill Automotive'. The welcome bell mounted on the inside of the door remained intact, pushed by the slight breeze to create a faint windchime sound in the night. For some odd reason, the tinkling sound irritated James...

CHAPTER 10

James drove from the Lakeview Hotel to Texxon Gas to fill up the Mustang's gas tank. From there he navigated back to Nathan Avenue, planning to take Lindsey Street down to the Flower Shop on Sanders to buy Mary a just-because bouquet of roses before dropping in on her at her place in the Woodside Apartments. At least that was the plan.

He drove past Rosewater Park, but before he even reached the T intersection at Neely Street, he heard the high-pitched *whoop* of a police car and saw flashing red and blue lights in his rearview mirror. Since he hadn't been speeding or been in the process of making a turn without signaling, he had no idea why the police had decided to pull him over.

Steering the Mustang onto the shoulder of Nathan, he shifted into park and turned off the ignition. The black and white police cruiser swung in behind his car, almost tapping his rear bumper before coming to a stop. With no sign of rain in the forecast, he'd put down the convertible top before leaving the hotel, so he sat there with his hands on the steering wheel and waited.

Observing via his rearview mirror, James saw a single occupant in the cop car, a middle-aged man with sandy hair. After a few minutes speaking on his radio, the uniformed officer approached the driver's side of the Mustang, right hand resting on his holster as if preparing for a duel in the old west. He wore a standard police officer's peaked cap and brown sunglasses. A nametag clipped to the breast pocket of his uniform shirt read TOLLESON.

"Good afternoon, Officer," James said as the man paused beside his door.

"Do you know why I pulled you over?" Tolleson asked in a flat voice.

"No, sir," James said, hoping his irritation wasn't obvious.

"License, registration, and proof of insurance."

James took his driver's license out of his wallet and told the cop the registration and insurance cards were in the glove compartment before reaching for them. After Tolleson gave a nod of acknowledgment, James leaned across the dash and retrieved the cards, handing all three pieces of information over.

"Don't believe I was speeding," James said, if only to fill the silence as the cop checked the items for expiration dates or authenticity, or so he imagined.

"No, you were not," Tolleson said. "Now sit tight."

He took the documents back to his patrol car. Based on what James could observe from the rearview mirror, Tolleson was punching information into his on-board computer, then making inquiries on his radio. James guessed he was checking for everything from unpaid parking tickets to potential parole violations.

After an interminable wait, Tolleson climbed out of his patrol car again, returning with James' documents. When he reached the side of the car, he handed everything back. Before James could put them away or ask a follow-up question, the cop said, "Everything checks out."

"That's good," James said. He hadn't expected any issues, but the longer the wait, the more doubt had crept in, wondering if he'd forgotten about something that could come back to bite him. "So, why…?"

"You have a broken taillight,"

"Really?" James asked, surprised. He was certain he would have noticed—unless it had happened recently.

"Calling me a liar, Mr. Sunderland?"

"No, Officer Tolleson," James said, trying to defuse the antagonistic vibe he was getting from the cop. "I was just… unaware."

"Of course, you were," Tolleson said curtly. He might as well have said, *That's what they all say.*

At that moment, a white Chevy Tahoe in the eastbound lane of Nathan, pulled over in front of James' Mustang, then backed up until its rear bumper was inches away, effectively boxing him in. James glanced at the cop to gauge his reaction, but the man's eyes were obscured by the sunglasses and his face remained stoic.

The Tahoe's driver side door opened and a woman in a black pantsuit with a shock of bleached blond hair stepped out. Dara, the detective. So, now it made sense. She must have heard the call on the radio with his identifying information and decided to check it out. After the lukewarm reaction from Mary's friends at Heaven's Night, he wasn't sure if Dara's presence was a good thing or not.

As she approached James' car door, Tolleson backed up a step, clearly deferring to a higher rank. She leaned over James, both hands pressed on the edge of the door, as if she might yank it open at the slightest provocation. And the smile she leveled at James never reached her eyes. "Heard you got in some trouble, James."

"Turns out I have a broken taillight," James said. "I was unaware."

"That so," she said, and turned slightly to address Tolleson. "Write him a ticket yet?"

"Not yet," Tolleson said. "But he was giving me a bit of lip."

"I wasn't—"

She held up a palm to silence him.

"I'm sure that was all a misunderstanding," she said, looking at James but addressing Tolleson. "I happen to know this young gentleman. New addition to town."

"Looked like a tourist."

"Not at all," Dara said. "But he's been staying at the Lakeview—for now."

"Noted."

"I think we can let him off with a warning, Tolleson," Dara said. "Don't you?"

"Well..."

"Assuming he gets it fixed right away, of course," Dara said. "You'll get that fixed right away, won't you, James?"

"Of course," James said. "I'll drop it off today."

"Splendid." Dara looked over at Tolleson. "Give us a minute, would you?"

"Certainly, detective," Tolleson said with a tip of his cap before striding back to his patrol car.

"Thanks for that," James said. "I really had no idea."

"Not at all," Dara said. "We're all friends here. As they say, any friend of Mary's and so on."

"Right," James said, slightly irked but attempting to play his part as grateful civilian and friend of a friend.

"Hear things are getting serious between you two," Dara commented. "Which is fine. I'm sure you know we're all just looking out for our girl."

"Of course."

"Know you have the best intentions and all that," she continued, "so I want to make sure we get off on the right foot. Wouldn't want things to get... complicated. Mary will always be our top priority. I hope you get my meaning."

"Wouldn't have it any other way," James said.

"Glad we see eye to eye," Dara said with a wink. "Tolleson's as by-the-book as they come, but that doesn't stop us from doing favors for each other. So, I wanted to get here before he wrote you up and made it all official. Just a little show of Silent Hill hospitality."

"I appreciate that."

"Good," Dara said. "Good, good. And, as a gesture of goodwill, take this..." She fished a business card out of her jacket pocket. "It's for Silent Hill Automotive. Tell Oscar that Dara sent you, and he'll give you ten percent off parts and labor. Sweet deal."

She slapped the card in his open palm.

"Also appreciated," James said and slid the laminated card into his shirt pocket.

"Drive safe now," Dara said, flashing her plastic smile. "We'll be seeing you around, I'm sure."

James nodded, forcing a polite smile of his own.

Dara returned to the Tahoe and drove away, her rear tires spitting gravel at his grille. A little power move on her part—as was boxing him in, psychologically cornering him, placing him at her mercy. Some kind of law enforcement head game that probably came naturally to her. But he was patient, not taking the bait. He waited until Tolleson drove away before starting the Mustang.

He had a sense the whole interaction had been a setup, from the broken taillight to Dara's arrival to save the day, letting him off with a warning. Probably took a hammer to the taillight at the hotel, then waited for him to leave to pull him over. Of course, there was the other possibility, that he was just being paranoid. But his gut had told him something was off with Mary's friend group from the start, and this traffic stop only increased his suspicions. After all, the real warning had come from Dara, and it had nothing to do with the broken light.

He took the business card out of his pocket and examined it. Basically, the shop's name and business hours. Nothing unusual about the card. And the issue was only a broken taillight, so it wasn't like some organized car repair scam designed to take a chunk out of his bank account. But it all made him wonder if Tolleson and possibly even Oscar had been at Heaven's Night, part of the crowd that had been overly invested in Mary's relationship status. The further he could get Mary from her so-called friends, the better…

CHAPTER 11

Looking away from the cracked Silent Hill Automotive sign, James glanced back the way he'd come to see how far away the Armless were. He scrambled to his feet, but immediately slipped on a mound of rotting food and fell to his knees again. Then he heard a new sound, a scurrying, fluttering rush reminiscent of a wave crashing on the shore. But it wasn't water. It was a wave of rats—meaty rats, like the one the scavenger birds had feasted on in the middle of the street—surging out of a narrow alleyway, clearly fleeing... something. Several of them bounded too close to James, who'd dropped his pipe club when he fell, and he swatted them aside with a nearby trashcan lid. But they weren't interested in him or the freshly spilled sewage. He just happened to be in their way. They scurried under fences, shot under cars, tumbled over each other in their haste, veered left and right, determined to get away, anywhere, as fast as their legs would carry them.

Then he heard squeaking and squealing, sounds of distress and pain, from the back of the stampeding pack. A struggling rat emerged from the alley, trailing a swarm of enlarged cockroaches flowing up from a sewer grating. At least a dozen clung to the rat's back, tearing into its flesh, leaving blood spatters in its wake. More besieged rats followed, some dropping in their tracks and succumbing to the ravenous horde of insects.

Within seconds the cockroach swarm had crossed to James' side of the street, latching onto rats and scrambling up their sides. The rats were oversized, but so too were the roaches. A few neared James, flowing around the trash mound, but one darted across a burst trash bag right onto his arm. He immediately swatted it away with the pipe. It flipped end over end, landing on its back.

For the first time, he saw the anatomy of the enlarged insects. Despite the cockroach carapace, the underside was vaguely humanoid, fat and pale, with an eyeless head, a mouth filled with needle teeth and a grotesque, darting, pinkish tongue. Disgusted, James crushed it with the blunt end of the pipe before it could right itself.

He climbed to his feet before the cockroaches had a chance to swarm him, glancing back the way he'd come to check on the Armless creatures he'd passed before he took a fall. Strangely, they held back, either waiting to see how the cockroach attacks played out or in fear of the cockroaches themselves. The Armless didn't advance, but neither were they standing still. Their necks and torsos twitched with frequent spasms. Grateful for the temporary reprieve, James climbed to his feet and fled.

Letting his cellphone flashlight guide him around the river of rats and the swarming cockroaches, he veered from one side of the street to the other, seeking the clearest route. But rats continued to bump into him or run across his shoes in their mindless flight. Concern for his footing kept his gaze downward and not on what was in front of him. Almost too late, he noticed four Armless spread out across the road. If not for the sudden squeal and squelch of the radio, he might have lined himself up to be sprayed with two or three streams of black acid.

He pulled up short, immediately feeling the weighty bodies of rats buffeting his calves, flowing between his legs, and veering around him as he stood his ground. Many of the rats carried cockroaches and, as they collided with the Armless, the ravenous insects clambered up the larger prey and tore into their unprotected flesh.

James swung his pipe back and forth to dislodge roaches that latched onto him and tried to climb up his legs. But the Armless had no defense against the small but fierce attackers. The radio crackled and squealed, emitting howls of distress and pain, almost overwhelming the small speaker. Then one of the Armless, in apparent desperation, opened its chest orifice and sprayed a fountain of black acid. It writhed and twisted, flinging the corrosive fluid in a half circle, like a rotary sprinkler watering a lawn. Though the acid had no effect on the cockroaches attacking its own body, the Armless managed to burn and dissolve many of the rats and cockroaches rushing toward it—and nearly struck James with the distressed attack.

A second later, James noticed the Armless closest to him was about to unleash its own deadly spray. He needed to move fast to avoid getting caught in the crossfire. Waiting a moment for a break in the flow of rats, he veered to the side of the road, leaping to the sidewalk as he realized he'd entered a familiar mixed-use neighborhood. Since darkness had fallen, he'd assumed his headlong flight had been completely random, but his subconscious must have been guiding him in this general direction all along. Running along a row of familiar storefronts, he shined his flashlight at the third building's fascia sign: *Fashion Boutique.*

Close to residences, the businesses in this neighborhood didn't have security gates. Crossing mental fingers, he grabbed the door handle and pulled—

CHAPTER 12

—the plexiglass door open, stepping inside the Fashion Boutique for the first time, hoping to surprise Mary at her place of employment and pry her away for lunch. He spotted her straight ahead at the checkout counter behind a clearance table. She wore a peach-colored sundress with a butterfly pattern, looking down at a stack of papers while engaged in an intense phone conversation. She pressed her free hand against her other ear to better hear the party on the other end of the line.

While he waited to catch her attention, he walked between featured displays on either side of the double doors, where mannequins stood on oval pedestals wearing matching skirt sets. The walls were painted a smokey taupe, almost gray, and all the clothing racks were uniform black metal, squared tubing. On the left side, along the wall, skirts and dresses were displayed, hats and handbags farther back. On the right wall, he saw jeans, casual wear, stockings and underwear. To the left of the clearance table and the checkout counter behind it, two freestanding racks held tops. These were closest to a dressing room in the back left, which was fronted by a gray loveseat trimmed in black, a convenience for those waiting on partners, spouses or children. A rack for pants stood on the right side, with a table for accessories behind that, with a restroom in the far right corner. Additional mannequins stood on elevated platforms near the two racks for tops, and bracketing the extended pants rack, the former had no heads, the latter lacked arms.

A mother with two daughters were the only patrons in the store, currently removing items on hangers in the jeans and casual wear sections. James spotted Kaitlyn by hats and handbags, ostensibly straightening the shelves, but she seemed as interested in trying on various hats and handbags herself. He noted that the skirt set she wore was similar but not identical to one worn by one of the mannequins at the front of the store. James recalled Mary's comment about her taking advantage of the employee discount.

While Mary was engrossed in her phone conversation, James circled around the left side of the store, intending to wait on the love seat and surprise her when she ended the call. But Kaitlyn was checking her reflection in a mirror as she tried on a wide-brimmed raffia hat and spotted him in the mirror. She whirled around to face him, eyes wide, about to call out his name, when he raised a finger to his lips, nodding toward Mary's back. Kaitlyn caught on and waved him forward. She stood between him and Mary, her wide-brimmed hat helping to keep him hidden.

"James, dear," she said conspiratorially, "what are you doing here?"

"Hoping to take Mary out to lunch."

Kaitlyn scoffed. "Think you can pry her away?"

"She doesn't take a lunch break?"

"Rarely," Kaitlyn replied. "Only child syndrome. Totally focused here. Hardly ever has time to socialize."

"Who's she talking to?"

"Had to guess, it's one of the independent designers whose stuff we agreed to carry on consignment," Kaitlyn said. "Trying to put incentives on top of agreed-upon percentages or some shit. Then there's this one vendor—gets cool stuff, but she misses dates, screws up orders—definitely has a few screws loose. Usual headaches."

"Yeah. Sorry I asked," James said with a chuckle. "But, hey, could you cover for her? If she'll go with me?"

"Well, I could," Kaitlyn hedged. "If she'll let me. Like I said, only child thing."

"She doesn't talk about her family much."

"Don't blame her," Kaitlyn said. "Poor girl."

"How do you mean?"

Kaitlyn glanced around, noticed Mary still preoccupied with the call, and the mother and daughters still engrossed in the casual clothing racks. "Her mother gave birth to three boys before her. All stillbirths," Kaitlyn said somberly.

"I didn't know that."

"Obviously, she wasn't there when it happened," Kaitlyn said. "I'm not surprised she doesn't talk about it. I heard from some of the others who knew her father before I did. But it got worse..."

"How so?"

"She didn't tell you?" Kaitlyn asked, eyebrows raised, almost as if it were a judgment and he'd been found wanting. "Her mother died in childbirth. Giving birth to Mary."

James was stunned. Mary had never talked about her mother. He hadn't asked, not wanting to pry. And when the subject of her father came up at Heaven's Night, she'd told him she'd rather not discuss the man, shifting the conversation to other topics. "Never knew her mother," James said. "So, I guess she was close to her father."

"Joshua worshipped her," Kaitlyn said. "His little angel." She took another quick survey of the store, then continued to speak softly. "He had big plans for her."

"Really?"

"He left her a trust fund," Kaitlyn said, "but she won't touch it." She sounded a little perturbed. Jealousy, maybe. "She's determined to live off the money she makes managing this place. Says she wants to prove herself. Independent woman and all that crap." She scoffed. "If it were me, I'd dig into that money with both hands." She chuckled. "But I have expensive tastes."

"Oh, my God," Mary called out, having set the phone receiver down. "James! What are you doing here?"

"Came to break you out of this place."

She hurried over, gave him a fierce hug and a quick kiss on the lips. "I wasn't expecting you."

"Figured I'd surprise you."

Kaitlyn shook her head. "Told him you chain yourself to this place," she said. "Bag lunch or delivery all the way."

"I'd love to grab a bite," Mary said, smiling up at James.

"Really?" Kaitlyn said, nonplussed. "Outside these actual walls?"

"Sure," Mary said, glancing at Kaitlyn before returning her attention to James. "Couple good places within walking distance." Mary noticed the mother and daughters heading to the checkout with a few items. She looked at Kaitlyn and nodded toward them discreetly. "You can handle things while I'm gone."

"I—yeah, sure. You bet," Kaitlyn said. "Although, you never want to grab lunch with me."

"If we both left," Mary said evenly, "I'd have to close the store."

"You know what I mean," Kaitlyn said, wagging a finger at her as she walked toward the counter. She stopped when she realized she still wore the raffia hat, darted over to return it to a detached mannequin head sitting on a shelf, then strode over to greet the customers at the register.

She took a moment to compose herself, then asked, "Find everything you were looking for?" Yet she kept looking over at Mary and James, as if trying to unravel the secret of their relationship.

Mary retrieved her bag from under the counter, paused to adjust a scarf on one of the mannequins, then nodded in satisfaction. She met James at the front of the store. "Ready," she said, purse clutched before her in both hands.

James held the door open for her.

Stuffing the purchased clothing in a plastic bag branded with the store name, Kaitlyn looked up to watch them leave. Despite wishing the mother and two daughters a good day, her hard gaze followed James and Mary. James couldn't shake the idea that she was resentful of Mary's departure.

"You surprised her," James said. "Almost left her speechless."

"Nah," Mary said with a crooked grin. "Would take a lot more than that."

"She implied you're a workaholic."

"Work helps me... stay focused."

"Know the feeling," James said, releasing the door.

Even with their blank, eyeless faces, the two mannequins standing guard on either side of the entrance seemed to stare down at him accusingly from their pedestals.

After leaving the Fashion Boutique in the probably-capable hands of a definitely-disgruntled Kaitlyn, James and Mary walked hand in hand several blocks to Gonzales' Mexican Restaurant at the corner of Sanders and Lindsey. Mary, looking lovely in her peach sundress with its myriad butterflies, smiled randomly as they neared the restaurant entrance.

"What?" he asked, grinning at her.

"This is... nice," Mary said. "Getting out. Feels—I don't know—liberating. Like playing hooky from school."

"Do I bring out the bad girl in you?" he asked playfully.

Mary squeezed his hand and smiled. "Oh, I'm sure Kaitlyn thinks so."

"Yeah, she wasn't too happy about it."

"She likes an order to things," Mary said. "Control issues."

"Well, I was happy to bust you out for the afternoon," James said. "Even if it's only for your lunch hour." He looked up at the fascia sign above glass doors. "Never asked before, but what's up with that sign?"

The sign read 'Gonzale's Mexican Restaurant'.

"Ah, the misplaced apostrophe?" Mary laughed. "Rumor has it, the sign maker screwed up. The owner demanded a new sign, obviously."

"Obviously," James said. "Who wouldn't?"

"But the sign maker offered to cut the invoice price in half if he kept it as is."

"And he took that deal?"

"So urban legend has it."

Fortunately, there was no wait. The hostess sat them at a table in the back, near a window, away from a large boisterous group sitting up front, and handed them menus. Before she left, she made a point of telling Mary to let her know if she 'needed anything, anything at all.' James' took it as another example of a town founder's daughter getting offered special treatment. He hadn't been to this restaurant yet, so he took a few minutes to look it over before turning his attention to his menu. The walls were painted in sunset colors, yellow here, orange there, rounded arches painted red. The tables were bare wood, no tablecloths, but the wooden chairs had laminated backs with depictions of Mexican life and scenes, from a simpler time, men riding horses or leading donkeys, a woman in a long white dress dancing near a bonfire, but also pictures of families walking on the beach at sunset, and Day of the Dead celebrations.

Mary ordered a house salad and shrimp tacos, while James had chori fries and grilled chicken fajitas. Away from the crowd, they were able to talk without worrying about casual eavesdroppers.

"So, how's life in the hotel room treating you?" Mary asked, mid-meal.

"Well, they don't want me painting in there, even if I throw down a tarp," James replied. "Claim it's a tripping hazard for their maids and for me and don't want to be held liable. Or so they say. I think they're worried about paint getting on the walls or furniture, even though I volunteered a security deposit."

"So, you can't paint," Mary said as she speared some lettuce on her fork.

"Not indoors," James replied after swallowing a bit of his fajita. "Lots of sketching. On the plus side, the view from my window is excellent."

Mary blushed. "I'm aware."

"You should come over more often," he said, smiling. "A lot more."

"Oh, I plan to," she said, "but the hotel staff might talk."

"I've sworn them to secrecy," James said. "Meaning, I tip generously."

"So, what were you and Kaitlyn talking about?"

"The workaholic stuff, you know," James said, unsure if he should bring up her family history since it was a topic she avoided with him and, besides, Kaitlyn may have been out of bounds discussing it with him. "That kind of thing."

"That all?" Mary asked with an eyebrow raised in suspicion.

"Not that I was digging or anything," James said. "But she may have said something about a trust fund."

Mary rolled her eyes and sighed. "Gossipy little bitch," she exclaimed. "Should fire her ass."

"Whoa," James said. "Touchy subject?"

"It's none of her business."

"She said you're too independent to touch it," James said. "I can respect that."

"Oh, so you're not looking for a sugar mama?"

"It's called a patron," James said, laughing. "Artists and patrons go way back. But I fell in love with you for who you are, not your vast wealth."

She scoffed. "I'll never touch that money," she said, her tone decidedly more serious. She leaned forward. "It's not money. It's a damn noose."

"What do you mean?"

She rubbed her mouth with her napkin, then clutched it between her hands on the edge of the table, clearly agitated. He'd stumbled on a topic that upset her and decided right then he wouldn't push the issue.

"I never planned to tell you about this."

"I understand," James said, hands up, palms out. "That's your prerogative. And none of my business."

"But I will tell you about it, since you'll probably think I'm crazy," she continued. "I never planned to tell you because it might as well not exist." She took a deep breath before resuming. "It's my father," she fumed. "Trying to control me from beyond the grave."

"I don't follow—"

"It's a conditional trust," Mary said. "Specifically, it's 'condition subsequent,' meaning I only keep the money if I fulfill certain conditions. And one of those conditions is…" She paused, took a deep breath and shook her head. "Well, it's a bunch of legalese about our family being town founders and needing to keep that legacy and heritage alive, blah, blah, blah. But that's *his* legacy, and it's no secret my friends kind of worship the ground he walked on."

"But you're not him," James said. "Don't you think there's a chance, they'll…"

"Grow bored with me? The pale imitation?" Mary asked, chuckling as she stared into the distance. "They are their own breed of… zealots. But anything can happen, I suppose. You wanna know the real kicker?"

"What?"

"My father made Cal the trustee."

"Cal, the lawyer," James said, nodding in understanding.

"So, what's the harm in humoring their… beliefs, as long as I get to live independently, as if the trust doesn't even exist?"

James hadn't noticed how much time had passed until Mary glanced at the clock.

"Guess you should get back."

She nodded and heaved a sigh. "Duty calls. Thanks for lunch. And one more thing."

Leaning across the table, she gave him a kiss. "I'm free to play hooky again any time."

"Noted."

The walk back to the Fashion Boutique was more subdued. She held James' hand, even swung it up and back in an exaggerated arc, but he sensed her mind was elsewhere, on darker topics, the trust fund that attempted to control her, to humor so-called friends who wanted to glom on to her as a substitute for their guru. And yet, James wondered why she continued to tolerate their displaced devotion.

When they turned at the intersection of Katz and Neely, James noticed a man standing by a window inside the Lucky Jade restaurant watching them intently, as if he had to file a report later about what he'd observed. Either Mary didn't notice or didn't care when strangers took interest in her comings and goings. So, James decided not to mention it. One touchy subject per lunch break was more than sufficient.

As James opened the door for her back at the Fashion Boutique, the cold mannequins, elevated on their pedestals, seemed to usher her back into the confines of the shop.

CHAPTER 13

When he entered the Fashion Boutique, the mannequins were gone from their pedestals. And not just those two. All the store mannequins had been removed from the store. Much of the clothing remained, covered in dust. A couple of the interior racks had fallen on their sides, clothing and hangers snarled around them. Who would steal the mannequins but leave the clothing?

James shoved the two pedestals against the double glass doors, hoping the added weight would deter the tide of rats and their cockroach tormentors from pushing their way inside. If they broke the glass or if the Armless decided to assault the entrance, he risked getting cornered. But he only needed a few minutes.

If Mary was hiding from the monstrous creatures that roamed the night streets, the Fashion Boutique was a likely place for her to seek shelter. She knew the store well, had spent long days there. It would be a familiar place to await help. More importantly, it was a place James associated with her, so she could reasonably expect him to check for her there.

"Mary?" he called, sweeping the store with the flashlight. "Mary, are you here?"

The wall racks on either side were too bare to provide a hiding place, so he checked behind the counter, then moved to the back of the store. Since the fitting room door was open, he started there, checking both partitioned areas. Several articles of clothing hung on hooks, forgotten, with stray hangers on wall-mounted benches and on the floor. Everything caked with the ubiquitous dust.

Every few seconds, rats thumped against the glass windows and doors, like the stylings of a hesitant drummer. The longer he searched, the less frequent the impacts. He tried to ignore the sounds, but worried that any moment a more resounding crash would precede a full scale infestation of the shop.

Next, he checked the enclosed storage area directly behind the counter island. He found numerous boxes, loose clothing draped here and there, a small desk with a dead computer, notebooks and pens, drawers filled with assorted odds and ends, tape measures, several pairs of scissors, shipping tape, charging cables, hair ties and a pack of playing cards. A corkboard in front of the desk was pinned with invoices, sticky note reminders, shopping lists… but no notes from Mary. If she had stopped here, she would have left him a note. Unless she had left in a panic. Or worried someone else might intercept the note. But so far, none of the horrors he'd encountered had the capacity to read a note or follow instructions. Simply mindless creatures, intent on destruction.

Lastly, he checked the unisex restroom. All he found were toiletries, cleansers, and sanitary products. No message hastily scrawled in lipstick on the cracked mirror above the small sink, which bifurcated his reflection vertically down the middle, showing his fatigued face in two unaligned halves.

Leaving the restroom, he made his way to the front of the store. He hadn't heard a rat bounce off the front door in almost ten seconds and hoped the worst of it was over. Shoving one pedestal out of the way, he pulled the door open and scanned the street as far as he could with the limited range of his flashlight. Rats scurried by, but their numbers had diminished significantly. The Armless were gone or had fallen under the mass assault of the cockroaches. He ducked outside and ran across a few streets until he saw the sign he was looking for, Katz Avenue, and farther down the street, the dark outline of a familiar building.

As soon as he turned onto Katz, the relative silence was broken by a chittering, hissing, clicking wave of cockroaches. A quick glance over his shoulder confirmed his worst fear. The ravenous mass covered the full width of the street, scrambling forward with deadly urgency. With no rats or Armless in sight, he represented their only potential prey. And they were closing fast.

He retained the pipe club for all the good it would do. He'd stand a much better chance surviving the next five minutes with a flamethrower. Even then, he wouldn't like his odds. So, he ran toward the building, hoping to find shelter. Every few seconds, he backhanded rain from his eyes, straining to see in the darkness. He imagined he could already read the sign: Woodside Apartments. But something was off—

Running too fast to stop in time, he crashed shoulder first into a cyclone fence barricading the street—and nearly fell on his ass.

"Shit!"

He staggered backwards and lost his grip on the pipe. Thought of climbing over the fence, but the flashlight revealed coils of razor wire that would slice through his flesh as effectively as the mutant cockroaches. He glanced back. The vanguard of the swarm had closed the gap to twenty feet. Seconds remained before they'd overwhelm him.

Frantic, he looked left and right along the fence, noticed a small gap and raced toward it. As he suspected, someone with a bolt cutter had parted the fence in a vertical line from shoulder to knee height. Wasting no time, he raised one leg to step through the gap, ducked his head and squeezed the rest of the way through.

Behind him, cockroaches raced along the base of the fence, attempting to squirm under it with their flailing segmented legs or squeeze through the small gaps between links. As wave after wave crashed against the fence, they piled on top of each other, layer upon layer, the horde forming a growing mound. The fence might slow them down, but it wouldn't stop them. Already several had squeezed half their bodies through the gap under the fence. Those in closest pursuit had followed him to where the fence was cut. A dozen or more popped through, dropping to the ground, scrabbling and spinning themselves upright. Noticing their success, the rest of the horde flowed toward the breach.

James had bought himself a minute or two, but that grace period was about to expire. Panting, he sprinted across the street, leaped over the curb, raced up the steps to the double glass doors of the apartment building and pulled them open. Once inside the lobby, he turned around and quickly closed the doors. Almost immediately, he heard the scratching and scrabbling of dozens of cockroaches flailing at the entrance. Within seconds, the doors trembled against the escalating assault. He wasn't sure how long it would hold. But he needed time to search for Mary.

Casting about, James spotted a pile of rubble and construction debris against the right side of the lobby. With the flashlight, he located two long pieces of wood, bent nails jutting out of them, and carried them back to the door. He wedged each of them through the double door handles, forming a compressed X, which abruptly decreased the play in the doors. One final adjustment and—

"Son of a bitch!"

He'd cut his hand on one of the crooked nails. Not a serious wound, but he paused a moment, trying to recall the date of his last tetanus shot. Nothing he could do about it now. He wiped his palm on his jeans and walked through the lobby, catching his reflection in a mural mirror as he swept his flashlight side to side.

Behind him, a sound like the clattering of hail against the front doors. The ferocious insects were hurling themselves against the glass. The barricaded doors held, but James wondered if it was a simple feeding frenzy... or if the insects were smart enough to know that glass broke if you hit it hard enough.

As he pointed the flashlight at the glass to check for cracks, the light flickered and died, plunging him into darkness. The cockroaches continued to pelt the glass, sounding even more destructive. Then the light flickered back on again.

He walked through the lobby, checking his surroundings for hazards while the light lasted. Mural mirrors on both sides of the lobby cast his reflection back and forth ad infinitum, like a hall of mirrors in a funhouse. He recalled Mary's story about Mia and Gia, how the twins found it amusing to see themselves duplicated so many times in their store. James found the idea creepy. He imagined one of his many reflections moving out of concert with the rest, becoming another self entirely. And what if that version of James took control, took over his life, supplanting the original? Pulling his mind and his eyes away from the mirrors, he located the staircase and hurried to it.

"Please be here, Mary," he said softly. If she had waited for him, her third floor apartment was the most logical place for her to hunker down to avoid the nightmares prowling the streets.

As he reached the stairs, the flashlight flickered and died again. He checked the phone display. The battery level was redlining, switching into low power mode before it shut down completely.

"Dammit."

After another nerve-wracking moment, the light came back on, noticeably dimmer. Out of the corner of his eye, James saw a lurid reflection in the mirror—

Mary, standing naked, blood dripping down her body.

Terrified, James swung the light around—but nobody was there. Only his own stricken reflection staring back at him. On trembling legs, he made a quick circuit of the lobby, shining the light in the darkest areas, but he was alone. After what he'd experienced since arriving in the transformed Silent Hill, he could hardly fault his imagination for getting the better of him.

"C'mon, James," he said aloud. "You need to calm the fuck down and find her before something—just find her already."

After that bit of self-admonishment, he returned to the stairwell but couldn't help notice his hands trembling. The stairs were uniformly coated with dust. No footprints. No scuffing. If anyone hid in the apartments, they hadn't come down the steps in a while. Probably a wise decision, considering what roamed the streets. But the steps weren't free of debris. He saw a random shoe, an empty wine bottle, plastic cups, a fashion magazine, balled up paper bags, and a brittle, yellow newspaper from a year ago. He steered clear of the detritus as he ascended.

Then the light died—

CHAPTER 14

Sunlight streamed through the windows of the Woodside Apartments.

James couldn't have asked for a better day to move in with Mary. The Lakeview was a modern, well-appointed hotel with a fabulous view of Toluca Lake, but no matter how long James had been there under his long-term rental agreement, he still felt like he was living out of a suitcase. Well, multiple suitcases considering how many times he'd made the round trip to his studio and back for more clothes, more painting supplies, more of his stuff, basically.

He had no immediate plans to get out of his studio lease, but the recurring trips back had become tedious after a while. Though he wanted to be where Mary was, he also hoped to pry her away from the provincial environs of Silent Hill at some point. And the studio figured into his escape plans, at least as an intermediate waypoint until they found something bigger while remaining close to the city. A place to call theirs. He needed to remain a familiar presence to the art galleries in the city and, if they moved too far from that scene, well, out of sight out of mind.

James ascended the stairwell yet again, carrying his larger painting case in one hand, several canvases tucked under his other arm. To make matters worse, there were no apartments on the ground floor, the lobby level, which meant the first floor apartments were one flight up. He'd been up and down the stairs so many times, he was beginning to feel like Sisyphus—at least enough to work up a serious case of empathy. Unlike Sisyphus, his moving trials would eventually come to an end.

At the top of the stairs, he walked down a long corridor, which led to the stairs to the second floor, where Mary lived. He glanced up and noticed a couple approaching from the opposite direction. As he stepped aside to let them pass, he realized who they were: the Meyers twins he'd met at Heaven's Night, Mia and Gia, never mind which was which. But they were deep in conversation, whispering conspiratorially to each other and barely took note of him. If he hadn't moved out of their way, they might have barreled into him.

Stunned, James stood there for a moment, deciding if he should greet them or not, but the moment passed, and it would have been awkward to call after them down the hall. Still, he wondered why they were here on his move-in day. None of Mary's friends had offered to help. Then again, he couldn't recall if she had mentioned telling them the moving date. They knew he planned to move to Silent Hill, but had she told them he was moving in with her? Maybe they thought he planned to rent a place of his own.

Shaking his head as he glanced back at the pair, he continued down the corridor, distracted by their presence and his own swirling thoughts.

"Head's up there, friend."

James almost crashed into a stepladder, catching himself at the last moment. He looked up at the man standing on the ladder. "Sorry, I wasn't—"

James instantly recognized the man, with his shaved head and glasses, but today he wore an open sweater vest instead of a blazer.

"Cal?"

"One and the same," Cal said amiably, with a friendly wink. He held a light fixture pulled down from the ceiling, dangling from its wires. "Took it on myself to fix this light. It's been flickering off and on for a few days. Figured it was loose wiring."

"Right," James said. If he'd been surprised to see the Meyer twins, he had now become suspicious. Mary must have told them. Or planned a surprise apartment-warming party or something.

Tightening the screws that held the wires in place, Cal said casually, "Wouldn't want the place to burn down."

"No," James said. "Wouldn't want that."

Puzzled, James walked to the next set of stairs. Before he began the climb, Mary leaned over the third floor railing and smiled down at him.

With a dramatic sweep of her arm, she said, "Hello, handsome."

Playing along, James looked left and right, then along the stairwell, as if searching for the object of her affection. Finally, he glanced down at himself.

"Yes, you, dopey," she said. "Get up here."

She had her hair tied back in a ponytail, wore an open dark long-sleeved shirt over a white camisole, along with cutoff jean shorts. She'd rolled back the cuffs on the dark shirt, which had a pattern of faux paint stains.

Smiling, he hurried up the stairs to join her, taking the stairs comically fast, despite his tired legs. Though his hands were full, he had the urge to drop everything, wrap his arms around her and lift her up in the air.

"How many times you get lost this time around?"

Boxes surrounded her on the landing from his previous trips. They'd negotiated a division of labor by establishing a drop zone on the third floor landing. He would bring everything there, then Mary would finish the trip to the fourth floor.

"Didn't realize how much stuff I had," James said.

"Come on," she said, patting his shoulder. "One last push—" Leaning in, she gave him a quick kiss. "—then you've earned the right to lie down."

"Never considered a first floor apartment?"

With a mischievous smile, she said, "Nah. Much better view up here."

Placing the paint case on top of the nearest box, he set the canvases upright on the floor, leaning against the box. Unless canvases were safely crated, he never stacked them horizontally. He'd learned that the hard way. As he stood, hands pressed to his lower back, he heard the neighboring door open.

"Hello, hello—"

James and Mary turned toward their third floor neighbor—

Kaitlyn.

She wore an olive green wrap maxi dress, her hair wrapped in a scarf again.

"Oh," James said, starting to wonder if he was having a bizarre dream. At any moment, he'd wake up and realize he needed to pack for the move. "Hey."

Grinning at his surprise, Kaitlyn said, "What is it, dear?"

"I just—I didn't realize you lived here."

Her outfit seemed a bit formal for the middle of the afternoon or for a trip to the grocery store. James wondered if she had planned a grand entrance to catch him off guard.

"We've always been right under Joshua and Mary."

James automatically looked behind her to her door. By 'we' he wondered if she was talking about her and Dara, assuming they lived together. But he had the uncomfortable idea that she had included Cal and his wife, Mitzy, as well as the Meyer twins. Just how many of Mary's friends lived in the same apartment building with her? Some of them were at least a decade older than her, so it made a certain kind of sense that she'd befriended a few of them simply by living in close quarters. At the same time, they all seemed to worship the ground her father, Joshua, had walked on, so it was also possible they had followed him here. A self-styled guru would want his acolytes nearby.

Visibly embarrassed by the situation, and without saying a word to Kaitlyn or James, Mary grabbed a few boxes from the pile and walked up the steps to the fourth floor, which was the third floor with apartments, leaving James to wonder why she'd kept the living situation a secret.

"What is this—?" Kaitlyn asked.

Ignoring James' discomfiture—or perhaps reveling in it—Kaitlyn edged past him to the canvases he'd set on the floor. Too late, he realized which painting faced out and instantly regretted not checking when he set everything down. He'd only had eyes for Mary then, but still—the painting was too intimate for casual public exposure.

Mary hadn't posed for this painting. He'd painted it from memory. A vivid memory of Mary from their first evening together, after their drinks at the Lakeview Hotel, after the thunderstorm that chased them from the rooftop bar, and after he'd rented a room at Mary's urging. The painting was his view of Mary's torso after she'd sat astride his hips, naked, her head thrown back in a moment of pleasure. The details were soft and sensual, cast in the shadows between flashes of lightning. The portrait implied more than it depicted, clearly showing her topless, if not explicitly so. But it represented a private moment, not something to be shared, especially without Mary's consent, because the nature of the moment captured was obvious even to a casual viewer.

"Just one of my—it was a gift—"

Entranced, Kaitlyn spoke almost absently, "We've known Mary for so long—always felt like she was one of our own. Like she belonged to all of us."

Standing between James and the painting, she bent at the waist and, with casual familiarity, reached out to caress Mary's face in the painting with her long, thin, pearly-nailed fingers.

What the actual fuck—? What the hell is she doing right now?

James cleared his throat, resisting the urge to tell her to get her fucking hands off the painting.

Chagrined, Kaitlyn pulled her hand back, then pressed both hands to her breast, flashing him an awkward smile. She slipped by him, avoiding eye contact all the way back to her apartment. She closed the door quietly behind her.

James stared after her, silently daring her to step outside her apartment again. He'd enjoy nothing better than to get right up in her face and tell her to mind her own damn business. But, always, he thought about Mary. These people were her friends and, like it or not, he didn't want to be the cause of a rift between them.

"Is she gone?"

James looked up the fourth floor stairwell, where Mary had been waiting—hiding—until Kaitlyn had left. Before answering, he went down the steps to the second floor hallway, saw the ladder still there, the light fixture remounted, but Cal had gone. Perhaps returning his tools before coming back for the ladder. Returning to the third floor, James picked up the portrait of Mary and set it behind a painting of a speedboat on Toluca Lake.

"All clear."

James met her halfway up the stairwell, close enough to talk to her without being overheard through thin walls. "Is this what it's gonna be like?"

Mary pursed her lips, remaining silent.

"Sorry. I just—I didn't realize we lived in a commune."

"It's so much pressure."

"What is?"

She looked away, silent, teeth tugging on her lower lip. When they were together, Mary avoided talking about her friends, even after he'd met them at Heaven's Night she hadn't volunteered much information. James had begun to assume the friendships were casual, more a consequence of their reverence for her father than something she sought out or encouraged. The living arrangements added a weird spin to his assumptions.

"It's okay," James said.

"He was so important to all of them. They see him in me. Everything he was to them."

"That's not what I see."

"No?"

"No."

James placed his hands gently on her waist and leaned in for a soft kiss. As he felt her body relax, tension melting away, he slipped his fingers through the belt loops of her jean shorts and tugged her close to him.

"Oh, my!"

At that moment, he didn't give a damn if her so-called friends were spying on their embrace through the peepholes in their doors. He wouldn't let them ruin a good thing.

CHAPTER 15

Hoping to keep his phone's flashlight working as long as possible, James switched off low-power mode. As a compromise, he adjusted the dimmer control to provide a faint light, enough to see the next step or two ahead of him but not much else. He navigated the first set of stairs, avoiding a few tripping hazards and proceeded down the hallway where, on move-in day, he'd nearly crashed into a ladder. The ladder was gone now, the lightbulb in the ceiling fixture Cal had been repairing at the time had been shattered.

Considering the extreme state of disrepair of the entire apartment building, a broken lightbulb was merely a footnote of concern. If he hadn't lived in the Woodside Apartments more than a few years ago, he might have guessed the building had been condemned long before then. Where the painted walls remained relatively intact, they were coated in grime. Rust-colored liquid had dripped from the ceiling as if from suppurating wounds. Mostly, the walls were brown and dingy, or cracked and split, bulging in some areas, concave elsewhere. Some sections had thick layers of plaster lathered over major fissures with no attempt at smoothing the surface, but simply to hold the wall intact.

Any carpeting had been ripped up and removed. Sections with tiling were just as bad. Tiles stained or split, some shattered, and in others completely gone. Generally, the floor was gritty with debris and crunched underfoot.

The air felt heavy and smelled sour. Now and then he felt a draft of air that carried the stench of decay. Somewhere in the building he expected to find an animal or human corpse left to rot. Not something he sought, but the idea of dead bodies awaiting discovery added another level of anxiety to his search for Mary.

At the stairwell leading to the third floor landing, the railing creaked when he placed his hand on it, leaning out of true. Rust had traveled throughout the railing and some of the weld points had come apart. One strong kick would dislodge the entire structure. Other than stains and small fissures, the stairs seemed intact, so he stayed in the middle, avoiding the railing and the stained and blistered wall. Past the landing, he could go no farther.

In the dim light of the cellphone's flashlight, he discovered the bars of a floor-to-ceiling metal gate blocking the stairs.

"The hell?"

He swept the gate with the light, looking for a latch or hinges or some kind of release mechanism but found nothing. He grabbed the bars with his free hand and tested their strength. Despite the decrepit nature of the rest of the building and the weakness in the walls, the gate held firm. No rust on the metal either. The gate must have been a recent addition. But why place a gate blocking access to the entire floor? Could the structural damage be that much worse above? Had they evacuated the fourth floor before blocking it off?

"Mary!" he called. "Mary, are you up there? Can you hear me? It's James."

He waited but received no response.

"I got your letter," he called. "If you're hiding up there, it's safe to come down now. We'll get out of this together. I promise."

Still nothing. But he couldn't be sure she wasn't up there. She might have been injured, hurt by one of those things roaming the street. She could be feverish, unconscious. He had come as soon as possible, but maybe he was too—

He stepped off the landing and approached the first apartment.

"Dara! Kaitlyn! You in there?"

Nothing. He rapped his knuckles on the door.

"It's James," he called. "I need—Mary needs your help. If you're in there, open the door!"

Again, nothing. About to turn aside, he stopped, then reached for the doorknob and tested it. Unlocked. If they hadn't locked the door, they were probably long gone. As he pushed the door inward, his flashlight flickered off. He checked the phone's display and saw the barest red sliver of a battery charge left. Before it completely died, he powered the phone down. Enough power left for an emergency call—maybe.

He shoved the phone into his jeans pocket.

"I'm coming in!" he shouted through the open doorway.

Dara was a cop. Probably kept a gun in the apartment. Wasn't beyond the realm of possibility that somebody was holed up in there, cowering in the dark and scared shitless, ready to fire at the first sign of an intruder.

Easing his way inside the apartment, he called out one last time, "Hello? Hey. Is anyone here?"

He expected total darkness in the apartment, but light emanated from the corner. The glow came from an old television set—the kind that still relied on vacuum tube technology—standing on four rickety wooden legs between two windows with shredded curtains. The room was devoid of any other furniture.

As he neared the television, he noticed the VCR on top of it, two wicker baskets on the floor, both holding VHS tapes, with several extra tapes lying on the wooden floor in front of them. The TV was the first sign of working electricity in the building, but what caught his attention was the television screen itself, the flickering images portrayed there via the tape player.

He crouched in front of the TV and stared at—

—some kind of ceremony being performed, captured by an unsteady hand with a camcorder.

James squeezed his eyes shut briefly, struck by a moment of wincing pain.

A string of bizarre images in closeup flash across the screen. Figures in hooded robes. Bare skin splattered with blood. Others licking the bloody flesh with eager mouths. An extended tongue, writhing as the tip laps at an eyeball rimmed in dripping blood.

Another surge of pain, crippling this time, like a spike through his forehead, dropped James to his knees. He could no longer look at the images on the too-bright screen. Instead, his gaze fell to the VHS tapes, each labeled by hand with only a month and a year, dating back several years, perhaps longer for the tapes in the baskets. Month and year. As if that's all that was needed—more of the same images before him. Images he couldn't bear to watch because of the pain throttling his skull.

He gripped his phone. Couldn't remember taking it from his pocket or turning it back on or dialing M. But the phone was ringing...

"Where are you?"

Her voice was concerned but calm. A calm in the storm of his mind. It took a supreme effort to respond, "It hurts so bad—my head—I can't make it stop—"

"It's gonna be okay," she said. "Just tell me where you are."

"I'm getting closer—I can feel it." He pressed his free hand to his temple, wincing, eyes squeezed shut again, trying to focus. "She's here—"

"Ja—"

The line went dead. The last sliver of battery life exhausted.

He shoved the phone back in his pocket.

On the television, the lurid images were gone, the recording ended. Only white static remained, a pulsing glow he could tolerate. The intense pain from his headache receded, making the light tolerable and breathing easier. He gathered himself and stood, ignoring the other tapes spread out on the floor before him. No need to subject himself to more of—whatever that was he'd witnessed.

Besides, an idea had occurred to him.

He lurched toward the nearest window, stumbling as he massaged pins and needles out of his legs. There was a way forward after all. The window squealed from desuetude as he lifted it high enough to climb through onto the fire escape balcony. And the fire escape, eroded by rust, creaked under his weight.

Outside again, his vantage point provided a wider view of the town, dark under an oppressive cloud cover, buildings coated with the strange rust, dark and shimmering from the steady rain that had replaced the ash of twilight. He stared for a while, caught sight of a few Armless, twitching and staggering aimlessly below, not a single human among them. They'd killed the homeless man. How many others? He wondered if Angela was still alive tending the cemetery or if she'd finally come to her senses and left.

M hadn't wanted him to come back to Silent Hill.

Unfortunately, when she called him back, she'd get the message that "the user's voicemail box is full" and, based on their history, she'd worry about him and request a wellness check. But there was nothing else she could do, except wait and fret some more.

James knew implicitly she worried about him. Of course,

that was the nature of her job. But she wouldn't be a true professional if she hadn't pursued a career that aligned with her own nature. She'd want to help him, have somebody come check on him. What he regretted was his inability to call her back and assure her he was fine, no assistance needed. The headache was manageable now. No more than a dull ache. The important thing was that he had a real lead on Mary. He needed to see it through.

Craning his neck upward, he squinted his eyes against the continual rainfall, to the fourth floor apartment level. Took a moment to locate the apartment he'd shared with Mary—and saw a light in the window.

CHAPTER 16

Energized with a sudden flare of hope, James crossed Kaitlyn and Dara's balcony and leapt onto the wrought-iron stairs of the fire escape. The staircase creaked and swayed under his weight. He felt the ubiquitous rust under his fingers as he climbed up to the next floor and wondered how much it had compromised the structural integrity of the fire escape. But it was a fleeting thought at best. His gaze kept darting toward the lighted window above.

His right foot slipped on a wet tread and his knee came down hard on the tread above, splitting it down the middle, as if it were cheap plastic. There were no risers for support and the wrought iron had become more brittle than he would have thought possible. He flung out his hand to catch himself on a higher tread and felt the entire section of staircase shudder under him. The thick bolts mounting the fire escape to the stone wall of the building were no longer secure. How many of those bolts could pop free before the entire structure toppled free and crashed to the street forty feet below? He'd rather not find out the hard way.

While the light in their apartment window beckoned, he climbed the rest of the stairs with what felt like agonizing slowness. Easing across the grated landing of the fire escape, he sensed the iron bowing under him. At the edge, he grabbed the balcony railing in one hand and swung both legs up and over, landing on the much firmer concrete surface. But even that was covered in the strange rust that had swept across every surface in Silent Hill when darkness fell.

Up close, the light in the window fell on drawn roller shades, casting a woman's figure in silhouette against the cream-colored vinyl surface.

James rapped on the glass. "Mary—it's me! Mary?!"

The figure remained immobile.

"Mary?"

Something was wrong.

Turning sideways, James braced his right arm with his left and slammed his elbow into the glass, breaking the window. He wrapped his jacket around his fist and forearm and knocked loose shards of glass from around the window frame. After shaking out his jacket, he shrugged back into it, swung his leg over the windowsill, ducking his head, and pushing the shade aside.

Without the shade acting as a filter, the light inside the apartment blinded him. He couldn't see anything, shielding his eyes with the back of his hand until he could step farther into the room and turn his back to the light. Finally, he saw the standing figure for what it was. A dressmaker's mannequin, clothed in a floral print dress.

The head and face were blank and white with a vertical seam down the middle. While the exposed torso was white as well, the arms and hands were wooden and segmented, posable. A large area of the torso was covered in black and, as he stared at it, he noticed movement. He stepped closer and realized the dark patch was a swath of black moths. When he leaned forward, the moths scattered, fluttering around the room, darting in and out of the beam of light.

He turned his attention to the source of the light, following it back to the closet. Empty hangers on a bar within had been pushed aside to expose a small cubby in the rear. He imagined at some point it had housed a wall safe. But a flashlight was propped in the cubby now. And behind it, a framed photo of a man standing behind a young girl, his hands placed possessively on her shoulders. To the right of the photo, a small bust of the same man.

James reached for the flashlight. It was about the size and shape of a pack of playing cards, with a clip on the back to slip over a breast pocket for hands-free operation. As he picked it up, he noticed an envelope at the back of the cubby, a corner wedged under the photo. When he turned the flashlight around to point toward the cubby, the black moths swarmed around his head, blotting out his vision with a dark stroboscopic effect—

CHAPTER 17

James had left Mary alone in the apartment to scout some landscape painting locations and run a few errands, ending up at the Grand Market on the corner of Neely and Katz for about a bag's worth of groceries. He charted a familiar course through the apartment building, opening the unlocked door to their apartment and closing it softly with the side of his foot. As he set the bag down on the kitchen table, he heard hushed voices coming from the living room. Mary hadn't mentioned she was expecting guests.

Curious, he walked down the short hallway, careful not to make a sound, and stood by the half-opened door, peering through the gap. It wasn't lost on him that he felt the need to sneak around in his own home. But he had the uneasy feeling he'd walked in on something he wasn't meant to see.

Mary sat on her heels in the middle of the living room, where all the curtains had been drawn, casting the interior in shadows, her hands clasped in her lap. She wore the same long-sleeved blouse with a dense floral pattern and jeans she'd been wearing when he'd left. Others surrounded her in a circle, sitting in chairs, looking down on her, as if she were a mere supplicant in this bizarre ritual. James identified the faces of Dara and Kaitlyn, Cal and Mitzy, the Meyer twins, and Claudette with her black cat Boo. Everyone she'd introduced to him at Heaven's Night, but there were several strange faces in the group as well.

Mary sat facing Dara. A small round table holding three burning candles stood between them. Dara, in a black vest over a dark plaid shirt, held a staff or a cane and seemed to lead the proceedings. She also wore a necklace James had never seen before. Some sort of geometric symbol. A horizontal bar with a skewed acute triangle hanging from it behind an open circle. They took turns speaking to Mary in hushed tones, almost reverent whispers, in a mix of compliments and passive-aggressive threats.

"We understand completely how you feel—" Dara whispered, her left hand clutching the silver head of the cane.

"Love's not an easy thing," Kaitlyn whispered in turn.

"It can get your head all twisted around—" one of the Meyers twins said.

"You lose yourself in it," the other twin added.

The twins wore similar cardigans—one gray, one pink—over blouses with Peter Pan collars, jean skirts and patterned hose, but James had given up trying to figure out which one was Gia or Mia on any given day. They didn't care, so why should he?

"But we have to stay focused," Mitzy said.

"Our work is not yet done," Cal said, nodding. "Remember, Joshua showed us the way."

"But warned us not to stray from the path." Claudette stroked the head of her cat. "You must remember your priorities."

"We have chosen a great undertaking," Dara said, twisting the cane for emphasis, its silver tip scoring the wooden floor. "The Return cannot be jeopardized by distractions or frivolities. You understand?"

Mary lowered her head, a slight bow of acquiescence.

Dara lifted her own head, as if acknowledging the gesture—and spotted James standing in the doorway. "And here he is," she said, without missing a beat. "Man of the house."

"What's going on, Jimmy boy?" Cal said, smiling.

At a loss for words, James nodded by way of greeting. What he wanted to say was, "What the fuck did I just witness?" But he bit his tongue. He was a private person and needed to talk to Mary before giving this group of so-called friends and several strangers the bum's rush out of the apartment. Instead, he acted as if he hadn't heard a good chunk of this weird intervention. "Mare—?"

Dara blew out the candles and tapped the tip of the cane on the floor as she stood. The others rose from their chairs and slipped into forced small talk, commentary on the weather, sports scores, compliments on clothing choices and accessories. While they milled around, pushing chairs aside, Mary climbed to her feet, avoiding eye contact with them as she brushed her palms against the thighs of her jeans.

James entered the living room, continuing to feign a casual, unbothered attitude. As he neared Mary, she looked at him and he read the question in her eyes. She wondered what he'd seen and heard but was too nervous to ask while the others were present.

He looked around the group, Mary's friends and the strangers, trying to place faces he may have seen before. He assumed some, if not all, had been in Heaven's Night when Mary introduced him to her inner circle. "Didn't know you were coming over," he said casually to no one in particular. Even so, he detected the accusatory tone in his own voice. He hoped his poker face was better than his voice.

Boo curled in one hand, Claudette passed close to Mary and caught her upper arm. "We don't have to finish this now." She exited the room after a quick nod to Dara.

The twins paused before them for a moment. "Enjoy the evening," said the redhead, wearing the pink cardigan. "See you soon," the twin in the gray cardigan added. They walked out together, whispering to each other.

After the others filed out, Dara remained, examining James' face for an extended moment, probably searching for tells that he'd overheard more than he let on. Then she gave him an overly friendly pat on the shoulder. "Take care of our girl," she said before leaving the room.

James waited until he couldn't see Dara anymore, listening as the group left through the kitchen and closed the door behind them. He crossed the room and peered down the short corridor. Satisfied they were gone, he returned to Mary, staring at her while he collected his thoughts.

"I'm sorry," she said. "They just showed up."

"Of course they did," he said sardonically.

She frowned. "What does that mean?"

"You put your life on hold for them. They don't get to just show up whenever they want."

Mary took a deep breath before replying. "They're like my family, James," she said, looking away for a moment. James sensed she wanted to say more. When she returned her gaze to him, she said, "What am I supposed to do?"

Tired of her excuses, even more tired of their weird behavior, James shook his head. For him, it was simple. He'd tell them, "*Get the fuck out of here and don't come back.*" It made no sense to him. She allowed them to have this weird hold on her out of—what? Respect for her father's memory?

Mary pulled him close, staring into his eyes, wanting to engage, but he couldn't dismiss the thoughts swirling around in his head, questions without answers, bizarre meetings that made no sense and, through it all, they had treated her with a lack of respect, as if she were subservient to them for some damn reason.

Over her shoulder, he noticed the open closet doors, clothing on hangers pushed aside to reveal a cubby within, a secret space that might have held a safe in the past. The cubby had twin metal doors that, when closed completed a stenciled design of a triangle within a circle, bordered by smaller symbols. The design reminded him of Dara's necklace. Currently, the doors were open, revealing a framed photograph beside a small bust of a man, with a few candles burning in front of it.

James slipped past Mary to take a closer look at the photograph. A tall, grim-faced man in a flat-brimmed hat and overcoat stood behind a ten-year-old girl in a dress, his powerful hands resting on her shoulders. The man in the photo had a port wine birthmark on his right cheek—and that same port wine birthmark was painted on the right cheek of the sculpture. James was certain the tall man was Joshua Crane with a young Mary. But he asked anyway, "Is that him?"

Mary remained silent.

James continued to stare at the photo. With the stenciled metal doors shut, the cubby would almost look like a baroque intake vent. Push the clothes on hangers in front of the double doors, and no one would even know it was there.

"Why'd you never put photos of him up?"

Mary spread her arms wide, then let them drop. "I wanted this place to feel like it was just ours—"

James had only glanced at her for a moment before returning his attention to the photo. He couldn't escape the odd feeling the dead man was staring back at him, that Joshua Crane was somehow in the room with them. *What did the others see in this man? And, just as strangely, why would Mary keep it hidden away? Maybe she only displayed the photo when his mentees—his acolytes—visited her.*

"What were they talking about?" James asked absently. "When I came in?"

"Oh, they're just—" She paused, flustered. "How much did you hear?"

"Definitely more than they wanted me to, I'm sure."

She strode past him to the cubby, blew out the candles and swung the twin doors closed. Then she returned to him, gently turned his face away from the cubby, forcing his attention back on her. He waited for excuses or maybe a lie to ease his concerns. For some sad reason, he didn't expect the truth.

"I know what they're like—how they seem—but I'm asking you to please—please—I want this to be about you and me. Always. Always just us."

She closed the distance between them, pressing her body against his, taking his face between her palms with the softness of a caress and kissed him on the lips. At first the kiss was soft and tender, but gradually her lips became insistent, and she moved one hand to the back of his neck, seeking more. Though he didn't resist, neither did he fully reciprocate. As far as he was concerned, nothing had been settled between them. The more she pushed him to ignore whatever the hell was happening with the people in her orbit, the more detached he became.

Movement caught his eyes—now open despite the kiss. The left stenciled cubby door had swung open quietly on well-oiled hinges. The grim face of Joshua Crane stared back at him. James had come to a decision.

Something had to change.

CHAPTER 18

James pointed the flashlight to the base of the cubby, reached under the photo and pulled out the white envelope. He adjusted the light toward the unsealed envelope as he pulled a letter from it. The black moths swirled around his head again, dipping in and out of the light. "Brookhaven Hospital Admission Request Form," he said softly. "Patient Name: Mary Crane..." His hand holding the flashlight trembled as he clutched the report in his other hand, pressing so hard the paper began to crumble in his grip.

A large black moth landed in the middle of the report, settling over the worst of it, the section that chilled his heart, its wings unmoving, as if frozen in time—as if it might never move again.

James heard a distant noise. A shout or some sort of human vocalization. Somebody else was in the apartment building. He swung the flashlight away from the medical report toward the other side of the room. The bright beam cast harsh shadows off the walls of the empty room.

Mary wasn't here in their apartment, but she had been. She had left the flashlight behind, knowing he would come here and find it. To help him find his way through the darkness to her.

He left the apartment through the front door, walking quietly down the stained and fissured hallway, listening in case he heard the sound again. With each step he took, the floor creaked softly as if his weight was almost too much to bear. A bitter, muttering voice led him down the hall with the promise of distinguishable words. Before he'd passed two apartments, he heard the sound, clearer now—retching.

Standing outside the open door of a dark apartment, James heard someone gagging a third time and entered, passing through a kitchen down a hallway that led to a bathroom. The door was ajar, far enough that he saw the worn soles of a pair of men's shoes. With his forearm, James brushed the door open the rest of the way.

An overweight bearded man, wearing a tan, sweat-stained T-shirt and cargo pants, kneeled hunched over the toilet, hands gripping either side of the stained bowl to control the paroxysms of his vomiting. He coughed and spat, then glanced up at the bright light flooding the bathroom, shielding his eyes with the back of one hand.

"What the fuck?"

Early thirties, James guessed. He had disheveled, shoulder-length hair, a full red beard and mustache in need of a trim.

"Are you okay?"

"It look like I'm okay? Turn that fucking thing off." He wiped his mouth with the edge of his hand. "Put it down. Put it down or it goes right up your ass."

"All right," James said, lowering the beam away from the man's face. "Take it easy."

"Who the hell are you?"

"I'm—"

"Wait. Wait, wait, wait," the man said, finger up as he began to gag. He resumed his position over the toilet, both hands engaged, convulsing—with nothing but dry heaves the result.

As he eased back from the bowl, James glimpsed half-eaten chunks of meat floating in the crimson water with strings and clumps of blood.

The man swung around, sat on the rough, tile-stripped floor with his back against the bowl, forearms hanging over his knees. Screen-printed on the T-shirt above an illustration of crossed axes was the word 'Lumberjack.'

"False alarm," the man said hoarsely. "All good. Who the hell are you anyway?"

"I'm James."

"Eddie," the man said. "James, huh? Don't know no James. Why are you not sick like everyone else?"

James had no idea how to respond. The only person he'd come across in town was Angela. As far as he knew, she wasn't ill. Then again, she seemed obsessed with the cemetery. "I'm looking for someone."

"Ain't nobody here."

"I think she might be at the hospital," James replied, which was a guess at this point. Mary hadn't been in her shop or in their apartment. But if she'd been sick, the hospital made sense.

Eddie cackled. A string of blood red drool dropped into his beard.

"What's funny?"

"Look around, buddy," Eddie said with a dismissive wave of his arm. "Won't find anyone at the hospital. City's one big cemetery."

"What happened here?"

"You should've seen it." Eddie took a moment to compose his thoughts, staring at his hands resting on his knees. He gave a listless shake of his head. "No one could get their ass in gear to react in time. Poor fucks. Whole town was rotten before anyways. But this... this was something else. Fires... the water... everybody going insane... bleeding, then out into the streets." He rolled his eyes, as if reliving the panic of those days in pure disbelief. "Stretchers of people. Stacked together in parking lots. Lines of morgue trucks on the highway..."

With a grunt of effort, he tried to climb to his feet but gave up and sank back down to the floor.

"Been days since I ate somethin.' You don't got anythin' to eat, do ya?"

"No, sorry," James said. "Keep going."

"It's like I told ya," Eddie said. "All that crazy shit happened and then these *things* started to show up."

"I saw a sign the well water was contaminated."

Eddie nodded. "Yeah, heard talk about the poisoned water supply." He stared at James in the reflected light. "Wow," he said. "You've been lucky so far."

"What?"

"Check this—" He pulled up his left sleeve to expose his shoulder, covered in blisters and open sores, like the flesh was rotting away.

James averted his eyes without turning his head, trying to hide his revulsion. "Jesus Christ," he managed to say.

"No shit, buddy," Eddie said with a bitter laugh. If he noticed James' disgust, he didn't show it.

"No treatment?"

"Pain meds, if ya can get 'em," Eddie said. "Dulls the pain. Does shit to fix ya."

"That's tough," James said. "Sorry, man."

"What about you? Got any signs yet?"

"No," James said. "Nothing... yet."

"So, what is it you do?"

"What do you mean, what do I do?"

"In life," Eddie said. "What do you do?"

"Uh—I'm a painter."

"No shit? Painter, huh? I ever heard of you?"

"I—uh—I really don't know—" James said. It was always an awkward question. "Not like I'm a household name."

Eddie was staring off into space. "Always thought I had the

goods to be an artist. You ever have weird dreams? Shit that goes on in there," Eddie said, tapping his index finger against the side of his head, "you couldn't handle it."

"No offense, but that smells really nasty," James said, indicating the befouled toilet bowl with a tilt of his head. "Courtesy flush?"

Eddie cackled. "These days, one flush is all you might get. Don't know if you noticed, buddy, but the infrastructure in this town ain't exactly aces these days."

From somewhere in the distance, James heard an infant screaming.

"Did you hear that?"

"Hear what?" Eddie asked. "You trippin,' man?"

"Sounds like a baby."

"A baby?" Incredulous. "There ain't no baby here."

James walked into the corridor.

"Fuck you going?" Eddie called after him.

Behind him, James heard Eddie slip and fall at least once trying to stand, then stumble into the bathroom door and curse before he caught up to him in the hallway.

"Wait up," Eddie said. "Where you going?"

"To find the baby," James said. "You really can't hear it cry—?"

The screaming ceased.

"It's gone," James said. "Can I ask you a question?"

"No, I didn't hear no baby crying," Eddie said. "May be sick but I'm not deaf."

"No," James said. "Not about that. Why did you stay there?"

"You kidding?" Eddie asked. "Place is rid of all these assholes. No more jerks calling me names, making fun of me, calling me 'fatso' like it's my nickname. No more bullies thinking they're better 'n me. No more high-and-mighty types looking down on me like I'm subhuman." He shook his head, smiling. "It's heaven now! Got the entire city to myself. Well, at least until you showed up. You're not an asshole, are ya, James?"

The baby resumed crying.

"There," James said. "You hear that?"

"I don't hear shit."

James pointed down an L-shaped turn in the corridor. "It's coming from over there."

They turned down the new corridor, with walls cast in a lurid reddish light from an unknown source. It seemed like emergency lighting, which was common during a power outage, but he saw no light fixtures to account for it. Instead, the light seemed to shine through the exterior windows, from the night sky.

Once again, the crying stopped.

If James listened carefully, he could hear the pattering of the steady drizzle against those same windows. The steady sound had become white noise, unnoticed unless he focused on it. But he no longer heard the distressed infant.

Not that he could do anything about it. Only a few steps down the new corridor, he had to stop. "What the hell is this?"

Floor-to-ceiling iron bars blocked their path. A security gate, like the one that had blocked his progress on the stairwell. He looked at Eddie. "Was this here before? When you came?"

"Don't remember," Eddie said. "I was feverish, wandering around, didn't know which way was up."

James examined the security gate with his flashlight. Rust had set in, but the bars remained sturdy. Again, he found no latch or release mechanism. But he noticed movement on the other side of the bars—

Close to the floor, the doors of what looked like a service panel swung open. From inside the crawlspace, a young girl peeked out, no more than eight or nine years old, with long blond hair parted in the middle, wearing a floral-patterned pink-hued dress with a rounded Peter Pan collar. Clutching an old gray doll to her chest, her face and hands were coated with grime. And her eyes were wide with fear.

"Holy shit—" James exclaimed. The last thing he'd expected to find running around the ruined town was a school-aged girl.

He crouched down, close to the wall, his flashlight directed toward her at a steep angle to avoid blinding her. But as soon as he'd moved closer, she withdrew into the crawlspace.

"Naw, naw," Eddie said behind him. "Be careful."

"She's just a kid," James said. "Hey. Hey—what's your name?"

He could see one of her eyes, reflected in the indirect light, peering out of the darkness at him, curious. But she remained silent.

"It's okay," James said. "I won't hurt you. Why don't you come on out of there. I'm James. This is—"

"Eddie."

"I'm Laura," said the little girl.

"You can't stay here alone, Laura," James said solicitously. He noticed an irregularity in the bars and examined it with the light. One of the vertical bars below the horizontal crosspiece was severed right beneath the crosspiece, and was bent to the side, creating a larger gap compared to the space between the other bars. "You're probably small enough to get through these bars."

"Let's get outta here," Eddie said nervously.

James wasn't about to abandon a little girl. He reached through the gap in the bars, offering his hand to the girl. "C'mon," he said. "You can trust me."

"I'm telling you, this is a bad idea."

James ignored Eddie. "C'mon, Laura," he repeated. "I got you."

Laura eased her way out of the crawlspace, continuing to clutch the old doll to her chest. After a few moments, she was completely out in the open, on her knees, and reached out a hand toward James.

"That's it," James said, nodding encouragement. "Come with us. We can help you."

Then his radio crackled and squawked, startling them all.

Laura froze.

He'd forgotten it was in his jacket pocket. The music had stopped playing a while ago and it had been silent since then. "It's okay—it's just—"

But now the squealing of the radio wasn't the only sound. James heard a loud, throbbing noise approaching from the far end of the hallway, then something heavy scraping the exposed floor, and thunderous footfalls.

"We need to get our asses outta here," Eddie exclaimed, his panic redlining.

James shook his head and directed his attention to Laura.

"Don't worry," he said, trying to project calm he didn't feel. "We're not leaving without you. Come on! Just a little closer."

But the little girl remained frozen.

James looked up, shining his flashlight into the distance, toward the strange sounds. Beyond the reach of the light, cloaked in frustrating shadows, he glimpsed a gigantic silhouette, a pair of large feet in heavy shoes, like gladiator sandals, and a long, serrated sword dragging on the ground behind the figure.

Shifting his focus back to Laura, her eyes wide with naked fright, he spoke urgently, "Come on, Laura!" She needed to hurry before that colossus came any closer.

"Shit! Jimmy, c'mon!" Eddie shouted. "We need to forget about the kid. We gotta go! Now!"

James strained through the wider gap in the bars, managed to brush his fingers against her shoulder. Another inch or two and he could pull her to him, then help her through the bars. His shoulder ground into the unforgiving metal bars, his fingers going numb from the sustained pressure, but he couldn't get a grip on her.

Eddie rushed close to the bars, bent at the waist and screamed directly at Laura, "Get lost, kid!"

Terrified, Laura spun around and ducked back into the crawlspace with her doll. Her trembling hands reached out to grip the twin doors and pull them shut.

James stood and spun around to face Eddie. "You asshole!"

Crippling pain shot through his head. Clutching his temples, he collapsed to his knees and dropped the flashlight, unable to breathe. Like a white-hot poker piercing his skull.

"Would ya look at that," Eddie said derisively. "You're all fucked up like everyone else. Mr. High-and-Mighty."

With that, Eddie swung his foot back and kicked James in the gut, dropping him to the floor.

Out of the corner of his eye, James saw the massive figure approaching, features slowly resolving out of the shadows. He heard each resounding footfall, felt the vibrations where his cheek pressed against the floor. But he felt helpless to move. Between the mind-searing headache and Eddie's cheap shot to his abdomen, James thought he might vomit.

"What did you call me again, Jimmy boy?" Eddie taunted. "An asshole?"

Hovering over James, Eddie punched him in the side of the head, knocking him down as he tried to rise. Eddie raised his fist for another blow, then froze, having caught sight of the behemoth, his blind rage evaporating in an instant as gut-clenching fear took over.

"Oh, fuck. You did it, didn't ya, Jimmy?" Eddie said, panicking. "You woke him up!"

Eddie retreated the way they had come, leaving James curled up on his side against the security gate.

Grimacing, James clawed the floor, wrapping his hands around the flashlight. He grabbed the flat crossbar of the gate to pull himself into a sitting position and swung the light around to illuminate the hallway on the other side. The colossal figure emerged from the shadows into the harsh light.

The first thing James noticed was the massive, red-tinted metal helmet the man wore, wedge-shaped, like a pyramid with steep sides, widest at his broad shoulders, rising to a point that made him stand nearly eight feet tall. The helmet extended downward nearly to his waist and half as wide with a flat base. The sides had many round vent holes, while the flat front had a zigzagging coarse metal mesh that hid his eyes and facial features. Unless, like the Armless, he had no face.

His muscular torso was wrapped in bandages, reminiscent of a mummy, while his lower half was covered by the shredded remains of a brown leather butcher's smock. His powerful arms were thick with veins and laced with scar tissues. He wore brown leather gloves and leather sandals. In his right hand he clutched the hilt of a massive, serrated sword. James had never seen a sword blade as broad as this one, nor as long. If a typical sword might be sharp and sturdy enough to decapitate someone, this Great Sword looked deadly enough to slice a full-grown adult in half—horizontally or vertically.

James couldn't know if this Pyramid Head was a man or a monster, but whatever his nature, his role seemed obvious. Executioner.

Fighting off waves of nausea and the pain throbbing in his head, James summoned his strength and tried to move away from the iron bars. He pushed off from the bars, falling from his seated position to hands and knees, facing away from Pyramid Head, supremely grateful for the iron bars separating them.

He glanced back just as Pyramid Head crouched and reached through the bars with his left hand.

"Oh, no," James said. "No! No! No!"

His attempt to scramble out of reach failed. A large, powerful hand wrapped around his left ankle, clamping down painfully.

James tried unsuccessfully to yank free of the monster's grip. Pyramid Head yanked him backward, pulling his foot and calf through the bars to the other side. Rolling onto his back, James raised his right foot and planted it against the flat crosspiece, bracing himself.

Pain shot up his left leg under the strain. James wondered grimly if his ankle would shatter before or after his femur was yanked from his hip socket.

When Pyramid Head heaved his sword upward, a darker thought intruded. He intended to sever the leg. James let his right leg slip from the crossbar to kick at the gloved hand gripping his left ankle. At the same time, he directed the flashlight beam at the meshwork of the helmet, right where the monster's eyes would be—assuming he had them.

The helmet turned aside abruptly and the grip on his ankle loosened just enough for him to kick it free. He felt a new fire burning in the ankle. Couldn't trust it to support his weight, so he didn't try to stand. He scrambled away on hands and knees. He hadn't gotten far when he heard a howl and a deafening clang.

He looked back long enough to see Pyramid Head had rammed the front of his helmet between the bars. The force of the blow had bent the bars aside. Pyramid Head reared back and slammed the helmet against the bars a second time, deforming them even more. He tried to squeeze through the gap, but it wasn't wide enough—yet. In this instance, his massive size worked against him. But James realized it wasn't a question of *if* the barrier would fall but *when*.

CHAPTER 19

At the turn in the hallway, James pulled himself to his feet, using the wall for support. The throbbing in his head had diminished, as had the nausea from the kick in the gut. His ankle remained tender, though he didn't believe any bones were broken. Gradually, he placed more weight on it, making sure it could support his full weight without buckling.

Behind him, Pyramid Head howled again, his helmet smashing into the bars of the security gate with the force of a sledgehammer. James heard a damaged bar fall to the floor, followed by a second, then the squeal of a third being wrenched free of its housing. A few moments of silence, then the clang and squeal of metal striking metal. And then the loud thumps of approaching footfalls, the scrape of the dragged sword. Pyramid Head had breached the gate.

Alarmed, James picked up his pace, battling a slight limp in his gait. The effort cost him. His head began to throb again, and his vision blurred. The hallway before him swam in and out of focus. The walls seemed to squeeze inward then expand as the floor sloped upward and down, as if the building itself were breathing. Nausea swelled inside him. He needed to sit down and rest, but a monster pursued him. If he stopped, he would die.

Hoping to lose Pyramid Head, he made a turn down an unfamiliar hallway. He ran his free hand along the sloppily patched fissures in the bulging walls to steady himself, yet he had trouble focusing on the way ahead. When he saw an obstacle on the floor, he stopped, trying to make sense of it. Without the dizzying motion, he focused on the figure curled up on the floor. A bald, naked woman with pale, mottled flesh, hands clutching her sides.

"Mary!"

Could she have been here all along? Had she left the apartment and been overcome by illness and pain, collapsing, alone?

At the sound of the name, the figure shuddered, a full body tremor. Her hands moved away from her side—

—and fell from her wrists, completely detached.

Stunned, James staggered backward.

Slowly, the pale figure struggled to rise from the floor, each articulated motion a separate act rather than muscles, ligaments and bones working in concert. More like a clockwork toy imitating human movement. Her head turned away from the wall toward him, continuing to twist until, impossibly, her face was directly above her spine and then the head—fell off its shoulders.

The disembodied head rolled along the abraded floor toward James, stopping at his feet. Its face—Mary's face—smiled up at him.

"*James,*" she said, delighted. "*You came back for me.*"

He stared in terror and fascination, unable to look away. "No..."

"*You came back,*" she said, unblinking. "*I knew you would.*"

"No," he said, rubbing his eyes frantically. "This isn't real."

"*I'm such a mess,*" she said, her gaze traveling down to her missing torso. "*Can you—can you help—?*"

The disembodied Mary head began to cough, unblinking eyes wide in alarm.

"Mary," he said, despite himself. The concussion—he was hallucinating.

The Mary head began to gag. A blackened tongue protruded from her pale mouth. James bent closer, squinting to focus. The black tongue split down the middle and erupted from her mouth.

Startled, he pulled back as—

—a dozen black moths escaped from the Mary head, fluttering past his face, momentarily blotting out the light. Then they were gone and the head on the floor no longer had Mary's face, merely that of a woman with similar features. Expecting to find her in the apartment building, he must have imagined it and her voice. A disembodied head couldn't—

Across the hall, the headless body began to twist and writhe, as if in unbearable pain, thrashing uncontrollably. Its arms shriveled to half their previous length and where its hands had been, twin crab-like claws formed. Both feet extended, bones crunching, flesh squelching, as they were absorbed into the ankles then narrowed to hard points. Then, horrifically, both sides of the woman's torso ruptured, three gaping holes on either side. Long, segmented appendages burst from these ragged openings. Three extra pairs of legs—but not human legs. The woman—the creature—was transforming into something else—a headless spider woman. The supine body rose into the air, primarily supported by her three new pairs of legs, while the withered arms waved around on either side of the neck stump like a spider's pedipalps.

Each of the eight legs rose and fell in quick succession as the transformed spider woman tested the strength and flexibility of her mutated body. The twin claws of the pedipalps opened and closed with sharp, clicking sounds. A moment later, the spider body was in motion, climbing up the wall briefly before dropping down to the floor and orienting on

James. Even without her head attached, she sensed him—and charged.

Circling away from her in the narrow space, James crashed into the door of an apartment on the other side of the hallway and staggered sideways, almost losing his balance. He spun around, backing away from the monstrosity illuminated by the wavering beam of his flashlight as she paused where he had stood. The clawed pedipalps reached down to the floor to retrieve the spider woman's dormant head. Carefully, she aligned the base of the head to the raw stump of her neck. Immediately, the head revived, its wide black eyes flashing white in the reflected light. The mouth stretched open to reveal jagged fangs sprouting from blackened, diseased gums. And with the mouth hanging open in the face looking upward at him, hundreds of tiny black spiders spilled out of the spider woman's maw, scurrying across her cheeks and forehead and scattering across the floor like a mobile plague.

Now that the mutation was whole, she turned her undivided attention to James. With eight powerful legs and the ability to climb walls, the freakish spider woman would have no trouble catching James in the confined space of the hallway. And if the hellish fangs produced venom in proportion to the size of her body, James had no doubt a single dose would be lethal. He needed to find a defensive position quickly or he would be overpowered. He spun around, turning his back to the spider woman to sprint down the hall. And, just as concerning, he heard Pyramid Head's heavy footfalls accompanied by the destructive scraping of his Great Sword. Too close. Hurrying down the hallway, he tried to tune out the rapid thumping of the spider woman's legs as she closed the distance between them.

With his blurred vision drifting in and out of focus, he lost track of his turns and found himself trapped—an apartment at the end of a long hallway. He glanced back the way he'd come but already the spider woman blocked his path, weaving side to side, multiple legs moving from wall to floor to wall again, as if daring him to try to slip past her. He shook his head, fighting off a bout of double vision. As the spider woman scuttled toward him, it almost seemed as if there was more than one of them, simply too many limbs moving at once—or he was suffering from double vision. He feared he was fighting his way through a concussion but had no choice but to push himself until he escaped the immediate threat.

Pyramid Head wouldn't be far behind.

Fortunately, the apartment door was unlocked. James slipped inside. He passed the kitchen and a dining table area into the living room, hoping to exit via the fire escape, but the windows were boarded up, planks nailed into the window frames. Grabbing the edges of one of the planks, he yanked on the wood. But whoever had boarded it up, had been overzealous in their use of nails. Even if he'd had a claw hammer handy, it would have taken a significant amount of time and effort to pry several boards free to squeeze through the window.

He returned to the doorway, switched off his flashlight and peeked through the gap.

The spider woman had closed the distance. Shadows of her segmented limbs stretched along the rough walls, making her appear even larger than she was, more agitated in her hypnotic prancing. The soft thumps she made as her legs struck the walls and floor contrasted with the alternating thuds of Pyramid Head's footfalls and the harsh scrape of its sword along the floor. Even if he could somehow elude the spider woman, Pyramid Head would see him coming and had already cut off his escape route.

James looked around the apartment, his gaze settling on the closet on the far side of the dining room, next to the living room. Taking care not to trip over a chair or kick anything on the floor and give away his location, he crossed the dark room and pulled open the bi-fold wooden louver doors, grateful when they didn't creak. He pushed several empty hangers aside and slipped inside the closet, closing the door behind him. Noticing a broken louver blade at chest height, he pressed down on the damaged side to create a gap through which he could peer into the room.

Seconds later, the spider woman burst through the apartment door, legs waving—so many legs! She navigated a rough circle around the kitchen, toward the living room and back toward the dining table. Sometimes she leaned forward, head low, exploring the area for hiding spaces. She bumped into a chair, backed up and circled around the table, moving dangerously close to the closet. One of her legs rubbed the wall and struck the closet's door jamb. The spider woman paused for a moment. Then she slid the tip of one leg down the row of horizontal louvers, eliciting a repetitive clicking sound until she hit the damaged louver which made a dull *clack*.

Inside the closet, James backed away from the louver gap through which he'd been spying on the room. Holding his breath, he ducked behind the hanging rod. He imagined the pointed leg crashing through the louvers to crush his face or impale him.

Two loud thuds sounded from right outside the apartment, followed by a crash as the door was nearly blasted from its hinges. The clothes hangers on either side of James' head trembled with the impact.

Pyramid Head had arrived.

Taking a risk, James resumed his position behind the broken slat. The spider woman had turned away from the closet to face Pyramid Head, who stood wide-legged inside the doorway, his Great Sword raised in his right hand. With an unobstructed view, James saw the spider woman raise and lower her eight legs in quick succession, but this time as if warming up for battle. She scrambled forward with that uncanny spidery grace and slammed the tips of her foremost pair of legs against the floor in a clear challenge. Then she hoisted a dining table chair with the same two legs and flung it at Pyramid Head with incredible force.

With a labored backhand of the Great Sword, Pyramid Head batted the chair aside. It sailed across the apartment and smashed a hole in the wall, knocking over a lamp as it tumbled to the floor in a shower of drywall. Pyramid Head stalked forward, and the spider woman rushed to meet him.

She scrambled over another chair onto the table, surging forward on all eight legs and leaped at Pyramid Head, who caught her by gouging leather-gloved fingers into her human shoulder and collarbone. He slammed her on the table on her back, virtually pinning her on the table.

All eight spider legs lashed out, pummeling Pyramid Head's arms and battering the long helmet to no effect. Ignoring the assault, he slowly raised his sword and brought the weighty blade down, embedding the tip into the wooden floor deep enough to hold it in place, freeing both his arms for his own assault. Then Pyramid Head curled his large hands into meaty fists and pounded them, one after the other, into the spider woman's exposed torso, determined to beat her into submission without the aid of his fearsome weapon.

Immediately, the spider woman switched tactics, abandoning her own assault in a desperate attempt to escape, but one striking fist was replaced by the weight of the next. She squirmed around on the tabletop, unable to break free and weakening by the second. James thought she sought the edge of the table. If she fell to the floor, the colossus might lose its hold on her. But it was clear to James that the spider woman, despite her additional limbs, was no match for the monster in the butcher's smock.

Another heavy blow landed, and the spider woman's legs sagged, twitching, almost lifeless at this point. With one hand pinning her in place, Pyramid Head circled the table, perhaps seeking a better angle to deliver the coup de grâce. And, as his back neared the closet, the radio in James' jacket pocket crackled to life. James shoved his hand in his pocket, attempting to pull it out and turn off the power before—

—Pyramid Head heard the radio.

His raised hand frozen mid-blow, Pyramid Head's long helmet turned toward the closet.

Perhaps sensing an opportunity in the distraction, the spider woman found a desperate reservoir of energy, and redoubled her efforts to break free, squirming, kicking and jabbing. Undeterred, Pyramid Head lifted her bodily a couple feet above the table, then slammed her down so hard the table split down the middle. The flailing legs sagged again, the spider woman's torso twisted at an unnatural angle, partially flattened. Dazed, she hung like a broken toy from the executioner's grasp.

Pyramid Head retrieved his weapon, turned and strode toward the closet door, dragging the limp spider woman behind him, as he laid the flat of the Great Sword on his right shoulder. Dropping the spider woman to the floor, the colossus grabbed the door handle and yanked the door open, dislodging it from the upper track.

Stunned, James looked up at the monster in the massive helmet, completely exposed to his wrath. At this close distance, James noticed the coarse zigzag metal mesh on the front of the helmet had been damaged from its recent use as a security gate battering ram. Behind the broken metal, a gleaming eye stared back at James.

Pyramid Head raised the Great Sword from his shoulder. The muscles in his powerful arm flexed and bunched as he prepared to strike.

James took a step back, banging his head on the hanging rod, before slipping back, pressing his body against the back wall. Trapped. Nowhere to run.

Then the siren *WAILED*.

Loud enough to be heard across the entirety of Silent Hill.

An insistent banshee scream that pierced the walls of the Woodside Apartments and drove a spike through James' skull—

Pyramid Head staggered backwards, dropping his Great Sword to the unfinished floor with a crash almost drowned out by the braying siren. His gloved hands rose to the sides of his pyramid-shaped helmet, fingers spread as if trying to plug the circular vent holes. But there were too many—

James knocked hangers from the rod and stumbled out of the closet, tripping over the limp form of the spider woman, veering away from Pyramid Head, hands clutching the sides of his own head, palms squashing his ears flat against his scalp—

Pyramid Head fell to his knees, wrestling with his helmet, desperate to rip it off his head but failing—

James dropped to his knees, an uncomfortable weight bearing down on his head. His eyes were squeezed shut against the stabbing pain, but he forced himself to look at the executioner kneeling opposite him, turned toward him, fighting to remove the ponderous helmet. James saw himself bearing that same burden, as if staring into a mirror—struggling to remove the same helmet from his own head—

...and the siren wailed...

CHAPTER 20

James opened his eyes—

—stared at the ceiling.

The world was hazy

but silent...

No siren blaring.

His head remained sore, but the intense pain had receded while he was unconscious. How long had he been out? Somehow, he was alive even though Pyramid Head was—

—gone!

He sat up and looked across the floor. No battered spider woman and no Pyramid Head. But wisps of fog eddied through the room. He climbed to his feet on unsteady legs to survey the immediate area. The walls seemed... indistinct, almost as if they might dissolve. His eyes had become accustomed to the dark but viewing the room now, in this twilight, the dimensions were wrong somehow. He bent to pick up the flashlight he must have dropped when he stumbled out of the closet and, when he looked up again, he realized the broken table was also missing.

Nothing about the room matched his memory of it.

How did I get here?

One wall was a floor-to-ceiling mirror with two barres attached to the mirror, one mounted horizontally, the other handrail at a slight angle. A studio for ballet dancers. And

James wasn't alone. A dark-haired woman lay on the floor with her back to him at the base of the mirror.

Her face buried in the curl of her arm, she said, "I told you not to come."

James approached cautiously, taking in his new surroundings. The rest of the walls were covered in blotchy maroon wallpaper with rumpled faux wood paneling covering the bottom third. At one time, the studio might have had a sprung floor to aid the dancers, but all that remained was wood planking painted white. Shredded curtains hung in front of a balcony.

Nobody else was in the open room, so the woman had been talking to him. He recognized her clothing. Dark gray baggy sweater over light gray baggy pants. *Angela.*

"What the hell's happening here?" he said.

Last time he saw her she was piling sandbags in the flooded cemetery.

She reached up to grab the horizontal barre and pulled herself into a sitting position. In her left hand, she clutched an eight-inch butcher knife, her knuckles white with the pressure she applied to the hilt. Why? What was she afraid of? They were alone.

She stared at him but didn't answer his question.

Then he noticed a pair of pink satin pointe shoes in the corner behind her, both bloodstained. The blood looked fresh.

James changed tacks. "Are you hurt? What happened?"

She avoided eye contact. "He always forced me to perform?"

"Who? Who forced you?"

"Doesn't matter," she said. "He's gone now."

James glanced at her feet. She wore thick black socks. And he couldn't see any blood leaking through to the floor under them.

"Are you safe now?"

"I do this to myself," she said miserably. "Why do we torture ourselves?"

James was unsure how to help her. But the knife in her hand was concerning. "I don't know," James said. "Guess we're too hard on ourselves."

"Sometimes," she said softly, staring at the knife, "it's all we know."

"What the hell's happening here?" James said. "This wasn't some flood."

"There are secrets," she said with a dark fervor. "They're all buried. They need to stay that way."

James crouched, trying to make himself look less threatening.

"What? What secrets?" he asked.

"What you're doing—it won't be enough to save her."

Stunned, James stared at her. How could she know about Mary's predicament? He tried to remember how much he'd told Angela in the cemetery.

"You can't save her, James."

The finality of her words scared him.

"Save her from what?"

Angela shook her head.

"Save her from what?!"

James rose, took a step forward. He wanted to grab her by her shoulders and shake the truth out of her. But she raised the knife in both hands, tilting the point toward his face.

"Stay where you are!" she shouted.

"I'm not gonna hurt you," James said, hands up, palms facing her in the universal I-mean-you-no-harm gesture.

"You don't know what kind of hell you have to face."

She was openly crying now.

"I didn't leave," Angela said. "None of us left. Look at us!"

James took a step forward, reaching to console her. But she thrust the knife in his direction, almost snarling.

"Don't touch me!" Tears rolled down her cheeks. "Nobody'll touch me ever again."

She backed into the corner past the edge of the floor-to-ceiling mirror, pressing her back into the corner, making herself smaller. But she continued to point the knife in his direction.

Her reaction baffled him. He'd never threatened her or touched her. They'd parted on odd but friendly terms at the cemetery, so her change of attitude made no sense. Then again, nothing made sense in the nightmare factory that Silent Hill had become. Whatever had happened to her, he didn't know her well enough to decode her trauma or ease her suffering.

"Go," she said softly. "Just go."

At a loss for how to help her and worrying that his continued presence would only agitate her, he acquiesced. He backed away with his hands still raised and left the studio.

CHAPTER 21

Unnerved by his brief interaction with Angela, James walked along the street in the twilight fog and falling ash again. Somehow, she knew more about Mary's plight than he did, but he'd had no success prying that information out of her. In her present state, he doubted he could reason with her. She'd only become more upset when he pressed for details. There was also a chance she was delusional. She'd been calm at the cemetery yet hysterical in the dance studio. He couldn't guess what she'd been through, especially considering the nightmares he'd faced.

No time to dwell on his unanswered questions. The darkness had passed, and he was back on the streets, he needed to be alert for the Armless. Fortunately, he hadn't come across any indoors. But they were plentiful out in the open. In the meantime, he needed to figure out where to search for Mary next. He'd come up empty at the logical places. But if she was sick, it made sense to look for her at—

A baby cried out.

James stopped to orient on the sound. He hadn't been able to find the crying infant inside the Woodside Apartments. Eddie had said he didn't hear anything, but Eddie clearly had no interest in helping anyone other than himself. He'd been more than willing to abandon Laura—had in fact chased her away to save his own hide.

He heard the cry again and turned back the way he had come. In the fog, he must have missed it. He'd chosen a path in the middle of the street to avoid an ambush or a dead end, but the sound came from the side of the road. He crossed to the sidewalk and walked along a brick wall, nearly six feet high, covered in stained and flaking plaster.

A child's graffiti covered one section of the wall just ahead, a drawing of a standing teddy bear facing a cat on all fours, with a flower and a few five-pointed stars between them. Beyond the drawings stood metal trashcans and a few trash bags.

When a third cry sounded, James looked up.

Laura sat on top of the wall, wearing the same knee-length vintage pink dress with the busy floral pattern, Peter Pan collar, and ruffles. She was talking to the worn, gray doll clutched in her lap.

"You don't have to cry," she said, swinging her feet back and forth over the edge of the wall. "It's okay. I'll never leave you."

"Hey, Laura," James called up to her. "Are you okay?"

She glanced down at him, then quickly looked to his left and right.

"It's alright," he assured her. "That other guy's gone."

Even so, she climbed to her feet as if preparing to run away.

James stood beneath her. "How'd you climb up there?"

He heard a strange chuffing sound and scanned the area. Whatever had caused the sound was shrouded by the enveloping fog. Out of sight but not out of mind. The radio would squawk if something monstrous approached, but that warning might be too late if it was an Armless spewing black acid at him.

"He was crawling on the ground," Laura said, mumbling to herself more than answering his question. "Slowly, slowly, slowly."

"Who?"

"A monster!" she shouted. "Nobody told me what to do, so I climbed the wall."

"That's good," James said. "That's really good."

Then she added ominously, "I think he's probably still here."

Another sound reached them through the fog, this time a scraping on the ground, something crawling along the concrete. Again, James scanned the area, looking left and right, then toward the middle of the street. Unlike when he'd faced off against the Armless with the section of pipe, he had no weapon now. He supposed he could use one of the trashcan lids as a shield, but a weapon had become a necessity on the streets of Silent Hill.

"I was very scared," Laura continued. "But I didn't cry. I smelled him. I hate that smell." Then, abruptly, "Catch me!"

She jumped off the wall.

If James hadn't been standing directly underneath her, he wouldn't have caught her in time. As it was, only his quick reflexes prevented a nasty fall. As he set her down on her feet, he finally had a close look at her doll. Made of flesh and bone, its skin was stained with mold. More disturbingly, he thought he glimpsed the remnant of an umbilical cord dangling from the doll before Laura stepped away from him.

"What is that?"

Laura shoved the doll behind her back. But he heard it giggle, as if it were alive.

Casually, he reached out his hand. "Show me your doll."

Playfully, she took his hand but kept the hand holding the doll behind her back. "Mary gave it to me."

For a moment, he thought he had misheard her. "What? What did you say?"

Remembering the mistake he made antagonizing Angela, he fought to calm himself. If he scared her or she freaked out and bolted, she'd be at the mercy of the monsters roaming outside. He took a calming breath before he spoke again.

"Who gave you the doll, Laura?"

"Mary."

"Mary Crane?" he asked. "That Mary?"

"Mary, Mary!" Laura said in a sing-song voice, matching the cadence of the old nursery rhyme, tilting her head back and forth mischievously.

"Lau—"

Crackle!

The radio in James' jacket pocket squealed a warning.

Suddenly, a swaying silhouette appeared in the fog.

"That's him!" Laura yelled, yanking her hand free of James' and running in the opposite direction.

"Laura!" James called. "Wait!"

James glanced back at the approaching silhouette. He still couldn't tell exactly what it was that had spooked Laura, but he was in no hurry to find out. Instead, he raced after the young girl, following the wall until he came to a corner and turned right where, a moment ago, he'd glimpsed her retreating form in the mist. A wide, straight path of stone pavers bordered on both sides by trimmed hedges guided visitors to the impressive stone staircase leading up to the entrance of Rosewater Park. When he reached the base of the stairs, he saw Laura waiting at the top, doll in hand. But she darted out of sight, swallowed by the fog before he climbed halfway up the steps.

From his time in Silent Hill, he knew that Rosewater Park overlooked the south shore of Toluca Lake. This close to the water, the fog thickened, making it hard to see more than several feet in any direction. Once he passed the stone Rosewater Park entrance sign, brick walls and higher columns surrounded him. Calling the place a park was a bit misleading, as the only notable greenery inside was squared hedges at various locations. Most of the park consisted of stone tile walkways at varying elevations connected by stone stairs bordered by the veritable maze of brick walls and staggered stone columns.

He remembered courtyards on the east and west featured memorials to two early residents of Silent Hill, one a soldier in the Civil War, the other a woman considered a saint and a martyr. The promenade featured a memorial commemorating the lost lives of sixty-seven people, from the days of the first settlers, victims of a deadly pandemic that ravaged the nascent community. In grim moments, knowing how the dead had been handled, James always wondered if those lost souls haunted the town.

Despite its rich history and scenic views of the lake on clear days, Rosewater Park truly felt like a maze in the dense fog. After a few moments, he glimpsed a child-sized figure dart down a narrow passage and moved to follow her before he lost sight of her again.

"Laura!" he called. "Laura, come back!"

He weaved through the fog, hands out in front of him in case he ran into a wall he couldn't see in time. Laura's shadow slipped in and out of view a few times before he finally lost track of her. James tried to get his bearings, but without any landmarks to guide him, he couldn't tell north from south or east from west.

He bumped into a familiar metal railing along a row of waist-high metal posts. Beyond that railing, if the fog ever lifted, he'd see a spectacular view of Toluca Lake and the Lakeview Hotel on the far shore. Although now, he might only see decay and ruin. But the view had been spectacular, back before whatever happened… happened…

CHAPTER 22

Not for the first time, James had been bemoaning a bout of cabin fever, which was arguably worse when the cabin in question was a hotel room residency in a long-term rental situation. The feeling of four walls closing in on him happened whenever he wasn't inspired by whatever he was painting. When it lasted too long, he needed to get out of the room, and out of his own head.

So, Mary had suggested a beach day. Wearing a big, floppy-brimmed sun hat, and a beige cover up decorated with a yellow shell moth pattern over a turquoise bikini, she met him in front of the Lakeview Hotel. She'd brought two beach towels and a small cooler with drinks, snacks and a bottle of sunscreen. Per her suggestion, they rented folding chairs and a shade umbrella from the hotel's beach stand.

James had come down from his hotel room wearing an unbuttoned beige linen shirt and swim trunks. In case inspiration struck, he'd brought a spiralbound sketchpad and a pouch with pencils, charcoal and erasers. They staked out a secluded area on the hotel's beach, far enough from people playing volleyball or throwing footballs and flying disks to stay out of the line of fire from errant spikes or throws.

"A sunny day, blue sky, puffy clouds, and a beautiful woman at my side," James said as he reclined on one of the beach towels, propped up on his elbows. "Who could ask for anything more?"

"If you're not too busy relaxing," Mary teased, "I could use some sunscreen on my back. I burn easily." After applying sunscreen to her face, arms and legs, she handed him the bottle. "If it's not too much trouble?"

"No trouble at all," James said, smiling as he sat up. Now that she'd discarded the cover up, he was really enjoying the view of her in the bikini, while trying not to be too obvious about it. He squeezed a dollop of sunscreen in his palm, then rubbed his hands together. "Have I mentioned how good you—?"

"I can tell," she said, giving him an over-the-shoulder seductive look that took his breath away. "I wanted to cheer you up, after all."

"Mission accomplished!" James said as he applied sunscreen to her shoulders and worked his way down to the small of her back.

While James enjoyed the hotel's beach and relaxing beside Mary on the oversized towels, he decided to try sketching some of the activity out on the lake, a family in a four-person pedal boat, the occasional speed boat or jet ski and, at one point, a speed boat pulling a water skier, all taking place beyond the protection arc of swimming buoys.

"I'm getting restless," James said. "Wanna stay here or...?"

She raised the brim of her sun hat above her eyes. "What do you have in mind?"

"Go for a swim?"

"This late in the season," she said, "water's kinda cold."

"Ah, wondered why almost nobody is going in above their knees," James said. "We could walk along the boardwalk. Maybe rent a boat?"

"Let's do the boardwalk," Mary said. "I'll think about the boat."

"Sure," James agreed. The boardwalk connected from the hotel's pier to the beach stand, for those who wanted to avoid walking across the sand, but barely went beyond the front of the hotel. Nevertheless, it gave them a chance to stretch their legs. They soon reached the end of the boardwalk where an open lot had a large sign announcing the imminent groundbreaking for the Lakeside Amusement Park.

"Coming soon," James said. "Another tourist attraction."

"The Lakeview is branching out," Mary said. "For the offseason. To keep the tourists coming. Although not everyone is a fan of bringing in more tourists."

"Before long your quiet little town won't be so quiet."

"Exactly," Mary said. "Now about that boat rental…"

Claiming a lack of Dramamine, Mary vetoed the idea of renting a speed boat, which was fine with James. Instead, they rented a sixteen-foot tandem canoe. James promised to do all the paddling, so Mary could relax and enjoy the water and the view. He took the bow seat, which was closer to the middle, but paddled with the stern forward so he could watch where he was going.

Once they pushed off from the pier, Mary said. "We can take turns. I don't mind a little manual labor."

"I'm not gonna be the reason you get blisters today," James said. "Just relax. We'll go out to the middle of the lake, and I'll sketch you."

"Sketch me?"

"Of course," James said. "I had a feeling you'd inspire me today."

"But you haven't heard my modeling fee."

"Your fee, huh?" he said, grinning.

"I'm not sure you can afford me," she replied. "Unless you have something else to offer?"

"Sure, we can work something out," James said. "I'm something of a handyman."

"Well, that's disappointing," Mary said and laughed, nearly losing her sun hat in the process before snatching it off the gunnel.

The spreading wakes of speedboats, jet skis, and water skiers created an abundance of ripples on the surface of the lake, flashing in the sunlight like a treasure trove of precious gems. When they neared the center of the lake, James lowered a twelve-pound bag of shot tied to a line over the side of the canoe to anchor them.

"This should be a good spot."

"Want to hear a scary story?" Mary inquired. "About this lake?"

"Sure," James said, flipping to a blank page in his sketchpad and reaching for the zippered pouch with his various drawing instruments.

"Back in the early days of the settlement," Mary said, "when immigrants were coming over from Europe, some of them unknowingly brought over an illness, a deadly pandemic, which they spread to other colonists and some of the local Native Americans. Supposedly, the seriousness of this illness was the reason for the early construction of Brookhaven Hospital. Even so, many people died."

"That's awful," James said. "But at least some good came out of it."

"True," Mary said. "But I haven't gotten to the scary part."

"No?"

"I imagine the colonists in the midst of this pandemic panicked," Mary said. "So, to stop the spread of the illness, they dumped the bodies of sixty-seven people in this lake, a mass underwater grave."

"No shit?" James said. "You're serious?"

"Obviously, there weren't regulations about that kind of thing back then," Mary said. "So, it was the quickest way to dispose of the infected. There were even rumors that some of the victims weren't quite dead yet when they were tossed in the lake."

"Are you gonna tell me this lake is haunted?"

"I'm not telling you it's not," Mary said, raising her eyebrows suggestively. "But there's a memorial to those people in Rosewater Park."

"Wow," James said. "Guess they wanted to appease the angry spirits."

Mary's face darkened, and her tone became more serious. "I don't think that was enough," she said grimly. "Not nearly enough."

"Well, at least now I can understand your reluctance to swim in the lake."

"That's not it," she said defensively. "The water really is cold!"

"Do you want to go back?"

"After you sketch me."

With the hotel and beach in the background, he positioned his sketchpad on his crossed knee and took out a pencil to begin the drawing. Mary attempted to recline against the thwart in front of the stern seat, using a couple of life jackets as cushions, since her cover up was flimsy at best, even balled up like a pillow. She didn't look remotely comfortable.

"You'll sketch fast, right?"

"Do my best," James said, attention divided between her and the sketchpad.

"Kinda hard to look alluring when your back is killing you."

"Alluring?" James said, with a mischievous smile. "Oh—didn't realize that's what you were going for with *that* pose." He looked in the pouch. "Now what did I do with that eraser—the big one."

Mary eased herself upright with a wince. "Hey! What do you mean by 'that pose?'"

"You're the pro," James teased. "I assumed you were going for something… unusual."

With her brows furrowed, she said, "Unusual, huh?"

"Well, odd, if we're being frank."

"Lemme see it!"

"Oh, no," James said, feigning outrage, as he held the sketchbook against his chest. "Not until it's finished."

"If you don't let me see it right now," Mary said with mock seriousness, "it's gonna be finished, mister!"

She pushed herself up from the thwart, standing shakily in the boat and made her way forward, reaching out with one hand as she attempted to steady herself with the other. In the process, the boat began to rock. "Now give it?"

"Just a peek," James said, lowering the sketchpad a few inches, then pulling it away again. "As long as you promise not to get mad."

"You haven't seen mad yet," Mary said, laughing as she attempted to snatch the sketchpad from his hands."

The canoe rolled back and forth alarmingly.

"You're gonna tip it—"

She lunged forward, slipping and falling to the side as the canoe lurched. James reached out to catch her, hands grabbing her upper arms, the sketchpad slipping down between them—and they both flipped over the gunnel into the frigid waters of Toluca Lake.

James surfaced and gasped for air, casting about for Mary, whose head popped up a moment later as she exclaimed, "Fuck, that's cold!"

Treading water, James said, "Always wanted to try an ice bath."

"Now you know—" Mary said, shivering, "—why I didn't—want to swim."

He caught her hand and helped her to the canoe, where she

grabbed the gunnel. When she started to lift herself, the canoe dipped toward her.

"Oh, no, I'm gonna capsize it."

"Let me swim around and hold the other side."

"Hey, your sketchpad is still in the canoe," Mary said, reaching to lift it away from the thwart. Bracing herself with one hand on the gunnel, she held the sketchpad. When she saw James getting close to her, she ripped the page out, dropping the sketchpad back in the boat. "Now I can see how you..."

James wrapped an arm around her shoulder as she examined the damp page. She looked from the drawing to him and back again, smiling.

"What?"

"It's... lovely," she said softly. "Thank you."

She wrapped her arms around his shoulders, hugging him while he treaded water, one hand on the gunnel to steady them.

"That's what I see when I look at you."

Long hair plastered to the side of her face, she kissed him, first a peck, and then more fiercely.

A gust of wind caused her sun hat to tumble along the length of the canoe, distracting her. At the same time, the page flew from her hand and dropped in the water.

"Oh, no, I ruined it!"

"Don't worry," James said. "There'll be plenty more."

She tucked a strand of hair behind her ear. "Promise?"

"Cross my heart," James said.

"There's still the matter of my modeling fee."

"Always a catch," James said, chuckling.

She pushed off from him, floating on her back, drifting away from the canoe with a gentle backstroke.

"Hey," James called, "you said the water was too cold."

"Strange thing about that," she said. "You get used to it."

CHAPTER 23

From behind him, a voice spoke.

"I've been watching you..."

James gripped the metal railing. The voice did not belong to Laura. It was a woman's voice, but whether it belonged to an actual woman or some new monster mimicking a woman—setting a trap—

Unsettled, he eased to the side. If an arc of black acid erupted from the fog, he didn't want to be in the direct line of fire. A silhouette approached, starting to solidify out of the fog. With each step closer, she revealed more of herself to him...

A woman with shoulder-length light blond hair, tinted pink at the ends. She wore a violet choker and a long, fake fur jacket with purple and black stripes. The jacket hung open, revealing a ruched burgundy crop top, a short violet pleather skirt with a snakeskin pattern, a gold waist chain, and knee-high black leather boots. Above her right hip, she had a colorful butterfly tattoo.

Her face remained obscured by thin veils of mist, as if they were reluctant to expose her.

She walked around him now, brimming with attitude and confidence, despite the ongoing nightmare that had swallowed Silent Hill, sizing him up. "You're not like the others."

Off his puzzled expression, she explained, "Place hasn't destroyed you yet."

To James, she seemed normal. But these were unusual circumstances, which made her, strangely, odd.

"You're not from here," she continued, coming closer to take his measure, maintaining eye contact, maybe to reassure him she was human by her directness. "Who are you?"

"James."

"I'm Maria," she said. "Who you looking for, James?"

"Just this lost kid. All on her own."

She stopped in front of him.

"Sounds familiar," she said with the hint of a smile.

For the first time, he had a clear view of her face. Other than the different hair color, and a more liberal use of makeup, she was a dead ringer for Mary.

The resemblance was striking.

If Mary had a twin sister, this woman—

"You just gonna keep on staring," Maria asked with an amused smile, "or are you gonna say something?"

"Sorry, I—"

"So, what's the plan?"

"What?" he asked, befuddled. "Plan for what?"

"Getting us the hell out of this place."

"I don't—" James began. "I'm not leaving. Not yet. I'm looking for the hospital."

"Why?" she asked, looking him up and down.

"I'm looking for someone there," he said.

"Other than the kid?"

"My girlfriend."

"I don't know how to say this to you—" Maria began, then paused to choose her words carefully. "Everyone got sick in Silent Hill. Really, really sick. What was she in the hospital for?"

"Not sure," James said.

"I thought she was your girlfriend."

"We've been apart."

"So, she *was* your girlfriend."

"I just need to find her."

"Alright," she said with a decisive nod. "Got it. Let's find her then."

James was taken aback by her willingness to help. Everyone else he'd encountered in this hellscape had been, to one degree or another, a source of frustration. Refusing to answer straightforward questions, giving vague answers, or simply running away rather than respond. Hell, Angela had threatened to gut him with a butcher knife!

Then Maria did something unexpected. She reached out her hand and caressed his cheek. James felt a strange rush of relief—and fear. Like he was balanced on a precipice with a decision to make. Fall forward or step back. But he couldn't decide which was the safer option.

She shrugged. "Just wanted to make sure you were real."

James had to smile. He'd been having the same thought ever since noticing her uncanny resemblance to Mary. That she questioned his existence somehow made it unnecessary for him to question hers.

"Let's get to it," she said. "Brookhaven Hospital or bust."

James glanced back over his shoulder. "What about the kid? Laura?"

"What about her?"

"Is it—is she safe here?"

"Seems to be one of the safer places," she said. "Reason I've been hanging out here. Maybe Saint Jennifer's statue keeps the boogeymen at bay."

"You believe that stuff?"

"As good a theory as any," Maria said. "Besides, if that girl wanted to be found, she would've stopped running and let you catch her."

"She is elusive."

"We'll come back for her," Maria said. "Maybe she'll be done playing games by then."

With one final glance back into the dense fog, James nodded in agreement.

They exited Rosewater Park and turned right on Nathan Avenue. Once they were in the middle of the street, the fog closed around them, muffling their combined footfalls. Ash continued to fall silently around them.

"I don't get it," James said finally. "Why are you helping me?"

"You're the first normal person I've met in weeks," she said. "Strength in numbers."

James eyed her skeptically. "You don't look like you've been here for weeks."

She touched her fingertips to her chest, just beneath her choker. "Why, thank you." Then she gave him a critical sidelong glance. "You on the other hand..."

"What?"

"You look fucked."

Despite himself, James smiled, relaxed. He could only imagine how he looked. Since arriving in the transformed town, he'd been put through the ringer. But equally remarkable was how at ease she acted with him. Like they already had a history together.

Crackle!

He flinched again, caught off-guard by the radio's abrupt warning.

"Shit. Every time this goes off, something's getting close."

"Something?" she asked, nervous.

"Something bad."

A moment later, an Armless burst through a passing fog bank, black acid pouring down its thighs, a trail of smoke streaming behind it.

"C'mon," James said, grabbing Maria's hand and running

with her down the street, looking for a place to hide. In front of Nathan Pharmacy, he spotted a black Ford F-150 pickup truck parked at the curb, coated in so much ash it almost looked light gray. He crouched beside the pickup, motioning for her to stay silent. Hearing shuffling, he lifted his head high enough to locate the monster.

Crossing the street, it would be on their side of the Ford in moments. He motioned her to stay low and led her to the rear of the pickup. Uneven footfalls approached. A glance under the truck revealed how close the Armless had come to the back of the vehicle. Its feet were past the rear wheel on the curb side, closest to James.

He leaned back against the tailgate. Just to his right, the monster's tortured fleshy body was a step away from the rear of the pickup. Without eyes or ears, could it sense them? If it took a step and swiveled, they would be within range of an acid attack. He waited, heart pounding. A quick glance at Maria, a silent warning. Her eyes were wide with fright, but she nodded.

Then the Armless stopped.

Acid leaked from the orifice in the creature's chest, dripping down between its feet to form a growing puddle, sizzling as it dissolved the layer of ash on the ground. A trickle of the black acid wound its way toward James' right foot. Before it got close enough to burn a hole in his shoe, he shifted his foot away. Held his breath.

A moment later, the acid drool ceased.

With a twisting spasm, the Armless continued forward, its awkward gait taking it past the back of the truck without noticing or engaging with them. Several steps later it was swallowed by the fog and the shuffling faded to silence.

James sighed, only realizing he still held Maria's hand as she pulled it from his grasp.

"There's a shortcut this way," she said, speaking softly even though the threat had passed.

James didn't reply.

"James..."

Her voice fell away, almost background noise as he stared across the street where a tall building with a green-grey roof rose from the fog. The ash falling gently in front of it reminded him of winter and falling snow...

CHAPTER 24

In a light winter snowfall, Mary stood alone near an intersection on Nathan Avenue beside the majestic columns in front of the Silent Hill National Bank. She wore a dark, three-quarter length coat over a black midi dress with a dogwood flower pattern and knee high tan leather boots. A long green-and-white striped scarf was wrapped around her neck, but her head was uncovered. A light breeze ruffled her strawberry blond hair. Her face ruddy from the cold, she brushed loose strands of hair from her face with the fingers of her bare hand.

People bundled up in winter coats, knit hats, scarves and gloves walked by her, running errands or shopping. But she stood there, unmoving. Obviously waiting for someone.

Across the street, standing under the awning of a sports collectible shop, his back partially turned toward her, James pretended to look interested in the signed memorabilia in the display window. He'd been following her for a while, since she left the apartment after she told him she had to run some errands of her own. Since she wouldn't tell him what was happening between her and her circle of friends, he'd decided to find out for himself. They had been living together for months, and he still had no idea why she tolerated their odd behavior. Things had changed. He hadn't stumbled upon any of their weird meetings after that first time. And Mary didn't socialize with them in public places, at least as far as he knew. They remained cordial when bumping into each other in the hallways of the apartment building. But more than once, he caught Kaitlyn or Mitzy staring after them, as if about to make a comment before thinking better of it.

Of course, Mary continued to work at the Fashion Boutique, sometimes long after closing, though she always gave him a call to tell him she was running late. Other times, he got caught up in his painting and lost track of time, hours on end, only realizing later that Mary had stepped out at some point and he hadn't heard from her in a while. She continued to stress that they focus on each other and not let outsiders come between them.

And yet, James had the distinct impression Mary was not as free and clear of her friends' weird behavior or... possessiveness as she would have him believe. Once or twice, he glanced out the window of their apartment and saw her on the street talking to Dara and Kaitlyn in hushed tones. Or returning from the Grand Market with Cal and Mitzy in tow, even though the married couple had no bags of their own. One time he visited Mary at the Fashion Boutique, well past the time when he might have dropped in to take her to lunch, and the Meyer twins were in the store, talking to Mary. And when they saw him, they made some excuse they had to run off somewhere.

His overall impression was that nothing had really changed about their relationship dynamic, other than the visibility of it. Occasional dissatisfaction with his painting tended to mask other emotional issues. But when he took time to center himself, he came to the realization that his discontentment was a symptom of his emotional unease. However true or loving her intentions, Mary's relationship with him was built on a foundation of secrets she was unwilling to share.

Were those secrets damning enough to destroy everything they'd built together? Not knowing was no longer an option. Either he could live with the knowledge and continue to live with her and love her… or what they had was a lie, nothing more than a pleasant delusion.

And so, feeling sick to his stomach, he became the guy who spied on his girlfriend. If she found out he didn't trust her—at least not in this one part of her life—she would be pissed, maybe worse. Maybe she wouldn't forgive the violation of her privacy. That was his burden to bear. But he couldn't live with the alternative. One way or another, he needed to know the truth.

Mary flashed a hesitant smile as a couple approached her.

Dara and Kaitlyn, the former walking with her silver-tipped wooden cane. They both wore three-quarter length coats over slacks. Dara wore a fedora with a curved brim, while Kaitlyn wore a dark head wrap. Kaitlyn wore gloves, but Dara reached up with a bare hand to stroke the back of Mary's hair possessively.

Mary spoke with them for less than a minute before Cal and Mitzy joined the group. Cal wore a flat-brimmed black fedora, navy blue overcoat, dark gray gloves, and black trousers. Mitzy had on a dark brown toggle coat with a tan lining and dark slacks. The discussion became more animated, with Cal pointing down Nathan Avenue. Mary pursed her lips, seemed reluctant to go where he suggested.

James felt a knot in his stomach. If they were pressuring Mary to do something she wanted no part of, he thought he should intervene on her behalf. Of course, that would 'blow his cover' so to speak. She would know he'd followed her. And he would be no closer to the truth.

Then Dara wrapped her arms around Mary's shoulder, smiling and, at last, Mary gave a brief nod. The five of them walked toward the intersection. On the far side of Nathan, James saw Nathan Pharmacy and Custom Signs & Lighting, but they turned without crossing the intersection. Only then, James noticed the Meyer twins had joined them, separating themselves from the other pedestrians. The redhead wore a red knit hat, a brown jacket and jeans with black boots; the brunette wore a blue and white knit hat, a tan jacket and jeans with tan boots. And she walked with her hand wrapped around the redhead's arm. Something always seemed odd with those two.

James followed at a distance, attempting to blend in with the other pedestrians. He regretted not wearing a hat, his face was completely exposed. He'd debated following Mary for a long time, but the final decision had been spur of the moment. Lacking the foresight to prepare an outfit that would render him incognito, he'd simply grabbed his dark gray wool jacket from the coatrack and threw it on over his navy blue sweater and jeans. Now he walked behind other people, keeping his head down as if lost in thought.

He turned the corner, glancing ahead every few seconds to keep the group in sight. They passed an official-looking red brick building and turned down an alley. A moment later, they were gone from view. James picked up his pace. He paused in front of the building, which had white double doors set back under a portico. Above the doors a sign read 'Silent Hill Historical Society'.

James turned into the alley—and pulled up short. Blocking his way was a tall cyclone fence thoroughly plastered with scores of overlapping band posters, many with smeared ink or faded with age. Even if there had been enough exposed sections of fence to provide handholds and toeholds, Mary's group never could have scaled the fence in the time it took him to reach the alley. And the vertical fence posts were too close to the alley walls on either side for anyone to squeeze through. He grabbed one post, then the other, pushing and pulling in case the fence functioned like a gate, but there was no give on either side. Both posts firmly cemented into the ground. Next, he pushed against the fence itself, moving right to left, high then low. On the lower left side, the fence bowed away from him. He plucked at the brittle flyers and slipped his fingers through the gaps to grip the chain link fence and pushed. Someone had taken bolt cutters to the bottom third of the fence in a vertical line, close to the left post, about four feet high, along with a horizontal cut at the bottom about a foot wide, creating a hidden flap, easy enough to squeeze through in a hurry if you knew where to look. With the rustling of stiff, glued paper and the clinking of the metal fence, he ducked through the gap to the other side of—the *blind* alley. A dead end.

It was empty. No sign of Mary or the others. Where could they have gone? Trashcans overflowing with garbage, a pair of rats enjoying the bounty, and a blue dumpster. He found a fire door for the Historical Society building, but it was locked. No other doors. Nowhere for them to have gone. Had someone been waiting to let them in through the fire door? If so, would an alarm have sounded. And, if they wanted to go inside the building, why not go through the front door?

Steam curled around the sides of the dumpster, filling the area with the sour reek of discarded and decaying food.

James crouched, tried to peer under the dumpster, but there wasn't enough clearance to see anything. Moving to the side of the bin, he lowered his shoulder and pushed it out of the way, exposing a steam grate—and a metal door.

A double door, with no handles. Decorated with raised symbols within squares lined up point to point, like religious iconography. Neither the symbols nor their significance meant anything to James, but he recalled Dara's necklace with the overlaid triangle and circle. Getting down on one knee, he tried to wedge his fingers between the doors to pull either side up, but he couldn't get a firm grip. Maybe they could only be opened from below. Again, he wondered if Mary's group had someone standing by, ready to raise the doors when they arrived.

He ran his palms along the cold metal surface, toying with the idea that the handle was recessed. The rows of squares and the symbols inside them were raised above the surface of the doors. He traced them with his fingers but found nothing that might release a handle. As he leaned back, his fingers trailed across the raised sections and, for a moment, he thought a section of metal wiggled ever so slightly. Backtracking, he found the spot with some give to it and pressed down. It was a button hiding in plain sight. Soon as he pressed it, he heard a slight pneumatic hiss, and the door rose about six inches on its own.

Intrigued, James grabbed the edge and lifted the door straight up.

Beneath the door, a concrete staircase descended into darkness. James felt as though he were staring into an abyss. And in that darkness, he heard an industrial pump, throbbing like a beating heart.

CHAPTER 25

"Hey!" Maria said, snapping her fingers in front of his face. "Hey!"

He shook off a memory, of secret doors, a stairway into darkness.

"Are you alright?"

"Yeah, yeah."

"We need to go," she said, alarmed. "Those things are everywhere."

James stood up behind the pickup truck and scanned their surroundings. His back to the truck, he saw three or four silhouettes taking shape in the fog.

"The hospital's close," she said. "This way."

She pointed beyond the front of the truck, away from the Armless.

"Good," he said, helping her up. "Let's go!"

But they'd only sprinted a half dozen steps when three more Armless materialized out of the fog in front of them. Another two shuffled toward them from the right. They were boxed in.

"Okay," he said. "Not so good."

"What now?"

James turned back toward the truck and thought about breaking into Nathan Pharmacy or Custom Signs & Lighting.

They could hide in either store or try to exit through a rear door into an alley or the next street over, where they might have safe passage. But a glance into the bed of the pickup truck gave him an idea.

"Hold on," he said.

He brushed off a thick coating of ash to reveal a dozen 2x4s, cut to half-length and tied in two bundles, each piece about a foot longer than a baseball bat. First, he tried to work the knot loose, but the ash made the rough cord slippery. He needed a knife to cut through it.

"Whatever you're doing," she warned, "do it fast."

"Need a few more seconds—"

"We don't have—!"

Maria shrieked in fear as a fountain of black acid splashed across the tailgate.

James yanked his hands away from the bundled wood. The paint on the truck sizzled and bubbled, producing an acrid smoke. Had the Armless been a step closer, the acid would have gone in the bed of the truck and all over his hands.

Maria backed into the street, away from the pickup but closer to the two Armless approaching from their right. "We need to go!"

"Wait!" James shouted, picking up the closest bundle of wood and pressing the rough cord against the sizzling acid dripping down the tailgate. The rope smoked, snapping as he applied pressure. The boards fell loose, but not before he snatched one and swung it at the Armless who had sprayed the truck.

It spasmed and twitched and leaned forward, right into the arc of James' swing, which collided with the side of the monster's head. As it staggered sideways, he hit it again, more of an overhand swing, and it fell to the ground.

Running past the fallen creature, he grabbed Maria's hand

and pulled her away from the two Armless behind her. Both of their chest orifices had cycled open with her well within their range. Twin arcs of black fluid hosed out from their torsos, but both missed by inches, falling harmlessly to the ground.

As James approached the three blocking their path to the hospital, he let go of her hand to get a two-handed grip on the 2x4.

"Get behind me."

Worst case, if his attack failed, the acid would hit him and spare her. But he could only be her human shield once. And there were three of the creatures shuffling and shuddering toward them.

"Stay back," he cautioned, "and follow behind me."

James chose to go wide right. If he took that one down, they'd have a clear path past the other two. As he veered right, he glanced back to confirm Maria's position behind him. Satisfied, he prepared to strike right to left, hoping to knock the rightmost Armless into the one in the middle.

"If I go down," he said. "Don't wait for me. Make a run for it."

"You better not go down!"

He swung the 2x4. Without arms to block the swing, the Armless was defenseless—assuming he struck it before it could douse him with acid. He bashed it in the head twice in succession, determined to take it out before it could launch a counterattack. It staggered backward and fell on its back, where it squirmed like a bug, trying to right itself. But the middle Armless had shuffled closer and, before James could get close enough to swing the 2x4 a third time, its chest had opened, and acid spewed from the deadly maw.

Instinctively James raised the board and ducked to the right. Behind him, Maria blurred into motion, but her view had been blocked and she reacted a second too late. The acid that had looped over and around the board struck her.

Maria screamed.

James saw the top half of the 2x4 was black and smoking. He rammed it into the gaping chest hole of the Armless, knocking it to the ground and tripping the third one. He raced to Maria, his eyes scanning her head, face, neck—

He reached for her—

"Don't touch me!" she shouted.

He'd been about to grab her arm, then noticed the black acid had struck the shoulder and arm of her purple-and-black striped jacket. The purple stripes had turned black and the whole arm was smoking, dissolving before their eyes.

"Get it off," James said. "Before the acid reaches your flesh."

"I can't—"

"Arms back now," he instructed. "Ball your fists!"

Wide-eyed with fear, she complied. He grabbed the jacket by the back of the collar and yanked it off her, instantly tossing it aside before the acid touched either of them. It fell to the ground in a sizzling, smoking pile.

She stared at him in shock, tears brimming in her blue eyes. Then, suddenly, she rushed into his arms and hugged him fiercely, whispering in his ear, "Thank you. Thank you. I thought I was—"

"You're not," James said. "You're fine."

She nodded.

"But we need to go now."

The remaining Armless were already closing in on them, undeterred by the fate of the others. James had lost his only weapon. Wasn't worth the risk to rush past several of the monsters to grab another board. One extremely close call was plenty.

"Okay," Maria said. "Follow me."

"I'm not leaving your side," James replied. "Just say when we need to turn."

They hurried into the fog together, the pursuing Armless fading to silhouettes— then shadows—then gone.

Minutes later they neared the end of Nathan Avenue. Maria directed him down a curved driveway, beside which stood a standalone stone sign that read Brookhaven Hospital. As they walked side by side along the driveway, the monolithic red brick building seemed to shimmer into existence out of the mist and ash.

CHAPTER 26

"And you're sure she's here?"

"Has to be." By the process of elimination, she had to be at the hospital. He'd checked everywhere else. "Do you want to wait out here?"

She reached out and grabbed his arm, turning him to face her. "That's a joke, right?"

"Kind of peaceful out here."

"It won't be if those things catch up to us."

"Whatever's waiting for us inside might be worse."

"I'll take my chances. Besides, there's no way I'm waiting out here alone," she said, shuddering. "Too damn creepy."

They strode together across the parking lot.

Veils of mist parted as they neared the courtyard, revealing dozens of stretchers filling the space. All were covered with a coating of ash. The sheets and padding were stained with blood and other fluids and spotted with mold. Rust coated the metal supports and rails. But there were no bodies on any of them. James recalled the Rosewater Park memorial to the mass watery grave. He wondered how many had died in this most recent contagion. Were they dumped in a mass grave? Cremated in the local morgue? He didn't kid himself that all the victims survived. More likely the caretakers had fallen ill as well. Nobody had stayed around long enough to clean up after the tragedy struck.

They entered the hospital through the front entrance. The lobby and hallways were eerily quiet, littered with abandoned wheelchairs, gurneys, hospital beds, IV pole stands, soiled bedding, and assorted medical carts and supplies. The walls were stained, blistered and cracked, covered with gunk, the floors covered with dust, littered with paper, food wrappers, used syringes and bandages, and the occasional clipboard. The ashy twilight filtered through windows—many stained with blood—casting everything in a hazy red light, like a portent of doom for all who entered.

At the nurse's station, James sat down in front of a dark computer screen, hoping to log in to the hospital's system and try to find a room number for Mary. He tapped a few keys to see if the computer was in sleep mode, but nothing happened. He checked the connections, data and power. Everything was plugged in, but the computer refused to power on. From one computer to the next, he shook his head in disappointment.

"Everything's dead."

From behind him, he heard a lighter flicker.

Maria sat on one of the nurse's desks, taking a drag from a cigarette. Her hands were shaking. Off his look, she said, "Sorry. When I'm nervous, these come out."

"No judgment."

James sympathized. He'd only given up cigarettes for good after his near miss with the lumber truck the day he met Mary. He envisioned himself bumming a cigarette from Maria, lighting up, and that first inhale—but he shook it off. Instead, he turned his attention to the clipboards hanging on the wall above the nurse's station. Judging by the stains on the paper and the rust on the metal clips, the information could have been five years old, maybe ten. Even the hospital itself looked like it had been condemned a decade ago. How could this level of rot and decay have happened in a short amount of time?

"So, walk me through this," Maria said, waving her cigarette around for emphasis. "You're looking for your kind-of-girlfriend."

"Yeah," James said, distracted by the notes and charts he hastily flipped through, looking for any mention of Mary or her room number.

"How long's it been since you've seen her?"

"I don't know. A long time."

"Wow," Maria teased. "And we're sure she's still your girlfriend?"

James lowered a clipboard to stare at her. Not that he couldn't weather a good-natured ribbing now and then, but he was not in a joking mood. Especially with Mary's life hanging in the balance. He had run out of places where he might find her.

"What?" Maria said with a shrug. "Girl can get into a lotta trouble in this town." She pushed off the desk, walked past him and down a dim hallway.

"Hey," he called. "Where are you going?"

"Need to stretch my legs," she replied without looking back.

James watched after her for a moment or two, then decided to give her some space. Her nerves were probably as jangled as his own. Returning his attention to the clipboard, he flipped through the last few pages, almost glossed over it, then returned to the previous page—Mary Crane.

"Toxicology unit," he said aloud. "So, where exactly—"

He found an emergency evacuation route hanging on the wall. Running his fingers along the map from the "you are here" dot somebody had placed on the representation of the nurse's station, he scanned for the location of the Toxicology unit.

Then he heard a recorded voice speaking from across the hall.

"—admitted at noon after collapsing in the street. On admission, she presented with severe anemia, high grade fever and significant subconjunctival and nasal hemorrhaging—"

James strode down the hall, following the sound of the voice, which became clearer as he approached an office with a nameplate beside the door that read 'Robert Wiene, Trauma'.

"—initial bloodwork revealed critically low platelet levels likely due to exposure to an unidentified substance—"

The door was already open, so James peered inside. The walls were as stained, cracked and blistered as those in the hallway. A freestanding bookshelf filled with medical journals looked as if someone had shoved the books around in haste, dropping some on the floor. In the opposite corner, a sink with a small counter was covered in grime, the faucet and knobs corroded with rust. Maria leaned over the doctor's desk, her right hand wrapped around a tape recorder in the middle of a scattered batch of dictation microcassettes.

"—patient remains stable but physically weakened."

"I found where they put her," James said.

But Maria was focused on the recording, too enthralled to respond.

"Miss, do you remember your name?"

Then a familiar voice spoke. *"Mary,"* she said. *"Mary Crane."*

The recording ended with a low hiss. Maria pressed the stop button.

Mary! *She* was *here*, James thought. He looked up from the silent tape recorder to Maria's face. "Does any of this make sense to you?"

"There were rumors—"

"Rumors?"

She stared at the sink in the corner of the office. The tap was leaking, one slow drop at a time, *plunk...plunk...plunk...*

"A hallucinogenic drug ended up in the city's water supply."

"What?" James said. Angela had mentioned the flood contaminating the water treatment plant. But this seemed different—deliberate. "How?"

... *plunk...plunk...plunk...*

Maria's gaze moved from the sink to James' face.

"There was this religious group," she said. "Old school Silent Hill crazies, founded by this preacher named Joshua Crane. Even after he died, they used to worship him as some kind of prophet or god. And his daughter, they would... Wait, she's who you're looking for, isn't she?"

As she spoke, her voice faded into unintelligible murmurs. James had trouble hearing her, had trouble focusing on anything, other than the sharp pain spiking through his head again.

"You really never heard about any of this—?"

Each word sounded as if it were uttered under water.

Maria popped another microcassette into the recorder and clicked play...

James pressed his hands to his head, wincing in pain as he dropped to one knee, leaning against the front of the desk for support.

Then he fell into darkness—

CHAPTER 27

James gripped the edge of the secret door he had opened after finding and pressing the hidden button release. Mary and her friends had turned down this dead end alley and disappeared. If they had left the alley, he would have seen them. They couldn't have gone anywhere else except down. Staring at the concrete stairs that descended into darkness, he told himself, "No turning back."

He took the first several steps, then reached up to close the door behind him. As he turned around, he bumped into a chain attached to the wall of the stairwell. The chain connected to a long metal rod with a hook on the end. He guessed the hook was how they pulled the dumpster over the doors just before closing them. They would only need a gap of an inch or so, the width of the rod. Once the dumpster was in place, they would withdraw the rod and let the door click shut. Though tempted to test this assumption, he thought he might need to make a quick exit to avoid detection if the group should double back before he reached the bottom of the stairs.

With the door sealed shut, the throbbing *whoosh* of the industrial pump far below filled the enclosed space, sounding like the labored heartbeat of a massive beast. James couldn't see his hand in front of his face, so he took out his cellphone and turned on the flashlight, directing it to the steps below and shielding the beam as much as possible to avoid detection. The walls were smooth on either side, with no handrail, so he took the stairs one at a time, avoiding small puddles of melted snow the others had left behind.

At one point, he paused and looked back up the stairs, but beyond his small pool of light there was only darkness above, same as below. As close to knowing as not knowing. A mote of light within the abyss. He could go back and choose to live in ignorance. But she meant too much to him, had become too important in his life to not know if it was real.

He resumed his descent.

At the bottom of the stairs, he found himself in a large tunnel made of bricks, like the entrance to a post-war atomic bomb shelter. The brick walls were dank, damp to the touch. Somewhere nearby water dripped. And the air wafting through the tunnel carried an unpleasant mélange of odors. He wondered if the tunnel was part of the sewer system or adjacent to the water treatment plant.

From around a bend in the tunnel, light flickered, providing enough illumination for him to turn off his phone's flashlight. Above the sound of the industrial pump and the continual dripping of water, he heard numerous voices chanting in unison. With each step he took, the chanting grew louder, but he couldn't make out individual words.

After one final curve, the broad tunnel ended at a large circular grate of squared iron bars, eight vertical bars braced with two horizontal crosspieces. The grate blocked access to the massive, vaulted room beyond. Beyond the grate, he caught his first glimpse of the chanting crowd, standing side by side, arms overhead, swaying back and forth.

Creeping forward along the edge of the rounded tunnel, James kept to the shadows. Up close, he examined the grate. The vertical bars were too close together to slip between, but centered in the grate was a rectangular, hinged gate wide enough to allow passage. Unfortunately, the gate was locked with no sign of a key or, for that matter, a keyhole.

Before he could investigate further, the chanting stopped, arms lowered and the crowd grew still. He looked through the bars into the vaulted chamber beyond, full of shadows, pierced only by burning torches placed at intervals in iron stands. Scores of people—perhaps a hundred or more—had gathered in the industrial space, all of them wearing hooded brown robes. He glimpsed several faces, some of them familiar—Cal and Mitzy.

Now that they had finished chanting, they stood together, expectantly, all swaying slightly in some kind of religious fervor fueled by alcohol or, more likely, narcotics.

Brick steps led up to an elevated platform, upon which Dara stood with a couple of hooded acolytes, heads bowed, faces hidden. Dara also wore a robe, but her hood was thrown back, revealing her bleached blond hair. She tapped her cane for attention. But this far underground the thunderous heartbeat *whoosh* of the industrial pump swallowed almost all sound. Only when the entire assemblage had been chanting together had their voices been strong enough to reach James' ears. The crowd was close enough to hear the rap of Dara's cane and the sound of her voice, but James struggled to make out individual words, focusing on gestures to make sense of their unfolding ritual.

"Joshua led us to this—" Dara said fervently, clearly feeling the effects of the group's drug of choice. "He guided us—" She held up her free hand. "I know—abandoned us—" She paused for dramatic effect, which was lost on James, as he shook his head, struggling to hear. Unfortunately, she lowered her voice, speaking more intimately to the enraptured group, finally smiling in satisfaction. "—fate provided—"

With her smile still in place, her gaze swept back and

forth over the expectant crowd. Then she raised her hand and gestured toward someone beyond the crowd. "Bring her—" Dara commanded.

Out of an archway to the right, two brown-robed followers entered the vaulted room on either side of Mary, in a translucent white gown. She wore a tiara with a spiky design resembling bare tree branches. Both her forehead and cheeks were decorated with elaborate gold leaf makeup.

Behind the iron bars, James felt completely helpless. Whatever they planned, he couldn't stop them. And if he left to get help, or contacted the police, it would be over before they arrived. He checked his phone—no signal.

As Mary approached them, all the cloaked figures had eyes only for her. James saw Cal and Mitzy—and Claudette without her cat. Everyone he'd followed had to be in the vaulted room, along with at least a dozen others who must have been waiting for them. As Mary walked into the assemblage, they stepped aside to let her through, but all of them reached out, straining fingers spread to touch her fleetingly as she passed, as if laying hands on a holy relic.

Mary's escorts stopped at the base of the stairs, but she ascended to the raised brick platform where Dara waited with the two hooded acolytes. With Mary standing before her, Dara reached into her robes and withdrew a small, ornate glass bottle filled with amber liquid. She held it up for all to see, turning the bottle back and forth so that it seemed to glow in the flickering torchlight. A murmur of excitement coursed through the crowd.

They've done this before.

Dara spoke but James couldn't hear her words. Instead, he heard a disembodied recorded voice speaking—speaking to Mary, "*Miss Crane, this drug that they've been giving you all these years…*"

Meanwhile, Dara continued to speak, her words swallowed by the indefatigable pump. She pointed her cane at a hooded figure at the base of the stairs and gestured for this person to join her.

The designated person climbed the steps with a processional slowness and stood behind and to the right of Mary.

After Dara said something, the figure nodded, reached up with both hands and pulled down their hood—Kaitlyn.

Dara then signaled the two hooded acolytes behind her to move forward. They took their places on either side of Mary. They too lowered their hoods, revealing themselves as Gia and Mia, the Meyer twins.

Then, in unison, the rest of the crowd reached up and pulled back their hoods, finally revealing their faces.

With a command from Dara, the twins wrapped their arms around Mary's arms.

Kaitlyn took her position behind Mary and wrapped her right arm around Mary's neck, locking it in place by gripping her wrist with her left hand.

Once the three of them had Mary secured, Dara stepped forward and removed the cap from the vial. With her left hand, she tilted Mary's chin back; with her right, she raised the vial to Mary's lips.

This time, the recorded voice speaking in James' head was Mary's. "*It made me feel whole...*"

James saw the anguish in Mary's eyes, sensed her reluctance to participate in this ritual, but her body language was neutral. She didn't resist. She dry-gulped before opening her lips, a lone tear streamed down her gold leaf makeup, glistening on her chin.

"*...it made me feel part of them.*"

Dara tilted the bottle back, pouring it into Mary's open mouth.

Dara continued to speak to the gathering, then she pressed her fingers to Mary's trembling lips.

Unable to contain himself as he witnessed Mary's apparent distress, James gripped the vertical bars of the grate that trapped him in the tunnel and shouted, "Mary!"

They stood with their backs to him, their full attention on the ritual, equally deafened by the roar of the pump. Nobody heard him.

The recorded voice continued speaking to Mary, words from another time, away from this madness, "*...it's killed your free will...*"

Mary's eyes rolled back in her head. She collapsed, falling backward, her body wracked with spasms. The Meyer twins and Kaitlyn bore her weight, shuffling down the stairs to join the crowd. Others moved in close, helping to raise Mary above them, as if she were crowd surfing at a concert. Almost glowing in her white gown above the sea of brown-robed bodies, Mary seemed to float over the believers.

"MARY!" James called even louder.

Neither Mary nor the cultists heard him.

Dara had followed the three servants down the stairs. She raised her arms and spoke, her voice no more than a murmur, lost in the throbbing bass of the industrial pump.

Still borne aloft, Mary's spasms intensified, turning into frightening convulsions. Blood leaked from her nose, splashing her face and neck as she writhed in the grasp of a dozen hands. Her head turned side to side, her gaze darting in all directions, like that of a wild animal trapped in a cage. Then blood trickled out of her mouth, then her ears, and finally from her eyes, as if her tears had transmuted to blood. And as the volume of blood increased, it began to rain on the disciples carrying her. Those nearby jostled nearer, nudging their way as close to Mary as possible, arms extended, hands straining for the random drops of blood.

Then, alarmingly, her translucent gown darkened with

splotches of red, blood oozing from her pores, transforming the white tunic into a crimson shroud.

"*...and it's caused permanent damage to your body.*"

James lunged futilely against the grate, and screamed, "Hey! Leave her alone!"

Blood covered her gown, mottled her face, dripped down her forearms and fell from her fingertips.

The convulsions ceased, with Mary in the grip of others, staring upward blankly, no doubt in a state of shock.

If only by the continued heaving of her chest, James knew she remained alive. But at what cost?

Her recorded voice seemed to speak to him while she, helpless below, could not, "*They loved me... I thought they did...*"

Impatient, filled with a literal blood lust, the hooded figures tore at her white gown, ripping blood-soaked patches from her body. Kaitlyn and the Meyer twins laid her gently on the hard floor. But when her bare flesh touched the cold bricks, Mary convulsed again.

"*MARY*!" James shouted impotently, unheard and unnoticed.

He gripped the iron bars and tried to shake the grate loose from its housing. He tugged the inset gate forward and back, side to side, determined to find a weakness or a hidden latch. Nothing worked.

Mary's eyes opened wide, her pupils darting around, tears of blood flicking from her eyelashes.

Kaitlyn held a small camcorder, recording the blood ceremony, the harrowing expressions on the faces of those feasting on Mary's blood. Those close enough to her body lapped it up directly from her flesh. Those who couldn't reach with their mouths smeared their hands in it then licked their fingers.

James caught a glimpse of Mary's face. Her blood-rimmed eyes remained open but seemed unfocused now. Then someone bent over Mary's face and stroked their tongue across her eyeball, lapping up the blood as it leaked out.

Once they consumed all the blood expressed from her orifices, they sat back, eyes wide as the hallucinogenic combination of the drug and her blood took hold. Their bodies swayed, almost in rhythm to the throbbing *whoosh* of the pump.

James' knees buckled. He dropped to the floor of the tunnel, his forehead striking the iron bars that prevented him from stopping the madness he'd just witnessed. Nothing that happened made sense to him, as if he'd been lost in his own wild fever dream.

Dara sat by Mary's head, cane across her lap. She pressed her hand, coated in Mary's blood, to her open lips. Her head lolled back in the weird ritualistic ecstasy the others had experienced. For a moment, she glanced in James' direction. Maybe she saw him kneeling there. More likely, a hallucination had taken hold of her mind, separating her from his tortured reality.

One last time, he heard Mary's recorded voice, *"All this blood… was it mine?"*

CHAPTER 28

The town siren wailed its warning.

Inside Dr. Wiene's office, the twilight faded rapidly, overcome by the rapid descent of darkness. The pale light that had pressed against the sole window behind the desk with little effect winked out as if a cosmic switch had been flipped.

Maria ejected the microcassette of Mary's session and dropped it on the desk with the others.

James wobbled on his knees, slapped a hand on the desktop for balance, as the visceral memory shattered, surrendering to the spike of pain from his neuralgia. He clawed his way back to awareness—

"We gotta go!"

Maria. Standing beside him.

"What—?"

"Look," she said, pointing at the floor. "Look!"

James glanced down, saw his other hand pressed to the floor and, seemingly from his own fingertips, the rust of the darkness—the otherworld of darkness—expanded in rapidly growing tendrils across the floor and up the walls like an infection chronicled with the fluttering acceleration of stop-motion photography. Except this was happening in real time. He climbed to his feet, taking a moment to gather himself and endure the spike of pain in his head. Across the room, the leaking faucet—now completely coated in rust—began to spurt red water—or blood, the hospital itself bleeding.

"Come on," Maria said, taking his arm.

Steeling himself, he nodded and followed her out of the office. By the time they were both in the corridor, the rust finished consuming the hall. Abruptly, the siren fell silent. Once again, the darkness had taken complete hold of Silent Hill.

Through the hospital's loudspeakers, classical music played. Bach's Aria from Suite 3, just as it had played on the small radio when he'd first come across the homeless man. James thought to question the coincidence, but the more he tried to understand what was happening in the town, the less it all made sense. He staggered toward a discarded wheelchair that looked as if it had been partially crushed and pried off one of the metal armrests. Stripping off the padding, he gripped it tight, assessed the weight and slapped it against his palm. Another makeshift club.

Determined, James said, "We have to find her now."

"Do you know where she is?"

"According to the nurse's records, she's in the Toxicology unit."

"You know how to get there?"

James nodded. "I traced a path on the emergency evacuation map."

"Lead the way."

James clipped the flashlight to the breast pocket of his jacket and switched on the light. Together they ran through the darkened corridor of the hospital. After a few seconds, the radio in his pocket buzzed to life with a loud *crackle*.

Out of the corner of his eye, James saw standing silhouettes in a dark room snap to life.

Maria noticed his momentary hesitation and slowed.

"Keep going!" he shouted.

With each room they passed, the scenario repeated itself. Preternaturally still silhouettes jerking to life the moment of their closest proximity, the radio crackling and squawking one warning after another. The sounds of their combined footfalls echoed through the deserted hospital, only slowing when they needed to avoid crashing into rusted gurneys and IV pole stands.

Their route through the hospital brought them right into the emergency room, which was situated at the side entrance. They slowed to a stop to negotiate their way around dozens of stretchers and wheelchairs. Now the abandoned gurneys left in the courtyard made sense. The hospital staff had run out of emergency room space to manage the influx of patients. While all the patients were long gone, the nurses remained—

Over a dozen, long-legged, faceless nurses stood inside the emergency room in frozen, broken-doll poses. Their heads were covered in what looked like pale flesh, with randomly spaced gaping black holes, instead of normal facial features. They wore traditional white caps and short white zippered dresses with red piping, which exposed garters above thigh-high stockings—the hyper-sexualized nursing costume typically sold at Halloween pop-up shops. Strangely, their bodies and clothing all gleamed with a glazed ceramic quality, as if they were figurines scaled to life size. Additionally, each motionless nurse held a weapon—knives and scalpels, pipes and bone saws, ice picks and crutches, broken test tubes and rusty syringes.

The cluster of nurses had been motionless before James and Maria burst into the emergency room. But as with the rooms they had passed on their way, the radio crackled and squealed again, more persistently this time. Slowly, the nurses snapped into motion like a battalion of dancers in an old Berlin cabaret. Those bent at the waist, straightened up. Those already standing twitched, heads swiveling toward the newcomers.

Hands holding weapons rose or twisted, brandishing those weapons toward James and Maria.

James scanned the wide room with the flashlight, looking for the exit back into the corridors. Past the row of small desks in the intake area, he saw a door. He signaled Maria to follow him. But the door was stuck. He looked through the window, pressing the flashlight to the glass to illuminate the dark corridor beyond. An abandoned gurney had been left outside the door.

"Shit," he muttered. "It's blocked."

Continuing to awaken from their bizarre hibernation, the nurses shifted their feet, heels clicking on the broken tile floor, covered with rust and signs of decay.

"Now would be a good time to get out of here," Maria said nervously.

James shoved the door, but it wouldn't budge. He redoubled his efforts, planting his feet and pushing harder with his shoulder. He heard a wheel screech, but the door only moved about an inch.

"Wheels must be locked."

"Do something, James!"

He raised the wheelchair arm and smashed the window, running the bar along the base to clear away dangerous shards. Then he reached through the window, gripped the gurney's siderail and heaved. It flipped over with a crash of metal against the rusted floor. After withdrawing his arm, he shoved the door again. This time the gurney skidded across the floor, easily pushed aside by the door. With a glance over his shoulder, he watched the nurses shove stretchers and wheelchairs out of their way.

"C'mon!" James shouted, clipping the flashlight back in his pocket to grab Maria's hand. They ran past the overturned gurney with a murderous legion of nurses in pursuit.

This time they sprinted down the dark corridor, the flashlight clipped to James' pocket arcing left and right, revealing abandoned stretchers and medical equipment with mere moments to avoid painful collisions. James' elbow knocked over an exam stool. Maria almost flipped over a medical supply cart and would have taken a hard fall if James hadn't caught and steadied her.

In addition to the nurses pursuing them from the emergency room, more nurses burst into the hallway from patient rooms, activated by their proximity, announced by the crackling radio. Soon a mob of maniacal nurses filled the hallway no more than a dozen steps behind them.

The nurses fought one another for position, to be the first to attack, shoving and jostling each other. The infighting grew worse as their numbers increased. One nurse tripped and fell. Its head shattered under the heel of another nurse. He recalled his earlier impression of their gleaming, glazed ceramic bodies, and realized it hadn't been a trick of the light. When struck hard enough, they broke like porcelain dolls.

Maria planted one booted foot on a plastic food tray covered in dust. The tray shot out from under her, and she tumbled to the floor, crying out in pain. Stopping abruptly, his moment having already carried him several long strides beyond where Maria had fallen, James turned back, about to shove an IV stand out of his way. His flashlight swept across the hall, revealing the clattering charge of the nurses as they surged out of the darkness to claim their victims. Too close!

Maria had climbed to her hands and knees.

"Just go," she shouted. "Leave me!"

"I'm not leaving—"

The pale head of the nurse leading the charge was canted at an odd angle, the irregular black holes that substituted for facial features were impenetrable to the light, a soulless void beneath the gleaming surface. In her right hand, raised high, she clutched an ice pick. If James bent down to help Maria rise, he had no doubts the nurse would shove that ice pick into his back up to the hilt.

Because the wheelchair armrest was too short for close quarters fighting against numerous combatants, he slid it toward Maria and, instead, picked up the four-legged IV stand and held it in both hands like a staff. He charged the lead nurse and rammed the top of the metal stand into her torso. It burst through her midsection with a crash. Pieces of her torso broke off and shattered on the floor.

Seemingly unbothered by the injury, she swiped back and forth with the ice pick, vicious slashing motions that, fortunately, remained out of reach. But the stand was jammed in her torso. James pulled her sideways, bringing her to the ground in front of the charging horde. The next few, packed into the hallway behind her, tripped and fell over her or the stand itself. Those behind pushed and shoved and clambered over the pileup in an unrelenting mass.

James had released the base of the IV stand when ice pick nurse went down. He hurried to Maria, who was back on her feet, rubbing her scraped elbow.

"You okay?"

"Fine," she said and extended the broken armrest. "Take this."

He took the improvised weapon, his free arm on her lower back in case she stumbled after recovering from the awkward fall. Behind them, the crowd of nurses fought their way past their fallen and shattered colleagues. Soon the only sounds were the clattering of their heels on the rusted floor, along with the occasional jostling of their hard shell bodies.

"You hear that?" James asked, staring ahead at the darkness beyond the reach of his flashlight.

"It's all I hear."

"But it's coming from in front of—" he said. "Oh, shit!"

The light revealed a second contingent of bloodthirsty nurses charging from the opposite end of the corridor. Somehow, they'd accidentally been caught in a pincer movement. He refused to believe the nurse creatures had organized a coordinated attack. But that made it no less effective.

Maria grabbed his jacket. "This way!"

She pulled him to the left. They had arrived at a T-shaped intersection. James looked down the cross corridor and had a bad feeling. From his brief study of the emergency evacuation map, he couldn't recall this section of the building.

As they took the detour, James shouted, "Don't know where this goes."

"Not like we have a choice."

At first, he feared they'd run down a dead end, but the flashlight finally revealed the open doors of a freight elevator. Panting, they rushed into the elevator. Maria stood with her back against the rear wall, catching her breath. James swept the light upward, noting the lack of a security hatch.

At the end of the hall, the two groups of nurses converged, losing a few of their numbers in violent head-on, body-shattering collisions, before navigating the turn and continuing their charge to the elevator.

Though rust covered the control panel inside the elevator, the buttons were illuminated. James frantically pressed the button to close the doors, then the buttons for any other floor of the hospital. The elevator ignored all of them.

"C'mon," he said. "Work!"

Nothing.

"Here," James said, tugging the clip-on flashlight free of his jacket and handing it to her. "Take this."

She held it between trembling hands, arms extended toward the hallway, as if the light itself might repel the killer nurses.

James stood in the middle of the doorway, determined to keep them out. Grimly, he recalled the story of the 300 Spartans who held off the Persian army at the Battle of Thermopylae. A tale of heroic resistance in tight quarters against overwhelming forces. But it didn't end well for the Spartans.

Only a few seconds elapsed from the moment he gave Maria the flashlight until the vanguard of the nurses reached the elevator. Taking a wide stance, James wielded the metal armrest like a truncheon, striking nurses with overhand blows and backswings. He shattered heads and upraised arms. Pieces fell to the floor like broken pottery. But they clearly felt no pain, experienced no fear, no matter how much damage he inflicted, and their numbers seemed inexhaustible.

As one to the right attempted to squeeze through the doorway, he had to shift his position to stop her. One blow broke her arm off at the elbow. The next one caved in her head, the right side tumbling away. But his right sidestep opened a gap on the left, and a nurse slipped by him, brandishing a long shard of rusty metal the size of a butcher knife in her right hand. Ignoring James, she rushed Maria in the back of the elevator, slashing at her with the sharp metal blade.

James recovered quickly and hooked his free arm around the nurse's midsection, hurling her off her feet back into the mass of gleaming bodies, many of them broken and stumbling around shattered limbs and torsos on the floor.

The elevator shuddered, the motor coming to life. The overhead light flickered on and then off again. James caught a glimpse of Maria, her face beaded with sweat, staring at the lights, no doubt willing them to come and stay on. The lights flickered on again, dimmed but stayed lit, and the elevator shuddered a second time.

Hope gave James a second wind. He fought feverishly to keep the horde of nurses at bay—just a few seconds longer and—

The elevator doors began to close, if haltingly.

The overhead light shone brighter.

James held the armrest horizontally toward the nurses in a double-handed grip, jagged end forward, and jammed it through faceless heads and torsos. As the gap between the closing doors narrowed, the nurses could only reach through with their hands. Swinging the armrest left and right, he shattered the exposed limbs. Debris rained down on the floor until, finally, the doors shut. With a lurch, the elevator began to ascend.

James turned his back to the doors, panting with exhaustion, trying to catch his breath. "Well, that was—"

Maria collapsed, sliding down to the floor, dropping the flashlight as she clamped her hands over her bleeding left hip. Her head was lowered in pain, her breathing shallow.

James dropped down on one knee beside her. Gently, he moved her hands, dripping with blood, away from the wound. By the light of the overhead lamp and the flashlight on the floor, he saw her blood-streaked left leg and the deep, bleeding gash in her hip.

CHAPTER 29

The Brookhaven Hospital's freight elevator creaked and trembled during its slow ascent. The metal walls were streaked with stains, covered with patches of rust and peeling paint. The dust-coated floor was now littered with debris from the shattered heads, torsos and limbs of murderous nurses. And in the back of the elevator, Maria's blood had formed a pool that continued to spread.

"I'm sorry—there were so many—"

"It's not your fault, James," Mary said, her voice strained as she pressed her blood-soaked palms to her bare hip. "I'm fine. I can handle it."

"You're not fine," James said. "We need to stop the bleeding."

He looked around the confined space, hoping to find an emergency first aid kit. The control panel looked fifty years old, even discounting the instant-rust, completely rudimentary, with no storage compartment under it. He would have expected a hospital to keep medical supplies in every nook and cranny, but it was probably just the opposite, with everything under lock and key.

The elevator shook violently.

"What the—?" James staggered, reaching out to the side wall to catch his balance.

Maria winced. A pained groan escaped her lips.

With a shudder, the elevator halted. A moment later, the interior lights winked off. The flashlight on the floor cast harsh shadows up the walls.

The elevator's hoist cable shook, jostling the cabin.

Staring up at the ceiling, James wondered if the cable might snap. The freight elevator only served five floors, and they were nowhere near the top, so the fall alone probably wouldn't kill them. Might hurt like hell. Even break a few bones. But considering Maria's fragile condition—

They needed to get out. Simple as that.

James wedged the metal armrest between the closed doors and pried them apart, at least enough to get a solid grip on them. Grunting with effort, he managed to get them half open, enough to squeeze through. Unfortunately, the elevator cabin was stuck between floors, so they'd have to climb up to get out. He bent down to pick up the flashlight—

Maria was unconscious.

One of her two hands had fallen away from the open wound, her bloodied knuckles resting on the sullied floor at her side. With a sweep of the flashlight, he confirmed that the corridor was currently empty. He clipped the light on his jacket and crouched down to pick up Maria. She moaned softly as he carried her to the elevator doors and transferred her to the floor outside the elevator, which was at waist height. He grabbed the broken armrest and prepared to climb out after her. For a macabre moment, he imagined the cable snapping while he was half in and half out of the freight elevator, the weight of the cabin in freefall ripping his body in half—

Shaking off the dark thought, he scrambled out of the elevator beside Maria. The sign on the wall facing the elevators read Psychiatric Ward. With the armrest pinned against his body, James scooped up Maria with his left arm under her shoulders, right arm under her knees and carried her down the dark hall. Along the way, he turned side to side, to shine the clip-on light at doorways, most of them offices. When he located a surgical room, he shoved one of the double doors open and carried her to a surgical bed.

Between the rust on the surgical bed frame and the dust and grunge on the padding, nothing was remotely sanitary. But desperate times required desperate measures. Her face was pale from blood loss, and the wound continued to drip fresh blood. He set her down gently on the bed, then roamed nervously around the room. Shelves were empty, but he found a portable medical supply cart with a broken wheel. Rifling through the drawers, he found a bottle of rubbing alcohol, a half-used tube of antibacterial gel, a box of gauze pads, butterfly bandages, and a spool of cloth medical tape.

When he returned to the surgical bed, Maria opened her eyes.

He gently wiped the area around the wound with alcohol and a couple gauze pads. "Gonna sting," he warned her.

She gave a brief nod.

Applying pressure to the wound, he cleaned the edges of the wound with more alcohol. She inhaled sharply, arching her back. With several butterfly bandages, he pulled the wound shut. Not as effective as stitches, but it would have to do for now. Next, he applied a liberal amount of antibacterial gel to a fresh gauze pad and pressed that against the wound, securing the pad on all sides with the medical cloth tape.

Hands shaking slightly, he looked into her familiar blue eyes.

She stared back at him, swallowed and said, "Tougher than I look."

His throat tight, he smiled, and she smiled warmly back at him.

He finally found his voice. "Never had a doubt."

"You can say it."

"What?"

Maria winced as she scooted up a little on the inclined top half of the surgical bed. "I look just like her."

"How would you know that?"

Maria's smile was bittersweet despite the evident pain. "It's how you look at me."

"That doesn't—you can't—" James shook his head in denial. It was not the same. It couldn't be. Of course, he cared about Maria. She was the first person willing to help him. They'd helped each other. Survived this unfolding nightmare. It was only natural to worry, to care—but she wasn't—

"Did—do you know Mary?" he asked softly.

"Am I wrong?"

James stared silently into the distance.

Maria reached up, placed two fingers on his chin and turned his face toward her. "Look at me, James."

He took a deep breath, then made eye contact.

"Am I wrong?" she repeated.

"Listen," James said, avoiding the question. Of course, she looked like Mary— aside from the hair, the makeup, the swagger. A Mary who didn't second-guess her decisions, a Mary who didn't always defer to the wishes of others at her own expense. "I'm going to go to the next floor," James said, placing a hand on her shoulder. "I want you to stay here and rest. Give that wound time to stop bleeding."

She took his hand in both of hers. "Please, don't leave me."

"You'll be safer in here," he reasoned. "I'll check for Mary, then I'll be right back."

"Okay," Maria said. "But promise me something."

"What?"

She brushed his hand against her cheek, then pressed it against her heart and held it there while she spoke. "If you find out she's gone, we leave. Together. We don't look back."

Belatedly, James realized all the panic he'd felt when they first met in Rosewater Park was gone. Somehow, spending time with Maria had drawn all the anxiety out of him. He remained determined to find Mary, but the crushing weight of imminent failure no longer plagued him. He simply needed to finish what he started and get out of the cursed town.

"I won't be long," he said at length. "I promise."

Outside the surgical room, James looked for a way to secure the doors. He found a broken patient monitor dangling from a wheeled stand on its side. Ripping out some of the loose wires, he knotted them around the door handles. As security precautions went, it was an elementary barrier but based upon his experience with the monsters inhabiting Silent Hill, he couldn't imagine them undoing knots. They seemed to react to movement and proximity, their attacks mindless fury lacking subtlety or strategy. If Maria kept quiet in the room, odds were good she'd stay safe.

As he stepped away from the door, he noticed Laura standing in the middle of the hallway staring at him, her weird gray doll held at her side.

"Who are you with?" she asked.

"Someone I'm trying to help," James replied. "Laura, you have to tell me where Mary is."

"She's not here."

"Then where is she?" At every turn he tried to protect this girl from the hellscape that Silent Hill had become, but all she did in return was taunt him. "Please, Laura."

"Doesn't look like you wanna find her," she scoffed.

Had this little girl—this kid—been spying on him?

"I do," he insisted. "It's all I want. Please. Tell me."

"My baby's sad," Laura said, holding the doll out for him to see—finally—in the light blazing from his flashlight.

Shocked, James realized the doll wasn't a doll at all. It was an unborn baby—a fetus—gray and pallid, eyes bulging. She'd been carrying that—thing all over town. Where had she found it? How was it even alive? Some kind of mutation? Was it even safe for her to be holding the damn thing?

"He's cold," Laura said, making a pouty face. "And sad. Sad because nobody loved him. Just like Mary."

"What do you mean?"

"He was left all alone, too."

The fetus-doll contorted itself in Laura's hand, squeaking, as if suddenly revived from death to bemoan its inhumane treatment—and to accuse James as well.

"You left her all alone!" Laura shrieked.

Stunned by the fetus' sudden revivification and by the implication of Laura's words, James felt the pressure inside his head building. *How could she—? There's no way she—*

"How do you know that?"

James took a step closer to her, only peripherally aware that he still held the broken armrest like a truncheon. Laura stepped back. He hadn't wanted to come across as threatening, but Laura didn't know him. Maybe she was fearful of all strangers.

"You have to get to her," Laura warned, "before it's too late."

Before he could reply, she turned and bolted down the corridor.

James ran after her.

He half expected her to lead him right into a crowd of murderous nurses, then duck inside a ventilation shaft too small to accommodate an adult. Instead, she turned left down a short hallway that ended with a pair of scuffed, windowless metal doors painted white and edged with rust, with a bright red sign above them.

AUTHORIZED PERSONNEL ONLY

With her doll-fetus clutched in one hand, Laura pushed the right door open and slipped through the gap into the darkness beyond. James followed her, proceeding more cautiously. With the door open, he heard the clanging sound of footfalls on metal and directed his flashlight down. Beyond the doors, the tile flooring had been replaced by industrial floor grating, almost as if he'd stepped onto a catwalk or raised platform in a factory. The walls were solid metal, marred with scratches and smears of grease. The nine-foot-high ceiling was metal as well, but with a rectangular network of grooves or tracks, also dented and grimy. His light wasn't powerful enough to illuminate the entire length of the corridor, but he saw a dark silhouette crouched beyond its reach.

"Laura," he called. "Is that you."

"I'm scared," she replied. "This is a bad place."

CHAPTER 30

"Stay there," James called to Laura. "I'll come get you."

James strode across the metal grating, playing the beam of light back and forth, making sure there were no gaps in the load-bearing bars or crosspieces he might fall through. Under his heavier weight, he felt the metal shift and rattle alarmingly. With the state of decay in the hospital, he couldn't be sure the grating would support him. He sensed the rustle of movement beneath him, staying just out of the light. Maybe only a trick of the shifting shadows or his own imagination getting the better of him.

Nearby, a metallic click startled him. He glanced up just in time to see a metal-framed cage swing down from the ceiling, with a pair of legs dangling through openings in the bottom. He jumped to the side to avoid being struck by the cage. The steel grating rattled under him. But the stark light shining into the hanging cage revealed a misshapen mass of writhing flesh. At the bottom of the cage, a grotesquely large pair of lips opened and closed, groaning as the dangling feet swung at him.

His evasive action kept him out of reach of the dangling legs, even with the cage rocking back and forth. But then he heard a metallic clicking sound. The cage shuddered sideways, moving along one of the tracks in the ceiling, sliding toward him. Ducking, he moved away, but one of the feet struck his shoulder with enough force to stagger him. The wall stopped him from falling, but already the mechanism holding the cage in the track was clicking and the cage was spinning with the changed momentum of the swinging legs to pursue him.

Its progress was slow enough for him to move away and run down the hall toward Laura, but then he caught another glimpse of movement beneath the floor grating. He looked down to see—something hanging beneath the floor with disproportionately large arms attached to a vaguely feminine body wrapped in a straitjacket-like canvas garment above atrophied legs. Both bulky arms ended in large lips instead of fingers. The lips on the face of the creature were hideously oversized as well.

"What the—?"

Overhead the cage rattled, sliding closer—

Beneath him, the wide lips on one of the arms opened and long tentacles protruded, reaching through the grating to ensnare his ankles.

James tried to pull his legs free, but the tentacles were too strong.

The cage swung toward him, as the creature inside tried to smash him against the wall. James had to drop to the floor to avoid the attack, even as the pressure on his ankles increased. Above him, the cage crashed into the wall and the feet flailed back and forth, seeking a target.

Swinging the metal armrest overhead, he missed twice before connecting with one of the legs. The animalistic groaning turned into a pained wail. And yet the tentacles throttling his ankles were too painful to ignore, so he turned his attention downward. He needed to free himself to get away from the hanging cage.

First, he tried whacking the tentacles with the side of the armrest, but his feet were taking the brunt of the blows. So, he switched to a more targeted attack, hammering the jagged edge of the armrest at individual tentacles. After two or three strikes, he cut away one of the tentacles. Then went to work on the next, ignoring the crushing pain in his ankle bone.

As he attacked the tentacles of one arm, the movement of his flashlight revealed a second dangling figure moving toward him. If the tentacles of the second creature managed to grab his arms, he would be immobilized and helpless. Redoubling his effort, he chopped away the remaining tentacles to free one foot and used that free leg to push himself upward—while still avoiding the hanging cage and kicking feet—to create a gap between the tentacles on his locked foot and the floor grating. That made it easier to chop away the second set of tentacles. With each dismembered tentacle, the dangling creature moaned and wailed. But it refused to retreat, so he attacked relentlessly until his second foot broke free.

Moments later, the second dangler had moved within striking distance. The first one, now that its tentacles were severed, gave ground to the second attacker. James had to sidestep continually to keep away from it. All the while, he moved hunched over to avoid the hanging cage, which continued to track him.

"Laura," James called. "Are you okay?"

"My doll doesn't like this place."

Her voice seemed far away.

"Stay low," he warned. "If you hear anything below, keep moving!"

"It's so dark here."

"I'm coming," James said a moment after he evaded another assault from the swinging cage. "Hold on."

"There's more," she said. "They don't want you to leave."

James shone the light down and, sure enough, dark shapes

were moving beneath the grating, drawn to his position like moths to a flame. Which made him realize that might be the exact nature of the problem. They attacked him, but not Laura. He had a light, while she crouched farther away in darkness. But if he turned off the light, he would be helpless to avoid their attacks. What if it was too late to turn off the light, now that they had a bead on him?

He backed away from the approaching danglers, taking care with each step, but then heard a metallic ratcheting from above away from the cage tracking him. He whirled around to face a squeal of metal. A second metal-framed cage swung down right in his path. Unable to avoid the collision, he reached up with his free hand and grabbed the bars of the cage. The momentum of the swinging cage lifted him off his feet, shoving him back the way he had come. He managed to hang onto the cage rather than falling to the floor on top of the mass of dangling creatures homing in on him.

The writhing, shifting mass of flesh inside the cage rolled across his fingers and it took him a moment to notice the oversized lips that groaned through the bottom of the cage were making their way toward his hand. Whether that obscene mouth contained tentacles or razor-sharp teeth, he didn't want to find out.

Releasing his grip on the cage, he dropped to a crouch and immediately checked his position on the grating. Metal rattled beneath him as half a dozen of the danglers swung in his direction. Some of them closed in around the sides, hoping to trap him in the center so he'd have no path to escape. Noticing the nearest pair of oversized arms less than a stride away from him, he waited a moment then, as it released one arm to close the gap, he swung the armrest against the other arm, which was momentarily supporting all its weight. Two quick strikes and the bloodied arm detached. The creature pinwheeled down into the darkness with a baleful wail, its body striking the next closest dangler before disappearing below, followed by a satisfying thud.

James had no time to celebrate his minor victory, because the loss of one of their own inflamed the other danglers. They rushed toward him and the grating rattled ominously. Ducking the cage that had tried to crush his skull, he ran in a crouch toward Laura's position. Ahead of him, a succession of metal latches clicked and squealed. He surveyed the ceiling and saw a row of alternating cages all the way to Laura's crouching silhouette. Each one, attached horizontally to the grid in the ceiling, detached at the same time, swinging down vertically, with kicking legs and a chorus of groaning lips. He had to stay low the entire length of the corridor, or the cages would knock him over. And if the cages missed him, he still had to avoid the feet.

Scrambling forward, he zigzagged between cages. Almost at once, the metal grating beneath his feet shook violently. Numerous danglers swung impatiently to catch him. He was jostled side to side, as if Brookhaven Hospital were at the epicenter of an earthquake. A cage struck the side of his shoulder, causing him to stumble into the next one's path. Kicking legs tried to lock around his neck to throttle him, but he swatted the feet away frantically with the metal armrest.

Suddenly, the grated flooring pitched upward, knocking him down. Metal rattled and shook and then, with a loud squeal, a section of the flooring broke free, falling under the weight of several wailing danglers, to a thunderous crash below. He heard rivets popping, metal squealing and shrieking in protest. In the glare of the flashlight, he saw the flooring falling into darkness, one section after another, a cascade effect, mere seconds away from reaching his position.

"Laura, run!"

He pushed himself up awkwardly, struggling to stay beneath the cages swooping back and forth or rolling along recessed tracks to reach him. With his light facing forward, he saw Laura rise, turn on her heels and race through the double doors at the end of the collapsing corridor. Seconds behind her, he felt the metal grating underfoot rising, like the prow of a sinking ship tilting skyward.

As he cleared the last of the dangling cages, he rose to his full height, took three long strides and launched himself at the double doors, striking the narrow gap between the two with his shoulder. The last section of flooring had risen high enough to clip one ankle painfully, before shrieking against one wall and crashing below. He burst through the swinging doors, rolling forward in an awkward somersault.

Grimacing in pain, he climbed to his feet, checking the hallway for Laura. The floor beyond the doors consisted of chipped and broken tiles, a welcome relief from the metal grating. He stood at a T intersection and checked both directions.

At the end of the hall to the right, Laura waited for him.

"Are you okay?"

"What took you so long?" Laura called. "You're running out of time."

With that, she ducked through a door to the stairwell. He ran after her, reaching the door before it closed and slipping inside in time to see her climbing the stairs. Her doll-fetus wriggled in her hand to look at him. And that wasn't creepy at all.

She exited one floor up.

He followed her, pulling the door open. On the wall facing him, a sign read Toxicology Unit. Was it a coincidence? Since checking the emergency evacuation map, he'd been attempting to make it to Toxicology and now, the final leg of the journey, led here by the little girl.

James stopped when he saw Laura standing at the end of the hall, apparently waiting for him to catch up.

"Why are you doing this?"

Laura gave a little shrug. "No one said it would be easy."

It's just a game to her, he realized. She teased him along and made him do her bidding if he wanted answers to his questions. He ran toward her, expecting her to turn and dash away again. But she simply walked into the room at the end of the hall. James followed her, reaching for the door handle, but stopping when he noticed the room number posted beside the door.

318

Same number as the apartment they had shared.

"How?"

Another coincidence? How much did Laura know about his relationship with Mary? She seemed to know Mary. Or at least she pretended she knew her. Was leading him to the same room number as their apartment number a childish joke?

He entered the dark room, beginning to walk in a small circle so the clip-on light would reveal his surroundings. Behind him, he heard a quick shuffling of feet, the sound of childish giggling. He spun around in time to see Laura slip through the doorway and slam the door shut behind her.

James grabbed the handle and tried to open the door, but she'd locked it from the other side.

"Laura!" He yanked the handle again, pounded his fist on the door. "Open the door!"

From the other side of the door, he heard her voice calling back to him, but with an ethereal quality. "Why'd you come here, James?"

Desperately, he pulled at the handle, yanking it up and down to no avail. All his calm and resolve was gone. He wanted out. Anywhere but there. He could—not—stay—

"Open the door!"

He was hyperventilating. Out of control. He clutched the handle in sweaty palms, trying to get his breathing and his heart rate under control—

As he quieted, he gradually became aware of a faint wheezing behind him, almost like the sound of a dripping faucet.

Placing his back to the door, he scanned the room with his flashlight. Nothing—nobody was in the room with him. But the wheezing, and the dripping sound continued to haunt him in the empty room. Then he remembered to look up—

The flashlight beam revealed a rusted hospital bed floating on the ceiling—upside down—with a bundle of sheets clinging to the mattress. Without the aid of a metal grid and tracks that had facilitated the ponderous movement of the cages in the corridor he'd just escaped, the hospital bed drifted across the ceiling tiles at the command of its own strange physics. Somehow, either by following the source of light or James himself, the bed flowed along the ceiling to position itself right above him. All the while, a dark liquid dripped from the bed, drop after drop *plinking* on the floor.

Horrified, James watched as someone—or something—writhed and moaned under the jumbled mound of bedsheets. The bed continued to hang suspended in the air above him, frozen in place. Wary of whatever moved on the bed and the possibility of the bed itself crashing down on top of him, James slowly stepped out from under it.

As soon as he moved, the bed reacted, trembling into motion to follow him, mimicking his movement to position itself directly overhead again. Without looking away from the bed, James cut across the room at an angle. Again, the bed moved, pivoting, then precisely tracking his movement.

James sensed movement by the locked door.

Directing his flashlight there, he saw an eye staring at him through the keyhole. But it wasn't Laura's eye. It was the dead eye of the doll-fetus staring at him. Nevertheless, Laura's voice called through the gap. "She waited for you."

The implication was clear.

Immediately, James looked again at the bed poised above him. The sheets had shifted enough for him to see they were wrapped around a pitiful, scrawny creature with a woman's emaciated face, blood dripping steadily from its nose.

"Mary—?"

A drop of blood struck his cheek and trickled down to his jaw.

As he wiped the blood away, two pairs of hands with long, claw-like fingers reached out from beneath the sheets on long, slender arms, stretching toward James' face. Two of the inhuman hands gripped each side of his face. One hand hooked into his mouth, tugging it open; the claws of the other hand pressed near his eyes.

James tried to swing the broken armrest at the creature, but a third hand latched onto his arm, holding it still. The fingers of the fourth hand squeezed together, a tight grouping of sharp claws, and penetrated his open mouth. Then the arm shoved that hand down his throat, forcing him to swallow it.

Paralyzed by the horror of the moment and by the utter monstrosity attacking him, James couldn't resist what was happening to him. Somehow, he felt like he shouldn't fight—that his fate was inevitable.

Again, he heard Laura's voice coming through the door.

"She waited," Laura told him. "But it was too late."

The bed creature's hands wrapped around his mouth and nose, cutting off his air, slowly suffocating him, while lifting his body off the floor. The flashlight, dislodged from his pocket, fell to the floor with a clatter. His tingling hands lost their grip on the metal armrest, and it slipped from his numb fingers—a distant *clang*.

The last thing James heard was Laura's distant voice, "Come back when you're ready, James. She's still waiting for you."

He dangled from the creature's writhing arms, a lifeless puppet, barely twitching as darkness closed in around him.

The creature pulled him closer, almost as if trying to kiss him before the end—

Helpless, he stared up into the gaping mouth, and saw only an all-consuming darkness, a chasm… an abyss… and deep within it—

—a blinding light. And a faint voice—

"Mr. Sunderland—"

CHAPTER 31

"Mr. Sunderland?"

James had been pulled into the darkness and fallen through only to find light on the other side. A blinding light—in his left eye, then his right. Once the light withdrew, he focused on the doctor leaning over him with a penlight. She had dark brown hair pulled back in a ponytail and wore cobalt blue scrubs, with a stethoscope looped around her neck. Her nametag read 'Helen W'.

"Are you with us, Mr. Sunderland?"

James cleared his throat, looked down to get his bearings. He was in a hospital bed, in a bright hospital room with sunlight streaming through three side-by-side windows, which somehow seemed odd to him after so much darkness in Brookhaven Hospital. Still groggy, he had trouble remembering what had happened to him. The last thing—the creature in the upside down bed floating on the ceiling. Clawed hands… lifting him up… Laura telling him something…

"Mr. Sunderland?"

James started to answer, then realized his arms were restrained, strapped to the bed. Was he a patient or a prisoner?

"Where am I?" he asked. "What is this?"

"Glad you're back with us," the doctor said. "You're in Brookhaven Hospital in Silent Hill."

"Silent Hill?"

That wasn't possible. Even in the fog world, Silent Hill and the hospital had been abandoned. And in the otherworld of darkness, it was corrupted, coated in rust, ruled by the murderous nurses that shattered like pottery when struck. All the changes he'd seen—

He scanned his room, the window wall that looked out on the hospital corridor. Nurses—normal nurses—striding up and down the corridor, talking to doctors or technicians, a man carrying a bouquet of flowers and a helium balloon on the way to visit a patient. A normal, busy hospital, his own room bright, clean and sterile. Nothing like—

James' bed was inclined, but he tried to sit up straight, fighting against the restraints that confined him. Why were they treating him like a prisoner, some kind of threat?

"Just tell me where she is."

The doctor frowned at him, confused. "Where who is?"

"Mary," James said. Wasn't it obvious? "Mary Crane."

A familiar face looked in on him from the open doorway, flashing him a warm smile before entering his room. If anything, he was surprised to see her not only outside her office, but in Silent Hill. She was tall, in her fifties if he had to guess, but her face had a youthful vitality. Foregoing her usual in-office pantsuit, she wore a taupe silk blouse and tan linen slacks, along with a gold pendant necklace of the sun surrounded by wavy rays. Composed and poised, as one would expect from a professional visiting her patient. To James, she was simply M.

As Doctor Helen W left his bedside, M took her place, like a changing of the guard. Idly, he wondered if they planned to keep him under constant guard. Not that he needed guarding if they planned to keep him strapped to the bed.

"Hello, James."

"I found her."

He couldn't help it, that was the first thing out of his mouth. Even before inquiring about the need for restraints. M had to know how close he was—

Her face fell, if only briefly, the composure he'd witnessed a moment ago transformed into momentary dismay. But she recovered quickly, displaying a sympathetic smile as she gently took his hand.

"James—"

"I know where she is—"

"You need to let go of her," M said. "She's gone."

James opened his mouth in protest, but nothing came out. He stared at her, really looking into those compassionate eyes. He was aware of his hospital room, aware of how normal—how natural—it was. The functioning equipment, the sun warming the clear windows, the hallway traffic outside his room. All of it was unlike everything he had experienced in Silent Hill over the past two days, the unrelenting fog and falling ash, the ever-present rust and rain that came with the darkness, the lack of people—normal people—and the proliferation of monsters, soulless creatures bent on death and destruction. And yet… somehow, this room with his therapist looking down on him… somehow this felt… real.

"She's dead, James," M said sympathetically. "Mary's been dead for years."

James stared at her, a lump in his throat, aching to tell her she was wrong. Mary had sent the letter to his studio. She needed him—she couldn't be gone, couldn't be—

—dead.

His vision blurred. He felt a tear slip from his eye and roll down his cheek. With his arms secured at his side, he couldn't even wipe it away, he couldn't deny…

"Why are you telling me this?"

She must have seen the resignation in his face. Quietly, she released his hand and walked away. At the doorway, she turned back to him.

"We've got some serious work to do," she told him. "But we'll get you through it. You just have to promise me something..."

James didn't reply, but neither did he look away.

"You need to want to see yourself get better as much as I do."

Tears welled up in his eyes anew. His mind was a confusing jumble of emotions. Confusion and fear, torn between two worlds, one filled with hope, the other with grief, one terrifying, the other intolerable, one threatened pain, the other delivered torment. But one was unsustainable, while the other offered at least the possibility of healing. Aware at least that something drastic had to change, he finally nodded at M.

"Rest," she said. "I'll be seeing you soon."

With a curt nod of her own, she departed his room, the sound of her footfalls on the tile rapidly fading. Dr. Helen W, the attending physician, came back to pull the curtains on all three of his exterior windows, casting James' room in shadows. Before she left, she gave James the same advice, "Rest now."

James stared at the new shadows on the ceiling of his room. He felt found, but lost, unsure of a way forward. Unshed tears filled his eyes, causing the shadows to twist and stretch above him. He lost track of time. At some point, the shadows above him grew wider and darker until they filled the room.

Foot traffic in the hallway diminished and the hospital became eerily quiet. Occasional voices in hushed conversations drifted by, the words indistinguishable from one another. Outside his room, a janitor wearing a cobalt blue scrub top over jeans pushed a dust mop along the hallway. *Dust is not tolerated here...*

Unmoving, James continued to stare at the dark ceiling, waiting for light...

CHAPTER 32

James lost track of time waiting for Mary to return to their apartment. He sat in the armchair by the window in his blue T-shirt and jeans, staring at the play of light and shadow on the ceiling from each passing car. His fingers tapped on the glass of white wine he held in his lap, between both hands.

He focused his attention on the animated chiaroscuro provided by street traffic, because the shifting shadows were the equivalent of visual white noise. If he closed his eyes, other images sprang to mind, haunting images he would never unsee. After the blood ceremony he'd witnessed from behind the iron grate in the secret underground tunnel, he'd fled in disgust. He'd retreated into the darkness, ascending the stone staircase to the double doors with the hidden release mechanism. He'd even returned the blue dumpster to its original position atop the doors, covering his tracks.

Briefly, before his retreat, he'd considered confronting Mary, confronting them all. But he didn't trust himself then. Could he trust himself now? That Mary had not returned to their home yet gave him time to get his temper under control. At the same time, he'd been drinking steadily, too far into the bottle of wine resting on the floor beside the chair.

Before today, he'd considered her circle of friends a bit eccentric, if he was being kind, odd if he was being truthful.

But nothing could have prepared him for what he witnessed underground. He didn't want to blame Mary for their behavior, but he couldn't understand why she would go along with the bizarre ritual. He always knew they had some kind of hold on her, but its nature remained a mystery. She behaved as if she owed them a debt because they revered her father. It seemed likely her father had been the head of the cult her friends belonged to, but was Mary a member as well? Was she some sort of legacy? Did they expect her to take over as the leader? She seemed reluctant to go along with their plans—and yet ultimately, she complied. No stronger evidence of that than letting those weirdos drink her blood.

His foot struck the brown leather duffel bag sitting on a throw rug at his feet. He'd packed a few essentials of his own in there, and he'd taken out a suitcase for Mary to do the same. They'd reached a fork in the road, so to speak, and the one path was no longer a viable option.

A key turned in the front door lock.

Mary entered the darkened apartment, closed the door, shrugged off her winter coat and placed it on a hook on the coatrack, then took off her green-and-white striped scarf and held it in her hand. She walked into the living room wearing her square neck black midi dress with the pink dogwood flower pattern. The same dress she'd been wearing on the street before she'd changed into the white ceremonial gown her friends had ripped to shreds during their drug-induced blood frenzy. As if none of that had happened.

She stopped when she realized she wasn't alone in the apartment, turning to where he sat in the shadows. "Why are you sitting in the dark?"

Mary's gaze flickered from his face to the half empty bottle. She realized he'd been drinking alone, in the dark, waiting for her to show up.

James emptied his glass before replying. Placing his heel on the top edge of the empty suitcase, he kicked it toward her. "Pack your things," he said, louder than he intended. "I want us out of here."

She looked down at the suitcase, inches from her tan leather boots, then back at him. "Why are you acting like this?"

"I want out of here," he said. "So, we're getting out of here."

Confused, she shook her head dismissively. "You're not making sense."

"Guess what I did today?" He heard the words coming out of his mouth, knew he sounded immature and sarcastic, but it was taking all his restraint not to yell. At this point, the alcohol in his system was more of a hindrance to remaining calm and rational. But he'd needed it to take the edge off the swirling emotions he'd experienced the whole way home.

He stood up and felt a wave of dizziness, needing a quick step to regain his balance before approaching her. She shot him a disappointed look, then her eyes darted toward the bedroom, as if she intended to flee. Her method of conflict resolution had always been avoidance. But he couldn't let this stand unchallenged. She did not have the high ground. "I saw this girl across the street," James continued. "So, I followed her."

Mary froze and James could tell she knew he knew.

"I went down this long flight of stairs—"

"Stop," Mary said, wanting to avoid the topic until the bitter end.

"What were you gonna tell me?" he asked, gesturing with the empty glass. "You were out for dinner with your friends?"

She remained silent.

"It's too late for more lies."

He kicked the empty suitcase across the room with the edge of his foot.

"I saw these monsters," he continued. "I saw them tear her apart—"

"Just STOP!" Mary screamed and slapped the empty glass out of his hands. It flew across the room and shattered against the wall.

They stood facing each other in silence.

James had never seen this side of her. She was always the accommodating one, the peacemaker, the one skilled in conflict resolution. But now she knew that her secret, the secret she'd fought so hard to keep from him, was out in the open, undeniable.

"How long?" he asked.

Mary looked away from him, took a deep breath, hands still trembling at her side. "Since I was a girl."

James was stunned. That was not the answer he was expecting. And it was so much worse than he had imagined. But then he thought about the photo of a stern Joshua Crane, standing with her as a child, his hands possessively gripping her shoulders.

"Why would your father do this to you?"

"I don't know," she said, her voice breaking as her eyes brimmed with tears. "I never had a choice."

He wanted to take her in his arms, couldn't stand seeing her distressed and in pain. For so long, he'd let the oddities and the evasions slide. He loved her, but he had reached a breaking point and, after what he'd witnessed today, he'd discovered that his fears were justified—more than justified—because he was horrified by what he'd seen. Things could never go back to the way they were.

"This is your last chance," he said, feeling the awful weight of his ultimatum, and hearing it in the brittleness of his voice. "Walk out that door with me now."

"Not when you're like this."

He could tell she never considered it. All she heard was someone else trying to control her, and she was digging in her heels.

"What am I like?"

"Scared."

"You think I'm scared?" He grabbed her upper arms, a far more violent gesture than he'd intended. His impulse was to shake some sense into her, to make her view the situation objectively, but the alcohol in his system robbed him of subtlety and understanding. She couldn't make him understand her irrational point of view, why she was complicit in her own abuse and debasement, so *she* was attacking *him*? "I am *not* scared," he raged. "I am not *scared* of any of you!"

Her arms were rigid in his grasp while tears formed in her eyes.

"But you were disgusted," she said, with a sob as she sensed the truth in his eyes. "Say it. Say I'm disgusting to you." She shoved him back, and his arms fell to his side. "Say it!" she repeated, shoving him again.

He remained silent, unable to form a denial. As much as he felt disgust for the ceremony, he was also furious that it had happened to her, that she had allowed it to happen. He was ashamed for her. His own vision blurred as his eyes filled with tears.

"That day," Mary said softly, a hitch in her voice. "I was leaving."

Struggling to understand what she meant, he shook his head in confusion.

"I was leaving," she continued. "And then you showed up."

The rest area—her luggage. More than a shopping jaunt into the city. He'd always known she lied to her friends about it. They'd seemed weirdly upset that she had planned to leave Silent Hill until her lie. James had always assumed she meant to get away for a few days, on her own, away from her busybody friends. And the more he learned about them, the more that made sense. But now—realizing she had planned to leave for good, to escape their madness. And that she had only stayed after he wrecked her luggage, after she'd become his accidental tour guide, and the start to a serious relationship…

James couldn't breathe. Felt like his chest was in a vise.

"Why—why didn't you just tell me?"

"Because I knew you'd walk away," she replied. "I see the way you're looking at me. That'll never change now." She sighed, resigned. "I told you there were things—you —you promised me—"

She was right. He had promised her. But he could never have imagined the truth. And now he had retroactively put conditions on something that should have remained unconditional. If you're only as good as your word, then he had failed to live up to her expectations—as well as his own. Even while asking her to leave with him, he'd undermined his own position by denigrating her. He might as well have admitted that she disgusted him. That wasn't an absolute truth—but a small part of him wondered if he could ever see her the same way again.

He wanted to say something, anything, but he couldn't find the words.

Her eyes were red-rimmed, and wet with tears, but now her shattered expression was helpless, silently pleading for him to relent, to change his mind.

While he couldn't defend himself, neither could he ignore his own ultimatum. She wanted him to tolerate something he had already decided was unacceptable. Their argument had been loud enough for the neighbors down the hall to hear, maybe loud enough for her cult friends to hear as well. But now there was only silence.

Despite the alcohol in his system, he was aware enough to know he'd played a desperate hand, and it hadn't gone the way he'd hoped. Finally confronting her about the lies and the bizarre nature of her friends and their cult hadn't, after all, brought her to her senses. It had only entrenched her in her long term—*since she was a child*—subservient behavior.

Choosing not to make a bad situation worse, he grabbed his coat, picked up his duffel bag, and left the apartment. When he stepped out into the night, snow started to fall. He made his way to the Mustang, chin tucked to his chest against the cold. It had snowed off and on most of the day, covering the black chassis and all the windows in a blanket of white.

He tossed the duffel on the passenger seat, circled the car and paused at the driver's side door to look up at the apartment building. Mary was silhouetted in the window, as still as her dressmaker's mannequin, with her arms wrapped tightly around herself. She was alone now, alone and as broken as he felt. Everything they had built together was over.

A moment later, his gaze fell to other illuminated windows, and the figures standing in them, watching him. He saw Cal and Mitzy in one window, Dara and Kaitlyn in another, and Claudette in a third, stroking the head of her black cat. He sensed an inevitability to the scene, wordless, unacknowledged goodbyes, as if they knew this moment was coming since the first time he met them at Heaven's Night. Maybe he should have known as well. The red flags were there all along.

He climbed into the driver's seat and shut the door.

Two pairs of eyes stared back at him in the rearview mirror.

CHAPTER 33

Heart pounding, he whipped his head around.

Gia and Mia sat in the back seat watching him.

"What—How did you get in?"

The redhead—possibly Mia—shrugged. "You gave Mary a key."

"We made a copy," Gia added, holding up a key fob.

He noticed they were wearing the same outfits as before, no sign of the hooded brown robes out in public. Only they had switched knit hat and jackets. Mia now wore the blue and white hat with the tan jacket; Gia wore the red hat and brown jacket. For some reason, he assumed they had also switched jeans, not that he'd be able to tell those apart.

"Okay, then, next question," James said. "Why are you in my goddamn car?"

"Dara thought she saw you down there," Mia said. "When we heard the argument, we figured this was… inevitable."

"And?"

"Just wanted to say—" They shrugged in unison. "—Goodbye."

"That's done," James snapped. "So, how 'bout you get the hell out now?"

Gia pushed the front passenger seat forward to reach the door handle, but then she paused and said, "She was never going to leave with you."

"You don't know that."

"You never knew the real Mary," Mia said.

"Only the version of Mary she wanted you to know."

"That makes no sense," James said, but had to acknowledge the kernel of truth in the statement. She'd always kept the dark side of her life hidden from him. But that alone didn't define her. She was so much more than that.

"Mary is alone," Gia said. "No family. All she has is us now."

"And whose fault is that?" James said bitterly. He had felt like a buffer between her and her cult friends. But ultimately, he had failed her.

Ignoring his accusation, Mia said, "All she's ever had is who we are and what she is."

"Can't wait to hear this cult bullshit," James said. "What exactly is she?"

"Just because you don't believe," Gia said.

"Doesn't make it untrue," Mia finished. "Not to Mary."

"She's our last connection to Joshua Crane," Gia said. "Blood of his blood."

"You're all certifiable," James said. "You know that, right?"

"Joshua was special," Mia said with a beatific smile. "Exalted among us."

"But that wasn't enough for him," Gia said. "He sought a higher purpose, an elevated state of being, no limitations, endless possibilities. And through him, us."

"And how'd that work out for him?"

"He struggled at first," Mia admitted. "But when the first of his three sons was stillborn, he saw the loss as a sign, that the blood of innocents was necessary."

"You're making even less sense," James said. "If that's even possible."

"Not at all," Gia said. "Joshua gave the next two sons voluntarily, but it still wasn't enough. His choices weighed heavily on Mary's mother. When she became pregnant again, this time with a girl, she said it was a sign to change. She urged Joshua to take mother instead of child."

"Wrong. All three boys were stillborn," James argued. According to Kaitlyn, anyway. "And Mary's mother died in childbirth."

"That's what the medical records say," Gia said. "Mitzy made sure those medical records were properly filed. She's worked at Brookhaven Hospital a long time. She's very—"

"—conscientious," Mia said with a knowing smile.

"Imagine Mary's mother, going through one childbirth after another and not getting to actually become a mother—"

"The situation was very difficult, as you can imagine."

"A noble choice," Gia added. "Choosing her daughter over herself."

"Mary was a child when Joshua first became ill," Mia said. "After sacrificing so much, he knew why Mary was chosen—why she was still with us. Though he faltered physically, her blood—as his legacy—was pure."

"And when his time grew short," Gia said, "he was blessed with a vision. That his own death was the final step—"

"Obviously," James said, disgusted by the man they somehow revered.

"You misunderstand," Gia said, ignoring his sarcasm. "For Joshua, casting off his flawed mortal shell was the path to achieving his apotheosis."

"You realize how crazy you all sound, right?" James said. "This is all—deranged nonsense."

"No, it was all part of the plan, finally revealed," Mia said. "From the start, Joshua guided some of us to... roles to facilitate the cause. Others he recruited. We are everywhere. The truth becomes what we say it is."

"When we taste her," Gia said, her eyes wide in a kind of

religious fervor, "we can *feel* him—what he finally achieved. What *we* can achieve through her. If we follow the plan."

Exhausted by their collective lunacy, James asked, "Why are you telling me this?"

"Why do you think?" Mia said, flashing her infuriating smile again.

"I have no fucking—" Then James had a dark thought. "Mary knows, doesn't she?"

"Mary is her father's daughter," Gia said. "She always knew who he was—"

"—since she was a young girl."

"She knows some of it," Gia said, "and suspects the rest."

"She never asks any of us," Mia admitted. "Especially the oldest among us. Those who were in Joshua's fold way back then. She pretends she doesn't know."

"But deep in her heart, she knows," Gia said, nodding. "She doesn't want her mother's sacrifice to be in vain. Her life here gives her mother's death purpose."

"She will always be here for us," Mia said. "Which is why she could never leave with you."

"We thought you should know."

"Because this—" Mia spread her arms inside the car, indicating James with his packed bag. "—was only a matter of time."

"Don't know which is worse," James said, shaking his head in pure loathing, "the ravings of an abusive madman, or the fact that so many of you nutcases fell so hard for his psychotic delusions." Leaning across the passenger seat, he shoved the door open. "Now, get the fuck out of my car, before I throw you out."

Without another word, Gia pushed the passenger seatback forward and they both climbed out of the Mustang.

"And give me that damn key."

Gia tossed the key fob on his duffel bag.

"Safe travels," Mia said, holding her hand beside her cheek and waving goodbye by curling her fingers.

As Gia slammed the door shut, James flipped them off.

He left Silent Hill the way he'd entered it, driving much faster than the posted speed limit, despite the slippery road conditions. All the while, he wondered about Mary and the ordeal she had experienced her whole life. A mother who sacrificed everything for her. A father who only saw her as a means to a delusional end. Her world had been warped by everyone in her life, and she remained trapped in their collective insanity. James had never felt so helpless in his life.

CHAPTER 34

James stood in the middle of the three windows in his hospital room wearing a lightweight robe over his hospital gown. He stared down at the courtyard and adjacent park, still sort of amazed by how normal and healthy everything was. No fog or ash. No darkness with never-ending rain. He'd observed dozens of birds, a stray dog, even a red fox during the last several days he'd been under observation in the hospital. But not one Armless, no oversized cockroaches, and certainly no Pyramid Head dragging a massive sword behind him. Plenty of nurses, but none of them showed any inclination to kill him. This was what the world was. But it felt empty…

The door to his room was ajar, with M and his attending physician standing on the far side of the glass wall. They thought he was simply taking in the view, but he could see them standing there, reflected in the window in front of him. And, standing quietly there, as if absorbed in his thoughts or the idea of being pronounced whole and released as a new man, he listened to their hushed conversation.

"How is he today?"

"Calm, I guess," M said.

"How long have you been treating him?"

"Almost a year," M replied. "But it's gotten worse. I've worked with vets. All kinds of trauma. But this is different…"

"How so?

"He won't let me in at all," M said. "His maladaptive defense mechanism, this dissociation from reality—" She paused, then tried a different tack. "It's like, he manifests these alternate realities, these characters in his mind that seem to represent the demons he's battling, the guilt he's coping with." After a moment of silence, she continued. "Mary died after their breakup and he just won't accept it."

James waited for Dr. Helen W to reply or M to continue, but they both stayed silent. Instead, M stared at him intently, as if trying to read his mind. Her concerned face was clear in the reflection, but he chose not to react to their exchange. Didn't want her to know he saw her doubt. And he wasn't sure how he felt about it.

Another day of normalcy passed in a normal hospital. Everything was bright, clean, dust-free, and antiseptic as possible under the circumstances. Nurses and, occasionally, doctors strode the halls every hour of the day. Visitors came to see patients. Other patients. Nobody came to see James, other than his doctor, therapist and whatever nurse happened to be on duty in his wing. The day was peaceful, like the day before. They were strung together like pearls, one after another for the past week.

James sat in one of the unnecessary visitor chairs, which he'd moved closer to the windows. Across the street people strolled in the park, many with leashed dogs, while couples walked hand in hand. An old man with a cane came every day to sit on one of the park benches and feed the squirrels. Normal people living normal lives.

She tapped on the doorframe. He'd been expecting her.

Glancing over his shoulder, he smiled and said, "Come in."

Today she was back in formal mode, dressed in a tan pantsuit, over a silk ochre blouse. She walked across the room and stood beside his chair, looking out the window to see what held his attention. He didn't think he needed to explain that outside was better than inside, trapped in a clean, bright and boring room. Anywhere outside.

"Seems like everyone's on the same page," she said at length. "You're ready to come home." She waited for his reaction and seemed surprised when he said nothing. "I mean—if you like—we could just strap you back into bed."

James forced a chuckle—the normal reaction—at her well-intentioned joke.

"What?" She wasn't so easily fooled. "James—?"

"I just wish—"

Knowing his true thoughts weren't what she expected to hear, he cut himself off.

"Nothing you tell me is going to take away from how far you've come this week."

Finally, he relented. "I still—it still feels so real to me, that I could see her again. I just wish I hadn't let her down."

This time she remained silent. She retrieved the second visitor chair from the far side of his bed and brought it over so she could sit beside him. The two of them stared out the window together for a while before she spoke.

"I know it feels like it could bring you some kind of closure. You're blaming yourself but… all this chaos in your mind, it's not real. It's not real and it almost destroyed you." She took a moment to let that sink in. Then she continued in a more ominous tone. "We can still fix this, but it's got to be *your* decision."

She'd never admitted the possibility of failure before. He'd become accustomed to her endless optimism on his account.

He wondered if she feared failing him or if her statement was designed to shock him into personal accountability. But he saw a vulnerability in her eyes that hadn't been there before in any of their formal sessions or more casual conversations outside the confines of her office.

"Thank you," James said sincerely. "For everything."

She nodded, gave him a small appreciative smile and squeezed his shoulder gently before she stood. The smile was fleeting, but he sensed a bit of uneasiness coming from her, a slight crack in her professional façade.

He turned around in his chair to watch as she slowly walked away, her footfalls barely making a sound on the polished tile floor. Then she closed the door softly behind her without looking back at him. Alone again in the quiet room, he resumed his former position, looking down at the world through the window.

As had become his routine, James sat in the hospital chair for hours, staring out the window, losing track of time the way he always had when painting. He liked to imagine he was scouting locations for one of his paintings, how he would frame certain landscapes or the people who came and went throughout the day. Sometimes he considered asking the hospital staff for a sketchbook. But he doubted they sold such things in the gift shop and wouldn't expect a nurse or the janitor to run errands for him. He might have asked M to pick one up for him. But again, she was a therapist, not his gopher. Ultimately, he visualized what he might sketch or paint from his confined view of the world on canvases he conjured in his mind. Since he expected his release from the hospital soon, that seemed to scratch the creative itch. For now.

A short while later, he noticed a young couple walking hand in hand, having an animated conversation, laughing and smiling. The woman had long, strawberry blond hair and a fair complexion. She resembled Mary.

James felt a poignant smile flicker across his face, accompanied by a welling of tears, he quickly blinked away.

But a black moth flittered by outside, finally landing on the window right in front of him. It spread its wings, blocking the woman's face. James' focus shifted to the moth, surprised by the coincidence. A second moth landed beside the first. James couldn't look away. This had to mean something.

More moths flocked to the window, one after another, an entire swarm of moths, each landing on another part of the window until their black wings blotted out the sunlight, with an effect like blackout shades, plunging his room into total darkness.

Once the window was completely covered, he finally tore his attention away from the moths, only to discover his entire room had transformed while he'd been distracted. The paint on the walls was peeling, blistered and stained. Every formerly polished metal surface was now riddled with rust. All the medical monitors and equipment were gone, except for some wiring and bits of metal and glass on the cracked tile floor. The sheets on his bed were ragged and stained, the mattress cracked and moldy. The window wall facing the hallway was fly-specked and coated with grime. Instead of doctors and nurses walking the hall, he saw only blurred silhouettes of things vaguely human.

Fortunately, his street clothes still hung in the small closet, undamaged. He changed out of his hospital robe and gown and put on his T-shirt, jeans and jacket, grateful they hadn't taken away his clip-on flashlight. With the power out in the hospital, he would need it to avoid the quasi-human things roaming the hallways. Something on the floor of the closet caught his attention, a silver gleam of metal with a dappling of rust—his makeshift weapon. The broken wheelchair armrest. Thankfully, that hadn't wound up in the trash.

As he pulled open the door to his room, he winced at the creak of rusty hinges. He squeezed through as soon as the gap was wide enough. He'd hoped to slip out of the hospital without drawing unwarranted attention to himself.

But first, he had to find the surgical room where he'd left Maria…

CHAPTER 35

James retraced his path to the surgical room. He breathed a sigh of relief to find his wire 'lock' around the door handles undisturbed. Leaving her alone, unarmed, he'd worried that the murderous nurses would stumble upon her and try to finish the job one of them had started in the freight elevator.

He dropped down to one knee, setting the metal armrest down on the dilapidated floor beside his foot, and reached for the knotted wiring. As soon as he began to undo the series of knots he'd made, he heard thumping to his right and left. Out of the corner of his eyes, he saw shadowy movement.

Standing, he turned one way and then the other. The flashlight revealed two mannequins closing in on him, one on either side. They each had two pairs of footless legs attached to their headless torsos. They hobbled around on ankle stumps, waving a pair of upper legs in place of arms. Though blind, they had no trouble homing in on his location. Again, he wondered if they could sense light or body heat or simply movement through vibrations in the floor.

By the time he crouched to pick up the metal armrest, they were close enough to strike. One upper leg slammed against his shoulder, stunning him with the force of the blow. He staggered sideways, losing his grip on the makeshift club. Before he could recover from the first blow, the second mannequin raised a footless leg and kicked him in the ribs, knocking him to the ground.

The first mannequin lumbered forward and tried to stomp on his face with an ankle stump. Considering the power of the previous blows, he had no doubt the leg stomp would shatter his nose, possibly embedding pieces of bone in his brain.

He rolled aside, bringing up a forearm to deflect the intended strike.

The mannequin lost its precarious balance and fell, crashing into the wall with its back. James scrambled on hands and knees to veer away from the mannequin that had nearly broken his ribs. It followed him across the hall, leg-arms waving frantically. When it tried to drill both upper legs down on his shoulder, he twisted away at the last moment, and its momentum caused it to ram into the wall instead.

Darting back to the surgical room door, James retrieved his weapon, rising just as both mannequins closed in on him. Their heads—if they had had heads—would have been obvious targets. Instead, he rammed the closest one in the chest, which caused it to stumble back a step or two, giving him the room he needed for a more powerful swing.

Without heads or vital organs, they had no obvious weaknesses. But their locomotion and bludgeoning attacks were possible only because of the limbs attached to their lifeless torsos. So, his plan was simple: attack the joints.

He swung the armrest overhead in a wood-chopping motion, striking the closest mannequin where its left upper leg was attached to the torso. The first blow staggered the mannequin, the second broke the leg free. Ducking fast to avoid a face strike from the other upper leg, James chopped at the nearest walking leg. The mannequin staggered back, but the leg held firm. James kicked the other leg out from under it, his heel striking just above the stump. It toppled over, falling flat on its back.

Another weakness noted. Without feet, the mannequins had poor balance.

While the fallen mannequin flailed on its back, attempting to rise, James planted a foot in the middle of its torso and attacked the left leg again, finally separating it from the torso. Now it had an upper and lower leg on the right side, no limbs on the left. Nearly impossible for it to rise from the floor.

Before he could work on detaching the remaining limbs, the ambulatory mannequin jumped onto his back, trying to drive him to the ground on top of its fallen comrade. The weight of the damn thing was more than he expected, but James managed to stay upright. He staggered forward, letting the momentum of the attack carry him and his assailant toward the wall. At the last moment, James spun and heaved backward so the mannequin absorbed the brunt of the impact.

Though it tried to throttle him between its upper calves, without hands, it couldn't retain any semblance of a secure grip, and it slipped free of his back, falling to the floor.

Before it could climb to its ungainly stumps, James struck the joints attaching the upper legs, back and forth, in a frenzy, breaking one free, then the other. He kicked the detached legs away from the torso. Unsure how these monsters assembled themselves from disparate limbs, he hoped they couldn't reattach body parts from a distance.

The two-right-legged mannequin had been flailing across the floor, almost snakelike, trying to reach him. James checked how far away it was before smashing the joints of the sitting mannequin's legs. After kicking those aside, he returned to the first mannequin and finished detaching the right side limbs. For good measure, he drove the sharp end of the metal armrest through the chests of the delimbed torsos, like staking a vampire. They had no internal organs and didn't bleed, but without limbs they became inanimate, which was as good as dead.

He leaned against the wall opposite the surgical room doors, taking a few moments to catch his breath and assess his injuries. His neck and shoulders were sore, and his ribs were tender, his own torso probably working on a wild color palette of a bruise, but they didn't feel broken.

After a minute or two to finish untangling the wires from the door handles, he went into the dim room with its cracked and peeling paint and debris-strewn floor, closing the doors quietly behind him. Maria lay on the surgical bed, sleeping. Belatedly, he realized he'd never cleaned the streaks of blood on her leg after cleaning the area around the hip wound. That blood on her left leg had dried, along with several spots on her violet pleather skirt and boots. He set a chair down beside her, noting the torn vinyl seat with exposed, crumbling foam swelling from the cracks.

As he settled on the chair, Maria's eyes fluttered open. When she saw him, her face lit up with a warm smile. Her left hand slid down to the gauze padding taped above her hip. He noticed the gauze was stippled with some blood that had seeped through, but it could have been so much worse. He had feared the gauze would be soaked through, that his hasty battlefield wound dressing hadn't stopped the bleeding.

"How are you feeling?" he asked.

"Good," she said. "Better. I think I was dreaming. A thunderstorm."

"Might have been me," James said. "In the hall, dealing with a couple unwelcome visitors."

"Oh," she said, alarmed, then looked him over quickly. "Are you okay?"

"Nothing a half dozen aspirin wouldn't fix," James said. "Might even be able to find some in this hospital, assuming they haven't expired."

"Could use some myself," she said. After a moment passed

in silence, she reached for his hand and gave it a squeeze. "You didn't find her."

Images flashed in James' mind. Being locked in the Toxicology Unit room, with that claw-fingered thing in the upside down bed floating across the ceiling. Whatever that was, it wasn't Mary.

James sighed before answering. "She's not here anymore."

Maria's face brightened, remembering. "So, we can leave. Together," she said buoyantly. When he failed to reply, she continued, "You promised, James."

He shook his head. He'd never promised that. Only that he wouldn't be long. He hadn't committed to ending his search back then, and he wasn't ready now. She'd heard what she wanted to hear.

Maria struggled to sit, pushing herself up from her reclined position on the bed, grimacing when her movements strained her wound. Once the flash of pain eased, she looked at him and he finally met her gaze in full.

"You look just like her."

"But I'm not her, James," she said. "I'm Maria."

She touched his cheek tenderly and caressed the side of his face.

Then she reached up with her other hand and pulled him in close for a kiss. At first, he hesitated to respond, but suddenly it felt normal and natural. He succumbed to the moment, reciprocating, and the casual kiss became something deeper. When their lips parted, she leaned her head on his shoulder and sighed contentedly.

"Or we could stay here together," she whispered into his ear, her voice soothing. "If you want. Just us."

James wanted to surrender, to accept the peace she offered. He was exhausted. It was easier to stop fighting and accept this compromise, a substitute for what he had lost, but he had not fought so hard for so long to settle for ease or comfort. More than anything, this felt like another test of his resolve.

He disengaged from Maria and stood, taking a step away from the surgical bed. When his hands began to tremble, he curled them into fists.

"What is it?" Maria asked, confused.

After a moment or two, he reminded himself that right decisions are often hard decisions. He couldn't succeed if he stopped trying. Turning his back on her, he strode purposefully to the doors.

"Where are you going?"

Through the doorway, he noted the still forms of the dismembered mannequins, the holes in their torsos remained. They were no longer a threat to Maria, so he had no qualms about leaving her again.

But she had hopped down from the surgical bed and pursued him into the hallway, running to catch up, her left palm pressed to the blood-stained gauze on her hip. "James! Wait for me!"

As he stopped in front of the freight elevator and pressed the service button on the rusted panel, Maria caught his sleeve.

James looked down at her hand on his jacket.

Reluctantly, she released her grip. "You won't find her down there."

James didn't reply. Despite the naysayers, he wouldn't give up.

"You know that, right?" Maria pressed.

The elevator pinged and doors slowly creaked open. James stepped inside and pressed the button for the lobby. Maria reached out and caught the edge of the doors, holding them open.

"James! Please."

He stared past her, refusing to make eye contact. There

was a weakness inside him, like a dying ember. He sensed it. But he'd made his decision. If he ignored that ember, it would eventually be snuffed out.

Finally, Maria released the doors and stepped inside the elevator.

"Not staying here alone," she said defiantly. "I'm coming with you."

The elevator jerked, its lift cables shaking, as if it had trouble bearing the weight of two people. They heard a deep metallic twang from overhead. A moment later, the elevator was in freefall, the overhead light flickering, the car shuddering, banging into the wall of the shaft, and continuing to accelerate.

Maria pressed her back into the corner, bracing for impact but staring at James, his face in shadow above the flashlight clipped to his breast pocket. "Why are you doing this!?"

Tortured metal shrieked as the elevator plummeted, seemingly into a bottomless pit beneath the hospital.

"You were free of all this pain!" Maria shouted above the squealing metal. "James!"

He remained silent.

"Oh, James," Maria said, tears in her eyes. "You shouldn't have come back."

A moment later, the elevator slowed, grinding to a rough stop. After a strangled *ding*, the doors creaked open. Maria stood still, catching her breath, obviously relieved the elevator didn't splatter them across the floor. But when she looked out into the darkness, illuminated only by the wedge of light shining from James' chest, her eyes widened in fear.

"You can't go in there."

Something told him to turn back, to heed her warning. Something visceral. He knew this wasn't about what she wanted. She only had his best interests at heart, but he couldn't stop. Each painful step offered the chance to give up, but he wouldn't let surrender be an option. He'd come this far. He had to see it through.

Taking a deep breath, he closed his eyes and steeled himself for what he must face. He stepped into the abyss…

CHAPTER 36

As soon as James stepped out of the elevator into darkness, he heard a protracted buzzing, and then lights flickered on. He was standing in an incredibly long corridor, with light gray cement walls. Mounted at equal intervals along both walls were massive canvases, each under its own black art wall sconce.

James walked hesitantly down the hallway.

Reluctantly, Maria followed him.

The paintings were all portraits he'd painted of Mary. There was one where she was illuminated by sunlight in front of the chapel. Another of her lying in the tall grass. One of her floating on her back in the lake from the time they rented the tandem canoe.

"Let's go back," Maria said beside him. "We can still go back."

Ignoring her, James continued.

After another few steps, the portraits became darker, more disturbing. One showed Mary with mascara streaked down her cheeks, lipstick smeared, her face emaciated. James paused, feeling a weight pressing down on him, making it harder to breathe.

Maria's voice was pleading now.

"Please don't go any further—"

James looked up at the next painting.

Mary was underwater, her hair floating around her pale, bloated face, eyes rolled back, showing only the whites—dead and lifeless. An image flashed in his mind, paintbrush in hand, standing before this painting in his studio. But he had no memory of painting her this way.

"It's over, James," Maria pleaded. "It's over—if you want it to be!"

James stepped forward.

Maria tugged on his arm violently. He stopped in his tracks but refused to look at her. He thought of the dying ember, deprived of oxygen, darkening.

"Mary's not dead," James said implacably. "Not to me. And you're not real. You're just in my way."

Before Maria could reply, they heard the harsh sound of metal scraping along the concrete floor of the gallery.

"No, no, no," Maria said, staring at him fiercely, though he refused to acknowledge her with a glance. "Look at me, James."

"Goodbye, Maria."

He placed his hands over his ears.

The metallic scraping became louder, impossibly close in the darkness beyond the reach of his flashlight.

"No—" Maria said disconsolately.

James looked back past Maria as Pyramid Head emerged from the shadows, swinging his Great Sword around in a slow arc so that the wide blade faced forward, directly behind her. Maria had no time to react as the colossus impaled her on the tip of the blade and hoisted her off the ground in one methodical motion.

She screamed in pain, a tormented wail James couldn't escape no matter how hard he pressed his palms against his ears. But it had to be done…

The monster rammed the tip of the blade toward the ceiling

even as it held Maria aloft. Willing himself not to relent, James stared as her body slowly slid down the impossible length of the blade, streaking it with her blood until, lifeless, she sagged against the hilt.

His resolve shaken, James turned his back on the carnage.

Standing there in shock, James heard the hoarse breathing of the monster behind him, closer now, impossible to ignore. Finally, steeling himself, he turned to face the nightmare. Pyramid Head stood before him, chest heaving. The long wedge-shaped helmet dipped forward, assessing James from a superior height. The crack in the middle of the narrow front wedge was slightly larger than James remembered. Through that gap, an eye glared at James. He stared back at the single exposed eye, and it was like staring at himself in a mirror. Because the eye was his own.

The realization hit like an electric shock.

James screamed, a howl that ripped its way out of his lungs.

All the wall sconces and his own flashlight winked out, plunging him into utter darkness. For a moment, he thought his mind had shut down but—

—he was sprinting down the corridor—

—bouncing off walls, hurtling into turns he didn't see, careening first left, then right, trapped in a maze that wouldn't release him—

Wall sconces started to light up each time he approached a new painting, then darken once he passed them. Liquid seeped down the walls, an oily brown sludge, as if the walls themselves bled. Each momentary glimpse of a painting left a disturbing image emblazoned on his retinas. Figures rolled up in hospital sheets. Emaciated bodies with tangled limbs. Nurses with disturbing, malicious faces, gathered around a bed. A hospital filled with horrors instead of healing. A hopeless place he couldn't escape—

CHAPTER 37

A flash of lightning turned the studio skylight into a blinding spotlight.

Wracked with grief, James painted feverishly for hours and hours that turned into days, and the blurred days daisy-chained into weeks. The images that wrung themselves out of his subconscious were from the nightmares he experienced during the odd minutes he managed to sleep before waking in a cold sweat. Alcohol numbed the whirlwind of emotions fueling his creative darkness.

He painted so he didn't scream.

Every day a scream built up inside him, churning in his gut. Only painting relieved the pressure. But some days that wasn't enough. He would bury his face in a pillow and scream at the top of his lungs. When he took time to leave his studio for painting supplies or alcohol, which he drank straight from the bottle while working, he wondered if any of his neighbors heard the muffled screams.

He bled onto the canvas.

Tears blurred his vision.

But his visions were terrible.

The early portraits weren't products of the madness of his grief. In one, Mary had a nosebleed. He remembered the first nosebleed, in the meadow by the chapel. But in other paintings, she had black blood leaking from her eyes, or black moths alighting on her face. In one painting, her face was bisected by a fissure, like a crack in plaster, from forehead to chin. In others, her mouth and cheeks were cut, black blood flowing from the wounds. Or one large portrait, her eyes were rolled back in her head, showing all whites, but her fingers were covered in blood, smearing her lips with it. In many, her eyes were clouded, milky white, apparently blind. In a few, her face was rotting away, as if a flesh-eating disease had taken hold. A disturbing portrait had the lower half of her face covered with a surgical mask, but her cheeks and even the mask were covered with putrefaction.

A few portraits on the floor came from the depths of his tormented mind. One showed a black fungus consuming her from the neck up to her face, her head surrounded by specter-like demonic figures. One had her emaciated face smothered by a sheet, with folds of cloth shoved in her mouth. Finally, one portrait showed her hairless head and chest completely rotted, her eyes nothing more than hollow black pits.

Everywhere he looked in the studio, the portraits gazed back at him. Even in the dark, he saw them. And with the raging storm bathing his studio in flashes of harsh light, they seemed to leap at him. Sometimes, when he turned on the light, he saw the rotting, hairless corpse sitting in a chair, as if posing for another portrait. But even in the dark, he glimpsed silhouettes in the studio with him.

In a lucid moment, during a time where he had slept for a few hours, and had remembered to eat, he attempted to paint something other than the series of portraits of Mary in various states of decay and death. As if staring into a mirror, he painted a self-portrait, something he rarely did, but he thought it might be a way to find himself, to get back to himself. And he captured a fair likeness of himself, but the closer it came to an actual mirror image, the more he rebelled against it. It was a lie, a likeness of who he wanted to be but could never be again.

In disgust, he opened a fresh bottle of bourbon or vodka, he hardly noticed what he drank anymore. He only required that it have a bite and, ultimately, numb him enough to forget. Dabbing red paint on a flat brush, he painted over the self-portrait in broad, overlapping strokes, creating a box around his head and upper torso—but not quite a box, more like a triangle, but he expanded it, made it a three-dimensional cage over the false image of himself, a pyramid. Suppressing another scream, he flung paint at the canvas before tossing the brush and his palette to the floor.

He stared at his hands, bathed in red—

Stained—

He grabbed a can of solvent and splashed some on his palms, scrubbing them with a spare rag dangling from one of his small tables. Scrubbing until his flesh was raw, he failed to remove all the paint. It was in his nail beds, in the creases of his fingers, on his shirt, and on his jeans. The stain would never come out. Some of it would always remain. Even if he couldn't see it, he would know it was there. There would never come a day when he wouldn't see it...

The bottle was empty. The room was spinning. Exhaustion swept over him. He staggered, kicking the accumulated painter detritus on the floor out of his way a moment before he dropped to the floor, fell back on his elbows, then laid down. Scratching his bearded cheek, he imagined it streaked red as well.

Flashes of lightning exposed him there, bathed the paintings in harsh, inescapable light, defying him to look away. If he had an ounce of strength left in his body, he would crawl out of the studio to escape the results of his frenzy. But he knew the images would continue to flash in his mind, unbidden, long after the storm petered out.

Tears in his eyes, he turned his head to the side.

Mary was there on the floor beside him.

Underwater…

Eyes all white in death…

Strawberry blond hair floating out and away from her pale face in a gentle current she would never feel again…

Next to that painting, propped against an overturned table, was a canvas depicting a cement maze with portraits on the walls under art wall sconces. In the center of the painting, like an inkblot, he'd painted a dark, amorphous shadow. He blinked and suddenly the black shadow appeared to grow larger, expanding and rising from the surface of the canvas. The shadow transformed into an emaciated specter of Mary, her face hollowed out by sickness and disease. As she floated toward him, the walls of the studio closed in on either side, the white brick transforming into slabs of stained, pale concrete…

CHAPTER 38

After a momentary lapse of consciousness, James continued to run through the underground maze, stumbling headlong in the dark, relying on the art wall sconce lights to guide him. But each light only turned on for a moment, winking off soon as he passed. They produced a stroboscopic effect that gave him a throbbing headache, yet he kept running. As he veered left and right to navigate sudden turns in the maze, he kicked over vodka bottles placed on the floor beside the walls. A few spun aside, shattering against the opposite wall, a few simply spilled their contents, leaving puddles and vapor in his wake.

He glanced over his shoulder; the emaciated specter of Mary soared behind him in quick pursuit. Her feet grazed the ground, leaving liquid vodka trails behind her, like arrows pointing toward him. With each stumbling step, the specter gained on him.

He heard something scraping the walls, which brought Pyramid Head and his Great Sword to mind. But looking back again, he saw the source of the sound. The specter's arms stretched to the sides, clawed fingers raking the concrete and slashing the images captured on the canvases in her path.

The specter emanated cold, which chilled his spine the closer she came, almost overwhelming him. Her clawed fingers began to knock the portraits to the ground. One spun along its edge and struck his calf, causing him to cry out in surprise. An icy chill blasted the nape of his neck. Another quick glance back and claws were inches from his shoulder, gleaming in the flashes of light—

—the floor fell away.

James dropped into darkness—and water.

Suddenly unable to breathe, underwater and sinking deeper every second, as if his body had no innate buoyancy. Down and down, and portraits of Mary floated beside him, the scarred, the bleeding, the disease-riddled, the decaying, the recently dead, the long dead. With each passing second, his lungs ached and the darkness closed in, robbing him of sight, until nothing remained...

CHAPTER 39

James woke up gagging and coughing, spitting out fetid water.

He was lying face down on a muddy shore, the still waters of Toluca Lake behind him. Reasoning that the maze under Brookhaven Hospital had an outlet into the lake, James assumed he'd stayed conscious long enough to reach the surface. What he couldn't understand was that he'd surfaced on the other side of the lake, near the Lakeview Hotel. Perhaps part of the maze was under the lake itself. That might explain the liquid streaking the walls. There were signs everywhere of decay and ruin, so it wasn't hard to believe the infrastructure had suffered as well.

Exhausted, he crawled up the mudbank, making his way under the rotting boardwalk. Specks of ash drifted down from the twilight sky, but closer to the hotel, the sky glowed yellow. As he edged out from under the boardwalk, he saw the source of the strange light. On the far side of a gently sloping garden, the Lakeview Hotel was on fire. Beyond the hotel, the derelict rollercoaster and Ferris wheel of the Lakeside Amusement Park rose like the skeletal remains of some prehistoric colossus.

Currently, the hotel fire was contained to the upper floors, but the damage was already devastating, well beyond the capabilities of a single person to extinguish. And he doubted a fire company would show up anytime soon. Silent Hill remained a ghost town, forgotten by almost all its former residents.

As he climbed up the embankment, the quantity of ash drifting down to him increased. The fire burned bright enough to light his way to the hotel. And despite the fire engulfing the upper floors, James was compelled to enter the hotel.

The acrid tang of smoke filled his nostrils as he entered the large peach-colored lobby, which had been decorated with large, fern green armchairs and sofas with walnut backs and armrests, enough seating for the hotel to handle a convention's worth of guests. Long octagonal glass top walnut tables were positioned between seatings groups, with a scattering of end tables holding boxy enclosed lamps.

The lobby was cavernous, rising at least three stories high, maybe higher, with smoke curling above the open mezzanine level like gathering clouds, while glowing embers of cloth and bits of wood fell to the green carpeted floor along with the rain of ash. Through the dark, roiling smoke, he caught glimpses of hungry flames devouring everything in their path. He heard unrelenting crackling and sizzling and popping, an ongoing quarrel between the fire and hotel that the hotel was destined to lose. At some point, the ceiling would come crashing down. It was dangerous to stay here too long.

Sudden movement to his right—

Laura jumped up from behind one of the roomy armchairs, laughing as she darted behind a sofa, out of sight. Her sudden appearance left him speechless. For a moment, he thought he had imagined her here, but then her voice called out to him.

"You're finally here."

No mistaking her voice. Had to be her.

He circled around the armchair and the sofa, trying to find her hiding place. "Laura," he called. "Where are you?"

Giggling nearby.

"I'm not playing anymore, Laura," he said. "This place is going up in flames."

More giggling from behind him—

He whirled around, scanning for her. She'd picked a hell of a time to play hide and seek. "Damn it, Laura!"

Then he thought he saw her, a shape moving behind another armchair, so he ducked around it, crouching down. A figure moved from one chair to the next, staying low. Though he followed the darting shape, he couldn't catch her. She'd vanished again. Shaking his head, he stood up, spread his arms and turned around—

From behind a sofa, a hideous face slowly rose into view, but it wasn't Laura's normal face. It was a distorted version of Mary's face, emaciated and ravaged by disease, the face he saw in his worst nightmares.

"Do you think you're ready to face it?" she asked.

James collapsed, falling into the seat of an armchair behind him. If the chair hadn't been there, he would have fallen to the floor. It took all his willpower not to look away from the tormented face. The warped version of Laura tapped skinny, clawed fingers on the back of the sofa, as if impatient.

The voice was pure Laura. No distortion. No mistaking it. If he closed his eyes, he could envision Laura sitting across from him speaking those words. But that wasn't what his eyes saw, the thing so unlike Laura.

"Do you think you're ready to face us?"

The hollow eyes in the ruinous face never looked away from him, as the mutated Laura crawled over the back of the sofa but, unlike her altered face, Laura's body appeared completely normal, wearing the same patterned dress with the rounded Peter Pan collar. She settled onto the couch opposite him, as if everything was normal.

At the plaintive sound of an infant crying, Laura reached

down and scooped up her hideous gray fetus-doll, which squirmed in her slender fingers, eyes bulging. Nothing about that doll could be considered normal.

Finally, James could no longer tolerate the disturbing vision before him and he squinted his burning eyes shut to block out the ravaged face, the living dead doll, all of it. In the darkness of his own mind, he could convince himself he had imagined it.

When he opened his eyes again, a few moments later, the Laura sitting before him was normal Laura, with her own childish face, smiling warmly at him, as if he were her favorite uncle bearing gifts.

With his arms spread wide in exhaustion, he asked, "Why are you doing this to me?"

"To help you remember," she said. "What's her name?"

"What?"

"Think—James!" Laura insisted. "What's Mary's full name?"

The familiar spike of pain seared through his skull. He gripped his temples in pain. Between almost drowning and smoke inhalation, he shouldn't have been surprised, but...

"Our full name, James," Laura persisted, her voice resonating with the overlapping voices of others.

The pain flashed like a whiteout in his mind and the dim twilight was replaced by—

—dawn, outdoors. James wore a black suit, a single pink rose clutched in his hand, the sun shining on his back as he stared down at a fresh tombstone in the Silent Hill cemetery. In the distance stood the chapel—the background for his first portrait of Mary—adjacent to Toluca Lake. James crouched to lay the solitary rose at the base of the tombstone. The name before him, even etched in stone, seemed impossible to him, a cruel joke played by a vindictive universe.

MARY
ANGELA
LAURA
CRANE

James remembered the chill that had gripped him in the cemetery, when he'd stumbled carrying a sandbag. He'd been standing in front of a tombstone but had only stared at the sandbag in his arms, refusing to focus anywhere else until he'd recovered himself. His subconscious had registered what was right in front of him, but he couldn't acknowledge it then.

He stood alone in the lobby, tears brimming in his eyes, streaming down his cheeks. The smoke billowed lower, filling the open space, blurring the walls from view. Disconsolate, he wondered how long he would have to stand there—remembering—before the ceiling collapsed on top of him, ending the pain. Already, the smoke burned his eyes and throat. Soon it would block the oxygen from reaching his lungs. The falling ash inside the hotel was darker than the gray ash outside, as if full of malevolent intent. The stinging, acrid black ash would not tolerate his presence for long.

Laura whispered in his ear, so close he felt her breath on the side of his face, "It's time now. To find her—"

He turned toward her voice, but he remained alone.

"—you need to forget how to lie."

Then Laura's voice was replaced by another, a hoarse male voice humming a contented, made-up song. The voice echoed throughout the lobby but seemed to originate elsewhere. James saw nobody nearby. Even though the lobby was hazy with accumulating smoke, he was in the cavernous room by himself. He supposed the person could be hiding behind the furniture, as Laura had, but after a few moments of listening to the humming, James thought he could detect the direction of its origin.

He left the lobby, entering a dim hallway, and arrived at a massive metal door with icy mist escaping from the base of it. Pulling the handle cautiously, he peered into what seemed to be a large cold storage room to serve the hotel's kitchen.

Inside, meat carcasses dangled from metal hooks. At the end of the row of hooks, a meat cleaver hung by its handle. James had lost the broken metal armrest he'd used as a club during his flight in the underground maze, so he grabbed the cleaver as a substitute weapon. Mist coiled around his feet as he strode deeper into the cold room. He realized the skinned carcasses were fetuses of calves. With each footfall he took, they shook and convulsed on their hooks, reminding him of the Armless that roamed the streets of Silent Hill.

Mist parted, revealing Eddie sitting on the floor, leaning against a cold metal wall, feasting on moldy meat he scooped out of a large tin can with his bare hand. Several emptied tins were scattered around his sprawled legs. In between mouthfuls, he continued to hum his contented little ditty.

Abruptly, Eddie looked up at him, but above James' head.

Turning, James saw his own shadow rippling across an icy pillar of mist, elongated, with a long distorted head coming down in a point, and the shadow of the meat cleaver he held down at his side had become elongated as well, its blade resembling a long, wide sword, almost touching the ground. For a moment, James imagined the sound of metal scraping along the steel floor.

Eddie's focus shifted to James' face, but his voice projected a tremor as he called out with attempted joviality, "Jimmy boy! You're back! Couldn't stay away, could ya?" When James didn't reply, Eddie continued, "Want some? Put hair on your chest."

He held out the tin can. Inside, mixed with the moldy clumps of meat were dozens of eyeballs, rolling in the muck, yet the irises all oriented on James. Looking away in disgust, James focused on Eddie's face, but with his straggly red hair, dirt-streaked face, and bits of spoiled meat clinging to his full beard, the view wasn't much better.

"You shouldn't listen to that little girl," Eddie advised, licking sticky chunks of meat from his fingertips. "She's gonna get you hurt."

When Eddie's gaze fell on the meat cleaver in James' hand, he flashed a knowing smile.

Shrugging, Eddie said, "I was only trying to help you."

"Oh, yeah," James said. "Help me what?"

"Help protect you," Eddie replied. "The things you saw, Jimmy. The things you did." He shook his head in admiring disbelief. "What was it like? Killing that bitch that wouldn't stop following you around."

"I didn't do anything to her—"

Eddie cut off his protest. "Oh, yeah, you did, Jimmy boy. You killed her. Admit it."

"I didn't—"

"C'mon," Eddie cajoled. "Just admit it."

"You only exist in my head."

Eddie scoffed. "Yeah, right! In the head of an asshole like you?"

James raised the meat cleaver overhead and the blade seemed to take on added weight by his threatening action. In his mind, he envisioned Pyramid Head raising his Great Sword. Eddie shielded himself, hands over his face.

"Nuh uh," he said nervously. "You wouldn't dare. You need me to lie to yourself..."

As if of its own accord, the heavy blade swung down, severing Eddie's fingers and embedding its cutting edge deep into Eddie's skull. Horrified at what he'd done, James yanked on the handle of the cleaver, straining to pull it from Eddie's head, an action that could never be taken back. Tears welled in his eyes and for a moment Eddie's face blurred and warped, resembling James' own face, with blood and brain matter dribbling down his forehead and nose.

Stunned, James stood there with the bloody cleaver at his side, watching in silence as Eddie's body slowly tipped over, crashing into a small, wheeled cart loaded with additional tins of meat.

"It needed to be done, James," Laura's voice said. He didn't need to look around the cold storage room to know she wasn't physically there with him. *"Now go. Mary's still waiting for you."*

James stood frozen in place. Despite Laura's instruction, he couldn't pry himself away from the corpse sprawled at his feet. The man he had murdered with so little provocation. He stared across the room—mist rolling across the floor as high as knee height—and saw his reflection in the shiny steel wall. But he didn't see himself. Instead, he saw Pyramid Head standing with his bloodied Great Sword, surrounded by flames. The bloodied meat cleaver slipped from James' numb fingers.

Finally, he turned away from the image—

—and found himself on a second floor hallway in the hotel, with flames burning the walls on both sides. The fire had worked its way down from the upper floors, in the accelerated process of consuming the entire hotel. Paneling burned beneath wallpaper curling away from walls, with sizzling embers breaking free and floating across the hallway. Several doors were aflame, the metal handles red-hot, like portals to hell.

With a quick glance up at the burning ceiling, James raced down the hallway, fearing an imminent collapse. A small table holding a bouquet of flowers beneath a mirror was ablaze, toppling over as one blackened leg gave out. Ahead of him an untouched door swung open, and James didn't hesitate to run through the doorway. As soon as he was safely inside the room, the door slammed shut behind him.

Inside this room, he could barely hear the crackling sound of the ravaging flames in the hallway. But the room looked less like a standard hotel room than the bedroom of a child long left untended. Next to a stained mattress on the floor without a boxspring, were two dolls near a row of burning candles. On the other side of the bed, stood a small bookshelf with books for young readers. The wood paneling was scuffed, and the wooden floor was stained.

But what stopped James in his tracks upon entering the room was Angela, kneeling on a soiled sheet, her dark hair matted and disheveled, her eyes bright with fear. And she wore Mary's black, square neck midi dress with the dogwood flower pattern. The same dress she wore the day he discovered the blood ceremony.

"Don't come any closer," she said tremulously. "It'll get you too."

CHAPTER 40

James could tell Angela had been sobbing and, when she spoke again, she was talking to someone he couldn't see.

"Leave me alone," she cried. "Haven't you had enough? Disgusting. You're disgusting—"

After a quick circuit of the room, checking the closet, moving a dresser, even tapping walls to detect secret doors or hidden passageways, James found nobody else there, just the two of them. He considered the possibility she was high or hallucinating. Her face was smudged, either from dirt or mascara smeared by her tears.

When he returned to Angela, she was feverish with confusion, enraged by it.

"Can't you see it?" she asked angrily. "Please tell me you can see it."

James was at a loss for words, unsure how to pacify her. If he knew what he was supposed to see, he could lie to calm her. But he doubted that would work.

Recognizing his confusion, Angela pulled up her dress, above her knees, revealing something horrifying under her. An indistinguishable shape writhed and moved under the mattress, like a massive parasite. But then a human face, with a gaping mouth stretched upward, its breathing labored and distorted as it strained against the surface of the stained mattress, like a membrane it couldn't puncture.

"He listens to me," Angela explained. "He always liked to hear me cry. He enjoyed hurting me. The power he always had over me. But they never saw that side of him. That's why they didn't understand."

Before the horror could escalate, James stepped forward, intending to pull her off the mattress where she kneeled above a monster.

"Don't!" Angela yelled, shaking her head. "Stay there."

"Let me help you," James said, tormented. "Please."

"How?" she asked plaintively. "How!?"

"I'll get you away from that—" James blurted. "Get you out of here."

Her head tilted to the side in resignation. "Don't you understand, James," she said. "It's too late for that."

"It's not," James said, urging her to move off the bed. "Come on—"

But it was futile—it had been all along. A man's large, grimy hands pushed through the soiled mattress—finally piercing the membrane—and clamped around Angela's exposed thighs. The hands flexed, pulling her down with a jolt. Then the powerful arms rose higher, the hands wrapping around her throat. Angela screamed as her legs sank beneath the surface of the bed. In moments, half her body had been absorbed by the mattress, like a python's head moving side to side to ingest live prey.

Belatedly, James stepped forward and grabbed her arm, wrapping it securely with both hands.

Angela's body was forced back into a reclined position, slipping deeper into the mattress, until only her head and arm remained above the churning surface.

He refused to let go. His feet skidded across the stained wooden floor, pulled by an undeniable gravity. "Hold on!"

Angela strained her neck, chin tilted back, gasping for air, eyes wide in terror. "It won't stop—!"

Her head disappeared beneath the surface.

Then the fight left her. The hand wrapped around his wrist loosened its grip. He held tight, refusing to give up on her. But whatever force was at work in this room was too powerful for him. He was pulled closer to the bed, inch by inch until, finally, he lost his balance and tripped forward. Focusing only on her descending hand, he ignored the darkness gathering around him, squeezing him, blotting out the light from the candles on the floor, until only the darkness remained—

James tumbled out of the darkness onto a soft, undulating surface.

Disoriented, he climbed to his feet and examined his surroundings. Instead of a normal room, he stood inside a chamber made of pale living flesh, its walls striated with pulsing, purple veins. Blood leaked slowly down the walls, and drops fell from the ceiling, splashing on the spongy floor around him. Alarmingly, he saw no exit from the room. No doors or windows. Unsure how he had fallen into the room, he also had no way to leave. But there was movement in the walls. Metal pistons pumping back and forth, penetrating the fleshy walls repeatedly without ever withdrawing completely. The room was like a living organ impaled by these cylindrical pieces of metal. The steady *whoosh* sound reminded James of the industrial pump he'd heard years ago when he discovered Mary's blood ceremony.

Hearing an irregular thumping sound behind him, James turned to discover a transformed version of the soiled mattress from Angela's room. Beneath the moldy covering, two bodies squirmed, moving the mattress forward. A membrane stretched over their bodies, as thin as an extra layer of skin, holding them captive within the mattress. The man was hunched possessively—obscenely—on top of Angela. Through the translucent membrane James saw the identifying port wine birthmark on the man's right cheek. Joshua Crane.

Savage emotions twisted Crane's face, a combination of ecstasy and anger, competing for dominance. The face of a man accustomed to control, a man who would brook no disobedience of his orders, nor suffer denial of his own desires. Angela's face, however, was twisted by torment and painful resignation, her eyes squeezed shut.

James watched the grotesque assault in shock, unsure what to do in that moment. The two bodies were almost merged into one within the confines of the soiled, undulating mattress. Angela's mouth opened, as if to scream or howl in protest at the primal violation, but her voice was silent as she was forced to suffer the odious coupling.

And as her face turned and twisted, desperately trying to pull away, her features distorted, at first resembling Mary, then becoming Mary. James could no longer see Angela's face in the meshed pair. Instead, he was forced to watch Joshua Crane assaulting his own daughter, and there was no escape for him just as there had been no escape for her, even after years of abuse. Abuse that had managed to outlive her abuser and had continued to scar her anew throughout her life.

Though Angela's voice had been silent, both before and after the transformation, James heard another voice, the familiar voice of Laura, speaking directly to him again, loud and impassioned.

"You never wanted to understand it, James!"

He felt his body trembling, wracked with guilt, unable to deny the accusation.

"You even hid it from yourself," Laura continued. *"The truth about the woman you loved."*

James raised his forearm in front of his eyes, shielding himself from the sight of the monster right before him.

"But you can fix it."

He squeezed his eyes shut, pressed his palms to his ears, but not to block Laura's voice, only to drown out the sight and sounds of the violation taking place.

"Face her pain, James," Laura said, her voice cutting through everything else he needed to endure in this hellish place. *"Face her pain so you can face yours—"*

As those words echoed in his mind, he realized he had denied this part of Mary's life for so long. He had been unwilling to face the brutal reality she had had to endure for years, since she was a child. Accepting only the parts of her he could handle and appreciate, while ignoring the dark side that had consumed her life. Even during their courtship, he had avoided treading in the dark spaces, too willing to let her brush his idle curiosity aside. For too long, he chalked up her overly protective and intrusive friends as odd or eccentric, rather than seeing their mistreatment of her for what it was. He had begun to split her into different personas, acknowledging the side of her he loved, and excluding every other facet of her.

And when he'd finally summoned the courage to find out what writhed beneath the surface, he had turned away, horrified and, yes, disgusted. She saw that in his eyes, the way he looked at her after seeing the rest of her, and she couldn't face the rejection emanating from him. Better to end their relationship than to always be seen as tainted, damaged goods.

So, he had run away. At the first sign of troubled complexity, the first hint of lifelong scars and enduring trauma, James had bolted out the door. Now, he had to acknowledge that he left not only because of what he had witnessed that day under the Silent Hill Historical Society, but because he had sensed a deeper darkness all along and, rather than stay and help her process that, work through it together and deepen their bond, he had scurried away.

Maybe the Meyer twins had been testing him after all with their back seat confessions and ultimate dismissal, laying Mary's trauma bare for him in all its ugliness to see how he would react. If they had wondered if it was too much for him to handle, they had their answer shortly thereafter. But he had failed his own test before he even got into the Mustang. Although he had felt broken at the time, he had also been relieved to flee the madness.

The realization that he had been Mary's last hope for a better life and that he had ultimately failed her drove him down to his knees before the monstrosity. Though tears streamed down his cheeks, the fear was gone. All that remained was regret. But Laura had promised him he could fix this at least.

He looked at Angela's face—which now only resembled Mary's face again without being completely replaced by it. Maybe it was that small mercy, but he was no longer terrified of the creature hunched over her. Instead of abandoning her again, he crawled across the fleshy, spongy floor toward the mattress atrocity on hideous display in the middle of the room. He ignored the relentless *whoosh-whoosh* of the pistons penetrating the fleshy walls and focused on Angela.

Her tortured face was turned away from Crane, while both her hands tried to shove his face as far away from her as possible within the confines of the mattress trap. But then she glimpsed James approaching her and some of the pain and panic left her face. She sensed the change in his demeanor.

Crane noticed the change in her and his snarling face twisted toward James, howling in anger, "She's mine! She belongs to me!"

James ignored the presence of the evil man as much as possible, along with the throbbing *whoosh* of the pistons surrounding them, to concentrate only on Angela. He reached out to the chimera and caressed Angela's face.

"I'm sorry—"

His voice, trembling with heartfelt sincerity, affected her like a healing balm, a tonic for her pain. Gradually, the indelible agony etched in her features and the torment in her eyes vanished.

Again, Crane reacted to the transformation occurring in Angela, howling in his own brand of agony at the loss of power and dominance, at the evaporation of the fear that he had spent years instilling in her, the fear that had ignited his depraved desires. Then he began to struggle in the mattress, trying to escape the hell he had created for her.

Angela's mouth stretched wide, but this time flames erupted from her throat and twin gouts of fire shot from her eyes, blasting Crane's raised face and chest, consuming him, and finally consuming the entire chimera.

James witnessed the monster's destruction with tears brimming in his eyes, as Crane was burnt to ash, and Angela at last was released from her agonies. The whole mattress monstrosity bubbled and charred, and dissolved into the spongy flooring, leaving only a dark stain rinsed away by the dripping blood.

Then the bleeding stopped.

The pistons fell silent.

And the light winked out…

CHAPTER 41

In the dark, James knelt on a wooden floor.

That was how he knew he'd left the fleshy room with the pistons. He never knew how he fell into that room, nor how he escaped. His hands pressed against the floor, felt the resistance of the wood, rather than the spongy surface of the room where the mattress chimera had burned and dissolved.

He turned on the clip-on flashlight to orient himself. As he suspected, he had returned to the neglected child's room where he'd found Angela kneeling on the mattress. The two dolls remained, but the row of candles near them had all been extinguished. The small bookshelf and the early reader books were also present but the soiled, moldy mattress was gone.

As soon as he climbed to his feet, the door opened of its own accord. The same door that had opened on its own to receive him. And now it seemed to tell him it was time to go.

With the door ajar, he could hear the crackling and hissing flames consuming the Lakeview Hotel. He hurried into the hallway, looking for an escape route. A virtual clock was ticking in his head, warning him to get out before the whole place imploded. But instead of an exit, he saw—

Mary!

She stood at the end of the hall, her back turned toward

him, with roaring flames on either side of her. Despite the direness of the situation, she seemed at peace.

"Mary—"

"I knew you'd come."

She turned to face him, wearing the black square neck dress with the dogwood flower print, and smiled warmly, a welcoming and loving look in her eyes. Heat waves shimmered in front of her, and reality seemed to ripple before his eyes. With each breath, her face remolded into a different countenance, transforming from Mary to Laura to Angela to Maria and back to Mary again. And he could see all of them in her.

Before he even took one step toward her, she turned away from him again and walked down the burning corridor, unfazed by the oppressive heat or the ravenous flames eating through the walls and ceiling. Even the hallway carpeting, with its repeating diamond pattern, began to smoke and smolder. James hurried after her, running in the center of the hallway to avoid the worst of the flames. But he couldn't escape the extreme heat, he simply had to endure it.

"Mary, wait!"

He wasn't afraid of the flames or the heat or the real possibility of the compromised floor collapsing under his weight. After everything he'd fought through to find Mary, he wouldn't let a fire stand in his way. She was here now. Nothing else mattered.

Mary turned a corner, momentarily disappearing from his view. Ducking and veering away from the worst of the flames, he came to a wide landing with a staircase leading up. For a moment, he glimpsed Mary ascending the steps before the flames obstructed his view. Crossing the landing, he took the stairs two at a time, attempting to catch up to her before she wandered into a dangerous situation. He feared for her more than for himself. If she was safe, he would deal with whatever hand he was dealt in this crumbling inferno.

No sooner had the thought crossed his mind, than he heard wood crack underfoot as the smoldering tread of a stair buckled under his weight. He yanked his foot from the split wood and felt heat rising through the gap, along with tendrils of caustic smoke. A burning picture frame fell apart, pieces crashing down the stairs. And above him, the ceiling shifted, blackened and bulging. Veering away from the split staircase, he kept his gaze on the ceiling, and almost brushed up against the flames dancing up the wall.

With a sudden explosion the ceiling buckled and burst, sending charred and burning pieces of wood down in a deadly shower of debris. James managed to get out from under the worst of it, hastily brushing glowing embers and bits of wood from his jacket and pants. Panting with relief, he reached the top of the stairwell and pushed open the metal double doors with the sleeve of his jacket to avoid scalding his hands.

He stepped out onto the roof of the Lakeview Hotel.

Rather, what was left of it.

The restaurant was engulfed in fire. Huge columns of roaring flame vented through big holes in the structure. He imagined himself standing in the caldera of an active volcano. Everywhere he looked, everything looked on the verge of collapse. All the shade umbrellas burned like oversized torches. The bar was completely burned, the stored alcohol having acted as an accelerant. The oversized Lakeview Hotel sign that overlooked the town was aflame as well. The 'L' and 'H' in the sign had either burned away or broken free and tumbled to the parking lot below. James wondered if the fire had started on the roof before progressively descending through every floor of the hotel. The spacious lobby had been relatively untouched when he arrived, but he doubted anything below was still intact.

Navigating a treacherous path around the torch umbrellas

and the holes in the roof spewing flame skyward, he cast about for any sign of Mary. She'd come up the same staircase and there had been no other path for her to follow. But he saw no sign of her.

When a table and two chairs shook in front of him, it took him a moment to realize the floor beneath them was shifting and sinking. Suddenly, the floor gave way, and the tables and chairs plummeted through the jagged opening, crashing below. Beyond the new hole in the ceiling, right in the middle of the rooftop restaurant, James saw something completely incongruous.

A hospital bed...

CHAPTER 42

So long after he spontaneously checked into the Lakeview Hotel on his first day in Silent Hill, James never imagined returning to the very same room. Certainly not for this. Instead of the original queen-sized bed, a partially inclined hospital bed had taken its place, currently empty, white sheets pulled down over a fern green blanket. On the near end table, next to a glass of water, and a bouquet of pink roses, a clock radio played Bach's Aria from Suite 3 in D major. The far end table held a modern lamp, metal with a white shade, a water pitcher, and several prescription bottles. Beyond the table stood an IV pole stand with a drip bag dangling from the hook.

Beyond the end table, against the far wall, there was an oblong mirror attached to a vanity table decorated with a glass vase of daisies. As he scrubbed a hand through his thick beard, James noted the reflection of his haunted eyes. He needed a moment to steel himself. The last thing he wanted was to fall apart in front of her. Though he hadn't seen her in a long time, his love for her had never diminished. If you lived with an ache long enough, it embedded itself into your personality. You forgot who you were before the emotional pain took up residence inside you.

On the far side of the room was a sitting area with a chrome and glass bar in the corner. The bar hadn't gotten much use lately, nor was it stocked. But she had not chosen this room for its amenities.

Mary was seated on a cream-colored armchair turned to look through the open glass balcony doors. White curtains on either side of the doors billowed gently into the room, flowing around the chair and giving her an ethereal quality as she took in the fresh lake air. Yet, even from where he stood by the door, James could hear the wheeze of her labored breathing.

When he'd knocked on the door, she'd simply said, "Come in."

The front desk had called ahead, and she'd told them she'd been expecting him.

Now he stood, at a loss for words, his heart breaking all over again.

"You came—"

James swallowed the lump in his throat. "Of course," he said, hoping his voice didn't betray him. Finally able to move, he approached her chair and kneeled beside her. As they spoke, she continued to look out at the lake and the blue sky. "Right when I got your letter. As soon as I could—"

"It's okay."

When she brushed her hand over her stringy, disheveled hair, gathered in a loose ponytail, he could see her arm tremble and the tremors in her fingers. She was dressed comfortably in loose clothing, a lightweight, pale green robe over a pale gray cotton nightdress.

"It's not, Mary. I should have never—"

His voice caught and he couldn't finish what he wanted to say, how he had lived with regret from the moment he abandoned Silent Hill—and her. He'd been too proud—and too afraid—to change course, literally and emotionally, to come back to her, to fight for her, to stand with her against everything she had had to endure.

"Whether you would've stayed or not," she said in a thready voice, attempting to absolve him, "I still would've gotten sick."

"But maybe I could have helped you."

"No one could've," Mary said with a slight shake of her head. "My father poisoned me. He poisoned me my whole life."

With a sniffle, she wiped away tears with the back of her hand.

James lifted her other hand from the armrest and squeezed it tenderly.

She turned to face him and suddenly her weakened condition became real, as if she was finally allowing him to see the toll her illness had taken. The pallor of her face, her sunken eyes with bruised crescents under them, her hollow cheeks, and her chapped lips were about what he had expected, and yet seeing how much of her youthful vitality had been stripped away was devastating to him. She had become a phantom of the woman he remembered painting in the chapel field, dancing with at Heaven's Night, boating and swimming with at Toluca Lake. He mourned the loss of time they could have had together if he had not fled in fear.

"I tried to shield you from it," Mary said.

"I know," he replied, but wished she hadn't, that they could have more time together before she had reached this weakened state.

She hunched forward in a coughing fit, pressing a wad of tissues over her mouth. When she took the tissues away, they were speckled with blood. Without comment, she shoved the tissues into a pocket of her robe.

James retrieved her water glass and pressed it in her hands.

After nodding her thanks, she sipped from the glass, struggling to swallow. He took the glass back to the end table before returning to her side in front of the balcony. She closed her eyes as the cool breeze washed over her face, stirring tendrils of her hair.

"How have you been?" she asked at length.

"Never the same," James said without hesitation. Fear drove him away, but guilt and shame had kept him away. "I've been going through the motions, but everything feels recycled, unimportant somehow. I've had some work in galleries and shows, occasional sales, but I don't feel the same joy in it, in the work. Compared to the time we had together—"

"Don't," she said, placing her hand over his. "Until they invent time travel, living with regrets is pointless. But if we learn from them, we'll make better choices going forward..."

Maybe true for small decisions, he thought, *but what if none of my choices in the future ever have the same gravity as the one I already screwed up?*

"Surprised the doctors let you stay in a hotel room," James said, if only to change the subject away from his own failings.

"My choice," she said. "I've had more than enough of hospitals. Besides, they know there's nothing more they can do for me. It's just a waiting game now."

"Don't talk like that," James whispered. "Maybe—"

"It's the truth," she replied. "No sense pretending it's not." She smiled briefly. "You know, there was a special clause in that conditional trust, to cover medical expenses. No strings attached for that. They wanted to make sure nothing happened to Joshua Crane's bloodline. My role in their delusional beliefs was always more important to them than I ever was as a person." Her voice had become hoarse, so she took a moment to clear her throat. "It was oddly satisfying to waste that money on what was, after all, a lost cause."

His throat tight with emotion, he squeezed her hand again.

When he found his voice, he said, "I never stopped loving you."

"Oh, James," she said, tears brimming in her eyes. "I love you too. But love was never a question—for either of us. That's the saddest part. My father managed to poison that too."

"It shouldn't have," James said. "I should have fought—"

"Stop," she whispered. "What did I say about regrets?"

He bowed his head, not wanting to argue with her. Not now. "I know."

"Sometimes the end is baked into the beginning," she said. "And we're just too blind to see it." She sighed. "They're all gone now."

James looked up. "Gone?"

"Well, not all of them, of course," Mary said. "But the inner circle, the most devout, the ones chosen to keep an eye on me. I managed to outlive them."

"What happened?"

"First, you must understand how important I was to them, to their faith in my father's vision. Me. I was—rather, my blood was—their ticket to their so-called apotheosis, some ridiculous pinnacle of perfection. God forbid any of them live an average or normal life."

"Never understood it."

She chuckled. "My father had this vision of some kind of heightened state of being, where thoughts could change reality, manifest success and happiness. I never questioned it. Never wanted any part in it. But I always tried not to trigger his anger. I experienced enough of his... dark side to avoid provoking more of it by expressing my doubts. I'm not sure they even knew what they would become. But the promise of apotheosis was enough for them to continue to subjugate me."

"I never understood why you—"

"Went along with it?" she asked with a wry smile. "My whole life... alone with my father... I never really had personal freedom. My choices were rarely my own. It was something I endured. Forever locked in a prison without walls. Finally, my doctor discovered the cocktail of drugs I'd taken my whole life—in addition to the severe side-effects—also made me compliant." She took a deep, shaky breath. "My only real choice was you, James," she said, wiping away another tear. "Being with you was the only time I ever felt truly free."

His chest heaved and he struggled to control his breathing without sobbing. "I'm so sorry…"

"No," she said quickly. "Being with you was a gift. I wouldn't trade that for anything."

After he regained control of himself, he said, "And they're gone now?"

"When they found out my condition was terminal," Mary said, "it shook them to the core. The news fractured their faith. I was dying, just as my father had. Somehow, I would achieve an apotheosis, just as my father had—without them. End of the bloodline. They took it as a sign—a test of their faith and devotion. Of course, most on the fringes simply abandoned the movement—I think most of them were in it just for the blood and drug high. But that wasn't an option for the inner circle." She cleared her throat, voice raspy. "I could use some more water, please."

James retrieved the glass, watched her sip, then held onto the glass for her as she continued her story.

"It started when Mitzy was diagnosed with pancreatic cancer," Mary said. "She died within eight weeks. The others began to speculate that she'd been called to the next level of *being*, as they believed my father had. It probably would have ended there, if not for Kaitlyn."

"What happened to her?"

"Undiagnosed brain arteriovenous malformation," Mary said. "An abnormal jumble of arteries and veins in her head that caused a massive brain bleed. She died before they could get her to the hospital." Mary shook her head. "This happened shortly after my condition deteriorated. That pushed the rest of them over the edge. Like a clock was ticking for those who remained. I believe they thought they needed to cross over before I—before the end—or they would get left behind. Cal's the one who proclaimed it a 'final test' of their faith."

"How did Dara take it?"

"She ate her gun," Mary said. "Isn't that the phrase cops use?"

"What about Cal and the others?"

"Cal put on a tuxedo and hung himself in his attic," Mary said. "The twins poured each other a glass of red wine, dosed with poison. They left one suicide note, something about 'achieving the unimaginable,' with both their signatures."

"And Claudette?"

"Left Boo with a neighbor," Mary said, "then drew herself a bath and slit her wrists."

"Wow," James said. "That's a lot."

"There were some others—from that group," Mary said. "The local news talked about suicide clusters for a while. Some other deaths that looked like accidents but probably weren't. I recognized some of the faces, even if I never bothered to learn their names. I just hope the madness my father started has finally burned itself out."

"Like to think they got what they deserved."

"Some of it—the evil perpetrated in the name of—nothing would be punishment enough," Mary said.

James thought about the Meyer twins' blithe recitation of horrendous acts performed by Joshua Crane and covered up by his chosen cult followers. Mary must have internalized that information to survive the horror of her childhood.

Mary had visibly sagged during her recitation of events. She looked at him now with exhaustion in her eyes. "Can you help me lie down?"

"Of course," James said. Rising, he returned her drinking glass to the table, then came back to pick her up, one arm behind her shoulders, the other under her knees. She winced in pain, but flashed a frail smile to let him know he hadn't done anything to hurt her.

As he carried her to the hospital bed, he was stunned by how frail she felt in his arms, the weight she had lost, bringing her bones alarmingly close to the surface. He'd always heard the expression skin and bones, but that was exactly how he imagined her now, with her flesh stretched uncomfortably tight over her skeleton.

He lowered her to the bed as gently as he could, easing her into the softness of the mattress as much as possible and helping her adjust her back and legs.

He kissed her forehead and asked, "Is that good?"

She nodded—and blood flowed from her nose.

"Hold on," James said, hurrying into the bathroom.

He glanced back briefly and saw she had wiped the blood from her nose with the back of her hand and was reaching a trembling hand for the glass of water.

In the bathroom, he grabbed a clean white hand towel and rinsed it under cold water. The face staring back at him from the mirror looked distraught, his eyes plagued by sadness and grief. Inside his head, the ticking of another clock was all too real. As he turned off the faucet, he heard a *thunk* from the other room.

Seeing the glass of water lying on the rug beside the bed and Mary's frail, weakened form leaning over the bed trying to retrieve it, he rushed to her side. For a horrible moment, he envisioned her falling to the floor and shattering her bones. He reached her in time and helped her back to a comfortable position. He sat on the edge of the bed and dabbed the wet washcloth on her face, cleaning away the blood.

"You need to be careful."

She scoffed. "Little too late for that."

"No need to make it worse," James said, rationalizing a situation he could never have prepared himself to face.

"There is no worse, James," she said. "It's taken everything from me, and all it gives back is pain. Every part of me is in pain, all the time. Nothing really helps. Today was a better day than most, but they are so, so rare. I wanted to enjoy the lake one last time. I remember that first night here. In this room. I'm glad you're here today, to see me this way, at least. The future is so much—I know what's in store…"

"Just tell me how I can help you."

"You know."

James stared at her, finally comprehending. The reason she wrote to him. Why she asked him to visit her in their special place.

"You know," she repeated, seeing it in his eyes.

A bead of blood formed and trickled from her nose. He quickly dabbed it away.

"He's lived inside of me for so long," Mary said bitterly. "This is his poison inside me, his cruel legacy. I don't want him there anymore."

"Please—I can't—"

He had no idea how he would endure the end of her, a world without her in it—but to do what she asked—he was paralyzed by grief—

"I want to be free."

He shook his head. It was too much. "No—"

She smiled warmly at him, a smile frail and fleeting, extinguished by pain. "I want it to be how we were when we met. Here. In this room. Just us. Please, James. Please."

Mary took his hand with the towel and held it to her nose and mouth.

His voice hoarse with emotion, James said, "I wish I could've helped you the way you needed me to."

She whispered, "Help me now."

Tears streamed down his face, no holding back now. Still

unable to comprehend the enormity of what she was asking of him. But he looked deeply into her pleading eyes. There was no doubt or hesitation in them, despite what she must see in his. She squeezed his hand tightly, but he felt the effort of will coming from her, the fleeting surge of strength that would soon abandon her body but not her mind and determination.

He hesitated, but only to look into her eyes again, to see her one more time, to see the love in her eyes for him and to let her see his love reflected to her in his eyes. A final goodbye between lovers separated and, at last, reunited. Then he pressed down on the cloth, never looking away from her eyes as raw emotions surged through him—gutting him with rolling waves of grief and despair. He clung to what had always been there, what would never change—his love for her. He stayed with her, connected to her soul through the love in her eyes, until the end.

She hadn't struggled at all, hadn't fought for air or tried to cling to the remaining life of pain that would have awaited her. She'd kept her hand between his until the tension left her body, and she found peace.

And at that moment, the bedside clock displayed 3:18

Still sitting on the edge of the bed, he removed the towel from her face and placed her hand at her side. Other than that, he couldn't move. He could only stare at her face, with the pain gone, finally relaxed in death.

Now, he was truly alone.

How do you survive, he wondered, *when you've lost everything that truly meant anything to you?*

He'd never felt more lost in his life.

A darkness flittered over the bed between them and flew away, drawing his attention toward the far wall.

And there, hovering directly in front of him, was a black moth…

CHAPTER 43

Surrounded by burning chairs and umbrella canopies, James stood on the unstable rooftop bar of the Lakeview Hotel and stared at the hospital bed in its center. He had followed Mary up the stairwell to the roof but saw no sign of her—only the hospital bed. An image of another hospital bed echoed in his mind, and he found it difficult to reconcile the two. All he knew was that Mary should be here with him now.

He felt the heat of the flames through the soles of his shoes. The surface had become tacky, and newly formed fissures vented dark smoke. With fire raging on all sides of him, and pieces of the roof collapsing and crashing to the floors below, time was running out.

"Mary!" he called. "Where are you?"

He looked left and right for any sign of movement. Flames shooting up from various holes in the roof, along with the black smoke issuing from them, obscured his view. She might be hiding behind a table or chairs, but that made no sense. Why would she hide from him?

The burning pole of an umbrella swung toward him like a flaming sword, crashing at his feet as he jumped aside.

"It's not safe here," he yelled. "We gotta go!"

A scrape of movement drew his attention back to the medical bed in the center of the roof. In the stark light cast by multiple fires, he saw the bundled sheets on the bed were covered in blood. Then the bed slowly rose up into the night sky, out of reach of the flames. James stepped forward to intercept it, but where the bed had stood, the roof shuddered, sagged, and then collapsed with a series of thunderous crashes, spouting a shower of sparks and thick plumes of smoke. When the smoke cleared, James stared down into the fiery abyss.

Now the bed was too far and too high for him to approach.

The tarnished metal bed frame turned on its axis, spinning so that the mattress and the bundled bloody sheets faced James. It hovered there for a few moments. Despite the flames surrounding him, he couldn't look away from the bed.

Suddenly, the bloody sheets swelled and burst. Clouds of black moths swirled outward from the bed and, like a murmuration of starlings, flew in unison, dipping and arcing toward James, spinning circles around him from head to toe. Through the maelstrom of black wings, James watched as the mattress tilted back, fully upright, and the sheets unfurled away from the mattress, two sets, each opening to the left and right, staying open like sails catching an air current—or like two sets of wings.

With the sheets unfurled, James saw a woman fastened to the bed, with a bowed hairless head and toughened, scarred flesh, upper arms crossed with clawed fingers draped over opposite shoulders, with a second set of arms hanging at her sides. Her torso and legs were bound tight together with strips of bandages. In some places, it appeared that the bandages had merged with the toughened flesh. With the bloody sheets as wings and the torso and legs bound to resemble a thorax and abdomen of a moth, the entity before him appeared completely inhuman. But, beneath it all, even though her eyes were closed as if in deep sleep, the face was unmistakably Mary's. In his mind, he thought of the floating creature before him as another manifestation of the woman he loved: Moth Mary.

Then the bloodied sheets began to flap furiously, like the forewings and hindwings of a moth. And these wings were so large, they fanned the flames around him, which surged almost high enough to meet the hovering figure bound to the mattress. The swarm of moths that had encircled James swirled upward, away from him and back to Moth Mary.

A moment later, the section of roof under James' feet collapsed, tumbling down to feed the burning abyss below. But James did not fall. He was suspended in the hot vent of air, swirling smoke and drifting ash. Beneath him, the raging inferno waited impatiently.

Looking up from the fiery oblivion that awaited him, James turned his gaze to Moth Mary. She floated down toward him, mighty wings beating at a slower rhythm. The black moths followed her down, circling her now. Her head tilted down toward him and, slowly, her eyes opened.

"I came so far to find you," James said quietly, his demeanor calm despite the imminent jeopardy he faced hovering above the roaring flames. He was resigned to whatever happened now that he'd finally found her. "I'm here now."

He stared into Moth Mary's eyes, which had begun to glow, and he saw himself reflected in them. Both sets of arms extended toward him, the lower pair around his waist, the upper pair around his shoulders. Gracefully, she wrapped him in those arms and pulled him close to her. At the edges of his vision the swirling moths were so numerous they resembled static on an old television switched to a dead station. They seemed to block out the outside world, the crumbling building beneath him, the consuming flames, even the unbearable heat, because all he experienced at that moment was the heat emanating from her body. Everything else was static.

"I can't live like this, Mary."

He referred not to that moment in time, but to everything

he'd needed to endure to reach that moment, the empty hours that faced him in the world, the monsters that haunted the nightly otherworld.

Incredibly, the moth swarm grew in intensity, swirling faster, so that static gray became encompassing darkness, a dark vortex completely blocking out everything except for the two of them, locked together.

Then James said the only thing that mattered.

"I can't live without you."

Daylight...

Disoriented, James stood in the chapel meadow. For a moment, caught in an odd daydream. He thought it had been nighttime, in another place and time. He shook off the reverie and took in his surroundings.

Mary approached in her short-sleeved white sundress with a bright floral pattern, bathed in golden sunlight. A gentle breeze caught and lifted her strawberry blond hair away from her face. She smiled warmly at him, a coquettish gleam in her pale blue eyes.

Flowing up from the grass, a dozen moths flittered around her and followed her, like a summer entourage courtesy of Mother Nature.

James was surprised to see her here. At the same time, he couldn't understand why her presence was unexpected. She had come with him to the meadow, to watch him paint the chapel, to enjoy a picnic together. Sometimes, he got lost in his own head, a condition common among creative types, at least most of the ones he'd ever met.

He smiled as Mary stepped into his arms, placing his hand on her hips as she reached for his neck.

"It's beautiful here," she said. "Don't you think?"

"No question," James said, but he only had eyes for her.

She sighed contentedly. "Wish we could stay here forever."

"Me too."

She leaned into him, head tilted up and pulled him in for a kiss. Her breath tickled his cheek, and then her soft lips pressed against his.

The moths multiplied in number and swirled around them both. Lost in the warm embrace, James hardly noticed that the swarm had completely covered them.

The maelstrom of black moths that had completely encircled James while in the arms of Moth Mary suddenly broke away, swirling up into the sky accompanied by myriad sparks and floating ash. Just as quickly, the swarm rushed back down to the Lakeview Hotel, flowing outward in a solid black wave to cover the rooftop. The rolling ebony wave shimmered and stilled—

—and the rooftop was completely restored, no more fissures and holes, all fires extinguished, the hotel's sign once again intact, all furniture undamaged.

James stood alone.

Moth Mary was gone.

The section of the roof where the hospital bed had stood seemed to ripple and swell. Then the darkness broke apart as hundreds of moths took flight, revealing Mary's supine body, gently wrapped in white sheets like a cocoon, only her face exposed, eyes closed. With the departure of the moths, the absence of the flames, and the restoration of the hotel, all was silent.

James kneeled beside the body.

He stared at Mary's face so long, he felt frozen in time.

Then, with tears in his eyes, he placed a hand gently on her cheek.

For a moment, he imagined her eyes opening, as if she were awakening from a pleasant dream. He imagined her looking up at him, a warm smile blossoming on her face. Anything but the silence...

After a while, he reached down and lifted her into a sitting position. But before he picked her up, a wave of emotion overwhelmed him. He wrapped his arms around her shoulders and gently kissed her forehead. Then he buried his face in her hair. His tears fell as he whispered her name.

This was not how he imagined their reunion.

Slowly, he placed one arm under her shoulders, the other under her wrapped knees and lifted her off the rooftop. Cradling her in his arms, he paused as the rising sun illuminated the rooftop, shafts of golden light scouring away the shadows with implacable efficiency.

No more sirens.

Or fog.

Or ash...

James carried Mary across the rooftop, through the double doorway and down the staircase. Everything had been restored. Everything was whole.

Except for him.

Though the Lakeview Hotel was undamaged, it was deserted. No guests or staff to question why he walked through the halls and down the stairs and through the lobby carrying the wrapped body of a woman they all knew but had never truly known. She was a stranger to them, as she had ultimately been a stranger to him. But that had changed. He finally knew her, all of her, only it had taken too long to secure that knowledge.

He stepped out of the hotel, solemnly carrying the body of the woman he loved through the courtyard and gardens, and down the steps to the parking lot. The only car in the lot was his black Mustang, with the convertible top up and the windows down, untouched by ash, facing the hotel's pier.

Carefully, he placed Mary on the passenger seat, securing her upright position with the seatbelt's shoulder strap.

Again, he imagined her fast asleep, face in deep repose.

He climbed into the driver's seat beside her and turned the ignition.

The Mustang roared to life.

Before shifting into gear, he turned toward her. Her head had tilted to the right and her face seemed peaceful. If her eyes had been open, she might have looked lost in thought, thinking about plans for another day, another outing, on the verge of asking him a question that might have caused him to chuckle or shake his head in pleasant surprise. He had the urge to reach for her hand, as he had held her hand on so many driving excursions. But the sheet wrapped around her body prevented this simple gesture of affection. Instead, he flexed his fingers and wrapped them around the steering wheel, taking a deep breath to steady himself.

Finally, he put the car in gear and drove from the parking lot onto the winding road that led toward the beach and the hotel's pier. At the broadest turn, he glimpsed the rollercoaster and Ferris wheel of the Lakeside Amusement Park. No longer a rusted ruin, the amusement park looked ready to entertain visitors to Silent Hill with assorted rides and games of chance heavily skewed in the house's favor. But the rides were still, the marquee lights dark, and nobody wandered around trying to decide if they wanted funnel cake, fries or ice cream before their next ride. No screams of excitement. No joyous squeals of children amped up on sugary confections, no ringing bells or buzzers, no endless loop of calliope music.

He swung around a gradual turn back toward the pier. At the unstaffed beach stand, umbrellas, folding chairs, and jet skis were lined up, awaiting the next hotel guest. The boardwalk was empty and the expanse of smooth sand between the lake and the hotel lacked any footprints.

As he made the final turn toward the pier, he gazed out across the still lake, the surface sparking under the blue sky and summer sun. Watercraft were assembled beside the pier, moored pedalboats, canoes, kayaks, rowboats, and a few speedboats for the more adventurous. All in pristine condition.

James did not find the lack of residents or vacationers troublesome. Even though the ash and fog that had kept the town in a hazy twilight had vanished, along with the strange creatures that roamed the streets, everyone had already abandoned the place. The road into town had been cordoned off by fencing topped with razor wire. Some time needed to pass before people rediscovered Silent Hill.

As with the hotel, the damage to the pier had been fully restored, no rot or decay to weaken the surface or compromise the pilings. He had doubts about the width of the pier, but up close those doubts evaporated. When he made a sharp right turn onto the pier, the planking rumbled underneath the Mustang's tires as if he were driving over cobblestones, a prolonged, percussive *rumpadumpa-rumpadumpa*.

Taking a deep breath, he squeezed the steering wheel hard and floored the accelerator.

The Mustang surged forward, racing across the rest of the pier in a blur—

—and plunged off the end.

CHAPTER 44

James lurched forward, his momentum arrested by the shoulder strap, as the Mustang struck the surface of Toluca Lake.

The heavy front end of the sports car immediately pitched forward, sinking like an anchor tossed from the bow of a boat.

Water gushed into the car through the open windows, swirling behind James' shoulders to fill the back seat even as the water level rose past his knees and hips in a matter of seconds. When the water reached the level of his chest, he unbuckled his seatbelt, then Mary's. As the water lifted her clear of the passenger seat, he hastily tugged at the wrapped sheet, lifting her arms clear.

Once the Mustang was completely submerged, James had only a small pocket of air to breathe. But bubbles rose to the surface, rapidly depleting this last store of oxygen. In the rearview mirror, he glimpsed himself, mouth closed after the last gasp of air. He saw no desperation in his eyes.

He turned his attention to Mary, taking in her peaceful face and the way her long hair floated around her in a slow hypnotic motion. Reaching along the length of her arm to her hand, he gripped it, interlacing their fingers. Then he let the air escape from his lungs, a sudden exhale before gulping only lake water into his lungs.

His body betrayed him, convulsing as it struggled to find oxygen no longer available. Lake fish swam peacefully through his final struggles, darting and gliding around the sinking car.

With Mary's hand in his, he looked through the windshield. The summer light from above had slowly abandoned him, growing hazy and gray, rapidly slipping into darkness.

A different darkness had begun to close around his consciousness, but as he stared down into the depths of the lake, the darkness split apart, and light bloomed. The bottom of the lake dissolved, transforming into a long winding road lined with New England pine trees demarcating the rise of lofty mountains.

On the winding road, nearing a hairpin turn to the south, a loaded logging truck roared along, gray smoke belching from its exhaust stack pipes…

CHAPTER 45

After discovering the glove compartment tin he used to stash a few pre-rolls was empty, James sighed, and patted his pockets, looking for the pack of cigarettes he'd yet to throw away. Kept promising himself he'd quit—until the inevitable backslide. His groping fingers found the crumpled pack of cigarettes in his left jacket pocket. About half a pack remained. When they were gone, he promised himself he'd quit.

A few moments later, he took his first puff in days. Any residual tension he'd been feeling began to ease away. "No, *this* will be the last one," he promised himself. "Might as well enjoy it."

Through an exhaled stream of smoke, he saw the winding road in front of him presented a blind turn, which probably meant another hairpin. With a brief tap on the brake pedal, he placed both hands on the wheel, confident the Mustang could handle the curve, and enjoyed the rush as the world spun on its axis around him. Smiling, he came out of the turn a bit wide, tires squealing in protest, kicking up some gravel on the right shoulder before he straightened out. Then he pressed down on the gas pedal.

Meanwhile, he needed the driving instructions Leo had scrawled on the coffee shop napkin to find his recommended out-of-the-way scenic spots. He reached for the glove compartment again as he was coming out of a wide turn. The right front wheel dropped into a pothole with a jarring impact, causing the cigarette to tumble from his lips, landing on his jeans. He glanced down to avoid picking it up by the lit end.

Sudden roar of a powerful engine—

Shriek of a truck horn—

Startled, James looked up in time to see he'd drifted into the lane of an oncoming logging truck, its massive grille bearing down on him with deadly speed. James spun the Mustang's steering wheel hard right, narrowing avoiding the head-on collision.

In his frantic attempt to avoid the logging truck, James hadn't dared brake, and the sharp right turn had steered the Mustang too far in the opposite direction. He struggled for control, whipping the wheel back again, swerving from the shoulder toward the oncoming lane. Out of the periphery of his vision, he noticed the blurred outline of a shabby bus stop.

Before he could roll the car or crash into something else, he slammed on the brakes. The Mustang fishtailed in a complete one-eighty before coming to a stop, punctuated by a loud crunch beneath the left rear tire. "Can't be good."

He switched off the ignition. Instantly, the car shuddered to stillness. After a few calming beaths, James located the burning cigarette on the floor mat and stomped on it. As the cloud of dust around the Mustang settled, James looked up at the rearview mirror, and noticed the reflection of a young woman—

Mary!

The sight of her overwhelmed him. Tears sprang to his eyes as he climbed out of the car on shaky legs. Walking past the rear of the Mustang, he saw the broken turquoise suitcase exactly where he expected it to be. But he quickly turned his full attention to Mary. She was exactly as he remembered her. Long, wavy strawberry blond hair, pale gray suede jacket, floral print camisole, short jean skirt, gold waist chain, and brown leather ankle boots.

He met her stunned gaze and said, "I'm so sorry. Are you okay?"

Flustered by the close call, she nodded, and answered rapidly, "Yeah. No. I'm fine. I'm fine."

The Intercity Coach bus drove past them, coasting to a stop at the shelter with the poster advertising Toluca Lake. The doors of the bus hissed open, engine idling.

Mary stared at James closely, as if on the edge of a realization. Despite the suddenness of their harrowing meeting, she smiled warmly at him, sensing something powerful between them. He could tell she was confused by her own reaction. Logically, she should be yelling at him for reckless driving, for destroying her suitcase and nearly hitting her, but her own pleasant reaction had her shaking her head in disbelief.

"Are *you* okay?"

James looked down, patted his thighs, spread his arms, smiled back at her. If anything, he felt invigorated—and grateful. Felt like he should pinch himself. "I think so."

Then he remembered the circumstances of the near-miss and their reunion and glanced down at the suitcase nearly split in two, clothing scattered everywhere. He darted from one side of the road to the other, gathering items of clothing, a cracked makeup case, even a pair of black high heels. He carefully placed everything back into the suitcase and swung the lid shut.

"Don't worry, I got it," he said. "The latch is broken."

Mary had retrieved her other bags while he cleaned up the mess he'd made. She had stood over him while he put everything back in the broken suitcase. "How do you know that?" she asked.

Of course, he had known before examining the suitcase, with a strong sense of déjà vu, but he simply showed her the dangling latch. "They usually don't leave the factory this way."

She quirked a smile. "No, I suppose not," she said. "You know what this means?"

With a squeal of metal, the doors of the bus closed, then the bus pulled away from the shelter, blowing a cloud of black smoke behind it.

Mary looked up, startled.

"Shoot," she exclaimed. "There's my bus.

"Hey! Wait!" she shouted at the bus driver, waving her arms overhead as she chased after it. She ran past the shelter, but the bus continued to pull away. Even if the driver had noticed her, he clearly had no intention of returning. Eventually, she gave up, standing on the shoulder of the road, hands on her hips in frustration.

She walked back to him, shaking her head.

"Can you believe that guy?" she said. "Had to see me standing here with my suitcases. Just left. No warning."

James' easel, canvases and painting supplies were stacked in the back of the Mustang, so he opened the trunk and fitted her other suitcase and toiletry bag inside before taking special care with damaged suitcase to avoid spilling the clothes again.

She frowned again, grinning at him. "So, now you're stealing my bags?"

James chuckled. "Where were you heading?"

"The next city."

"Well, I just ruined your day," James said. "Wouldn't be much of a gentleman if I didn't try to help fix it."

"A gentleman?" Mary said with a raised eyebrow. "Didn't know they made those anymore."

"Gentleman named James," he said, holding out his hand.

"I'm—"

"Mary."

Both her eyebrows rose in earnest this time.

"Saw it on your case," he said, patting the undamaged suitcase in the trunk. He gave her an inquiring look, waited for her nod, then slammed the trunk lid. "Well, we should probably get going then."

Hesitant, she stood there for a moment, examining the car, which was easy enough with the top down. She noticed the easel leaning to the side in the back. "You're a painter?"

"Yeah."

"People might think I'm crazy," she said, "getting in the car with a complete stranger."

"We've exchanged names," he said with a playful grin, "so we're not *complete* strangers."

She poked a finger at him. "That's a technicality."

He circled around and held the passenger-side door open for her. "Well?"

Mary stood there, considering, almost glowing in the golden light. James couldn't take his eyes off her. All he could do was smile. She stared back at him, half suspicious, half-amused. Suddenly, the wind lifted her hair. Dead leaves fluttered all around her.

"I have this weird feeling we've met before," she said. "Like I already know you."

"Same here."

Finally, she shrugged and flashed an amused smile. "Call me crazy."

She jumped into the passenger seat, brushing a loose strand of hair back from her face while he closed the door and hurried around to the driver's side. As James settled into his seat and started the Mustang, she laughed and asked, "What do you paint?"

James gazed at her lovely face and grinned before slipping

on a pair of sunglasses. He turned on the radio and, surprisingly, had no trouble finding a clear station. One of his favorite classic rock songs came on, so he cranked up the volume. Mary smiled at him, bobbing her head in time with the music.

He put the car in gear, checked his mirrors, then swung the Mustang around in a U-turn, and floored the accelerator, leaving Silent Hill in the dust.

THE END

ACKNOWLEDGEMENTS

At Titan Books: I'd like to thank my editor, Daquan Cadogan, for giving me the opportunity to adapt this classic story in novel form; thanks also to Valerie Gardner and Lukmon Ogunbadejo for helping things go smoothly; additionally, I'd like to thank Kiran Rihal, Christine Duggan, and Claire Schultz.

At Evolution, I would like to thank Travis Rutherford and Kirsti Tichenor. Also thanks to Lisa Perkins for facilitating an early look at the trailer, which really set the mood, for giving me access to thousands of set photos, without which writing this novelization would have been at least a thousand times more difficult, and for shepherding this project through the process on the filmmaking/production side, your work has been invaluable.

Of course, none of this would have been possible without the wonderful script written by Christophe Gans, Sandra Vo-Anh, and William Schneider and stunning film directed by Christophe Gans and produced by Victor Hadida, Molly Hassell and David Wulf.

Music Department: Thanks to Tangerine Dream for helping this author focus by providing the soundtrack to long writing sessions, with *Raum* and *Sorcerer* in heavy rotation this time around.

Finally, I'd be remiss not to thank the developers of the *Silent Hill* 2 video game, Team Silent, a group in KONAMI Computer Entertainment Tokyo, and published by KONAMI.

ABOUT THE AUTHOR

John Passarella won the Horror Writers Association's prestigious Bram Stoker Award for Superior Achievement in a First Novel for the coauthored *Wither.* Columbia Pictures purchased the feature film rights to *Wither* in a prepublication, preemptive bid.

John's other novels include *Wither's Rain, Wither's Legacy, Kindred Spirit, Shimmer* and the original media tie-in novels *Supernatural: Night Terror, Supernatural: Rite of Passage, Supernatural: Cold Fire, Supernatural: Joyride, Grimm: The Chopping Block, Buffy the Vampire Slayer: Ghoul Trouble, Angel: Avatar,* and *Angel: Monolith. Halloween,* based on the 2018 movie starring Jamie Lee Curtis, was his first movie novelization. *Halloween* and *Grimm: The Chopping Block* were both finalists for IAMTW Scribe Awards. In January 2012, John released his first fiction collection, *Exit Strategy & Others. Return to Silent Hill* is his fifteenth novel.

A member of the International Association of Media Tie-In Writers and the International Thriller Writers, John resides in southern New Jersey with his wife, children, a dog and a cat. As the owner of AuthorPromo.com, he is a web designer for many clients, primarily other authors.

John maintains his official author website at *passarella.com*, where he encourages readers to send him email at *author@passarella.com*.